ACT OF JUSTICE

A NOVEL

BY DICK COUCH

BOOKS

Aura Libertatis Spirat

ACT OF JUSTICE

Copyright © 2022 by Dick Couch

Braveship Books
www.braveshipbooks.com
Aura Libertatis Spirat

Cover design by Rossitsa Atanassova

ISBN 978-1-64062-150-3

Printed in the United States of America

ACT OF JUSTICE

PRAISE FOR DICK COUCH'S WRITING

"Couch...is a well-qualified guide to this class (Navy SEALs) of men."

Wall Street Journal

"Sure to keep you on the edge of your seat."

Clive Cussler

"Exceptionally nuanced and insightful."

The Washington Post

"The complex plot never seems contrived, thanks to the author's careful attention to his story's human dimension."

Publishers Weekly

"No psychological or mushy stuff. Lots of pep and some nifty new gadgets."

Kirkus Reviews

ALSO BY DICK COUCH

FICTION

SEAL Team One
Pressure Point
Silent Descent
Rising Wind
John Moody, Navy SEAL
The Mercenary Option
Covert Action
Act of Valor
Op-Center; Out of the Ashes
Op-Center. Into the Fire
Act of Revenge

NONFICTION

The Warrior Elite
US Armed Forces NBC Survival Manuel
The Finishing School
Down Range
Chosen Soldier
Navy SEALS; Their Untold Story
The Sheriff of Ramadi
A Tactical Ethic
Sua Sponte
Always Faithful, Always Forward
By Honor Bound

This one is for Julia

CONTENTS

FOREWORD

BY GEORGE GALDORISI

Over the past several decades, the United States and its allies have been engaged in a global war against terrorism. This war has been a primary focus of the U.S. intelligence and military organizations for almost a generation, and it has cost the United States thousands of lives and trillions of dollars.

Soon after the 9/11 attacks, the U.S. military, as well as the Nation's intelligence agencies, recognized that this war on terrorism would not be won by conventional forces and their tanks, ships, and fighter aircraft. Instead, it would be the U.S. military's special operations forces—Army, Navy, Air Force and Marines—who would do the heavy lifting in this fight. In 2002, the U.S. military began a drive to substantially increase the number of special operators.

While there are many components of the U.S. national security establishment that have been making inroads against stopping the terrorists who threaten us all, perhaps none have been more prominent than the U.S. Navy SEALs. Among the SEALs many noteworthy exploits, none is more well-known and celebrated than the takedown of Osama bin Laden at his compound in Abbottabad, Pakistan, in May of 2011.

While other special operations forces and three-letter agencies have made valuable contributions in this effort, it is likely that the attributes the SEALs bring to the fight—talents that are embodied in their very name, which stands for sea, air and land—are the ones that make them the Swiss Army Knife of special operations and the entity most called upon to take on some of the most dangerous missions.

While other entities in the U.S. Special Operations community bring awesome capabilities to the fight, the reason the SEALs were directed to take out bin Laden likely stemmed from their past success in similar operations; their ability to coordinate their missions with other parts of the U.S. military, as well as with U.S. intelligence assets; and, most importantly, because they were in Afghanistan in numbers and were the closest Tier One Special Operations forces available for the mission.

Because of the high profile—but mostly covert—success of the Navy SEALs, as well as other U.S. military special operations forces, many writers have written about the special ops in magazine articles, online postings, and books—both nonfiction and fiction. The quality of these writings has varied wildly: from rather good, to so-so, to egregiously bad and inaccurate. Because of this, it's wise to look at anything written about U.S. military special operations with a high degree of skepticism.

That is not the case with retired Navy Captain, former SEAL, and former CIA operative Dick Couch. He is universally recognized as the most authoritative voice when it comes to understanding the special operations mission and conveying it accurately and fully in both nonfiction and fiction. He stands alone as the one writer who not only explains the intricacies of the SPECOPS mission, and especially how U.S. military special operators leverage the capabilities of the nation's intelligence community, but also does so in an entertaining and convincing way.

Whether it is one of his earliest books, *SEAL Team One* (still recognized as one of the most compelling novels of SEAL action in the Vietnam War), *Rising Wind*, or *Act of Valor* (a *New York Times* best seller), Dick Couch is unique in communicating just what it is that special operators do as they stand on the front lines in the global war on terrorism.

This brings me to his latest book, *Act of Justice*, which completes the trilogy he began with *Act of Valor*. Knowing that he is the author, it goes without saying that what you are about to read is highly accurate, breathtakingly compelling, and relentlessly entertaining. But this book is more than a military thriller. It is a book that makes you think, and think deeply, about our national security.

Famously, in 1939, Winston Churchill defined Russia as "a riddle, wrapped in a mystery, inside an enigma." If he were alive today, Churchill likely would call *Act of Justice* an alternative history, wrapped inside a mystery, wrapped inside a military-intelligence techno-thriller. In chronicling—in a fictionalized narrative—the events surrounding the decades-long hunt for and takedown of Osama bin Laden, Dick Couch makes the reader not only think about, but also question, many of the levers of our national security enterprise.

Hold on. Reading this book will be more than a thrill ride. It will make you think deeply about how the United States deals with not only the global war on terrorism, but also how we deal with our place in the world. And it, no doubt, will leave you with a deeper understanding of, and respect for, the U.S. special operations and intelligence professionals who stand ready to do violence on our behalf so we may sleep peacefully in our beds at night.

INTRODUCTION

I've been associated with American military special operations and American intelligence operations for close to fifty years. The two—special operations and intelligence—have often worked at cross-purposes or at least independently, each seeking to keep the other in the dark about what they were doing.

That began to change after 9/11. The CIA Special Activities Division and Army Special Forces (the Green Berets) combined their talents and resources to mobilize the Northern Alliance and sweep the Taliban from power in Afghanistan—or at least send them into Pakistan and into hiding. Their respective domestic headquarters commands were not always in accord, but the operators in the field found a way to work together.

Over the course of the last decade and a half, the special operators and the CIA field case officers have continued to build on the cooperation that began during those early days in the Hindu Kush. I have been in tactical operations centers in Iraq, embedded with SEALs and Special Forces, and have had the opportunity to observe this working relationship. "Those are our special friends," one special operator told me, referring to a group of civilians across the room. "They're a great bunch of guys, and they're very good at finding targets for us."

There is a name for this symbiotic relationship: it's called operations-intelligence fusion, more commonly, ops-intel fusion. The intelligence officers in the field have become very good at generating what is known as "actionable intelligence," and the special operators have become very good at getting out the door quickly to act on this valuable, and sometimes perishable, intelligence product.

It was this kind of cooperation that led to the successful takedown of Osama bin-Laden in 2011. On that day in May, when the SEALs stormed bin Laden's compound in Pakistan, there were eleven other concurrent special operations raids conducted on hard intelligence to capture or kill Taliban or al-Qaeda leaders. Not all of them were successful, but the hit rate was well over fifty percent—the average during recent years. Our special operations forces worldwide conducted close to three thousand of these operations each year, most of them driven by well-defined and sophisticated intelligence collection efforts. That number has recently declined, but on any given day...anywhere, anytime.

Our special operations forces have taken their game to a new level since 9/11. SOF, as it is often called, is a growth industry; since 9/11, their size has doubled, their budget has tripled, and their deployment posture has quadrupled. Yet, their evolution and emergence as the direct-action arm of our military in the Global War on Terrorism has been more one of perfecting their existing tactical expertise. Their radios are smaller, more reliable, and more secure; their insertion platforms more refined and technically capable. Their night-vision goggles are several generations better than they were only a short time ago. Yet, their mission set has changed little; they still kick down doors, and they still capture and kill bad guys. They just do it a whole lot better than they did fifteen years ago.

Our special operators have simply grown more proficient in the business of conducting combat assault and using emerging technologies in their operations. They are courageous to a fault and highly professional, but the operations side of this ops-intel fusion pales in comparison to advances in intelligence collection—both human intelligence (HUMINT or agent-sourced information) and the vast array of technical collectors now available to our intelligence and military services.

We may never know the extent and scope of the intelligence efforts that tracked bin Laden from 9/11, during the "first" Afghan campaign, through Tora Bora, and into Pakistan; but we can be sure there were some sophisticated and, perhaps, even unorthodox measures employed. And what was aired in the media about how we "got him" is, at best, the tip of the iceberg and most probably part of a disinformation campaign to fool the press and our enemies. These tactics, techniques, and procedures need to be protected.

As someone who was both a former special operator and a CIA case officer, I've had to ask myself: why did it take so long to get bin Laden? Why, on that particular day in the spring of 2011, did we decide to launch an operation into Pakistan to make a martyr out of this man? And just how closely were we able to monitor his movements all those years when he was in hiding? Could he really have eluded us all that time—unless, of course, his freedom served our purposes? Could it have been that we intentionally allowed him to live?

Aside from bin Laden's surprising, decade-long run of freedom, there remain a number of unanswered questions about this mysterious architect of the 9/11 attacks. One of them is his health.

It was widely reported that bin Laden suffered from both Marfan Syndrome *and* kidney disease, but the extent of his afflictions has never been documented. While he may or may not have at one time been on a dialysis regimen, he did suffer from bouts of fatigue and kidney-related issues going back to the early 1990s. He was also said to have been wounded twice, once at the hands of the Russians and again as he made his escape from Tora Bora in 2002, after the collapse of the Taliban in Afghanistan.

Bin Laden was also known to be something of a hypochondriac and dependent on any number of medications. In 2006, during his infrequently released video clips, he began to look more vigorous and robust in his appearance. He appeared to be more fit. Bin Laden was a vain man and took to dying his beard, and the media simply attributed the new, healthy look to the man giving more attention to his makeup and on-screen appearance. Or, he indeed may have somehow found a way to better health.

The year 2006 also marked the beginning of a decapitation process within al-Qaeda. A great many lieutenants and key leaders began to disappear or be killed. Many others left the cause or announced their disassociation with bin Laden on political grounds. For a great number of Islamic militants, their goal was the overthrow of monarchies like the House of Saud and constitutional monarchies in Kuwait and Bahrain—secular governments that catered to a ruling elite. These western-leaning regimes also spurned *Sharia* law. These militants felt al-Qaeda simply made these governments more entrenched and less disposed to theocratic transition.

Whatever the reason, those who remained loyal to al-Qaeda and bin Laden began to be killed off, marginalized, or driven into hiding. For the most part, they were targeted and killed. It was also in the 2006 to 2008 timeframe that the inner circle of al-Qaeda began to shrink dramatically.

Faced with so many senior al-Qaeda leader killings, primarily at the hands of the Americans, bin Laden suspended the promotion of junior leaders to senior leadership positions for fear of penetration. This paranoia of outside penetrations, in effect, paralyzed the organization. As the remaining loyal lieutenants continued to be killed, al-Qaeda Central, bin Laden's governing entity, gradually ceased to be a functioning, top-down, coordinated organization. Leadership fell to zealots like Abu Musab al Zarqawi in Iraq, who brutalized and subjugated in the name of al-Qaeda, which made the movement unpopular with the people. The rise of regional tyrants like Zarqawi, who was killed by the Americans in 2006, marked the decline of a "centralized" al-Qaeda organization, a decline that bin Laden seemed powerless to halt.

Certainly, there were scattered, local al-Qaeda franchises in Yemen and North Africa, but these were spontaneous, militant-Islamic power grabs that ignored any direction from bin Laden's shrinking al-Qaeda Central organization. As a result, the decline of al-Qaeda Central paved the way for the emergence of ISIS.

Finally, there was the near-absence of terrorist acts against the West. With the amateurish attempts at hijackings, the splashy-but-ineffective attacks at Heathrow, and the not-so-amateurish attacks on the American embassies in Kenya and Tanzania in 1998, al-Qaeda had little success in spreading terror to western nations in general and the United States in particular. The one notable exception was the attack on Mumbai in 2008, but since that time, there have been few global incidents or terror engineered by bin Laden or al-Qaeda Central. And the Mumbai attack had ISI (the Pakistani intelligence service) fingerprints all over it.

The attacks of 9/11 made bin Laden and al-Qaeda players on the international stage. They seemed poised to bring down a reign of terror and to keep the West on the defensive. Our initial moves, first into Afghanistan and then into Iraq, were something they did not expect. From their relative safe havens in Pakistan, as well as other pliable Southwest Asian nations and East Africa, one would have thought they would have been more aggressive, especially once we became bogged down in Iraq. Yet, it didn't happen, and one has to ask, why? After the dramatic success of the 9/11 attacks, the remarkably secret organization built so carefully by Osama bin Laden in the 1990s seemed to crumble during the middle and latter part of the last decade. Again, why?

I'm a fan of cowboy movies and a fan of Paul Newman. The late Mr. Newman made some great ones. There was *Hud* and *Butch Cassidy and the Sundance Kid*, but my favorite is *Judge Roy Bean*. I particularly like the disclaimer that opens the film: "This may not be the way it was, but it's the way it should have been."

I think a variation of this phrase is appropriate for this novel: This may not have been the way it was, but it certainly *could* have been the way it happened. We will probably never know for sure, but the unanswered questions about the life and death of Osama bin Laden leave room for a great deal of speculation.

I *do* know from contacts in my former life that on more than one occasion we knew *exactly* where he was but elected not to take action. Some say we didn't strike for reasons of potential collateral damage. Others contend that it was an effort not to offend the tribes in the semi-autonomous Federally Administrated Tribal Areas in Pakistan, where bin Laden was—at one time—their guest. With the exception of the Abbottabad raid to get bin Laden, we have gone to great lengths not to offend Pakistan, whose help we continue to seek to counter the resurgence of the Taliban.

Or, just perhaps, there was another very good reason why we waited for close to ten years to end his life. Maybe it served our interests for Osama bin Laden to continue in his leadership role of al-Qaeda Central.

Act of Justice is but one version of what might have taken place.

Dick Couch
Ketchum, Idaho

CHAPTER ONE: GARRETT

The circumstances that brought Special Warfare Operator First Class Michael Montgomery, or M-Squared as he was known to his teammates, to this time and place were a matter of chance and premeditation. The place: landing in front of a door to a room on the top floor of a three-story compound near Abbottabad, Pakistan. The time: Monday morning, May 2, 2011, at 0311 hours—some three hours before dawn.

Behind Montgomery were three other special operators, attired much like he was—in ceramic body armor, Kevlar helmets, M4 assault rifles, and advanced night-vision goggles. As they cleared the rooms on the lower two floors of the building, they followed their standard operating procedures, or SOPs. They were a four-man fire team charged with room clearance. In accordance with these SOPs, the last man in the door of one room would be one of the first to enter the next room. This rotation had its variations depending on room configuration or opposition, but it was a formatted, free-flowing progression that these SEALs had done hundreds of times.

So, it was this purely random leapfrog rotation that put M-Squared at the head of the stack before this door on this particular night. The fact that Special Operator First Class Michael Montgomery was a veteran of this particular SEAL special-mission unit was wholly premeditated. He had trained for over a decade to be where he was at this very moment. His country had been at war

1

for most of that time, and he had kicked in many a door and killed many of America's enemies. SO1 Montgomery was a very experienced warrior.

Physically, he was a wiry six-footer with thick red hair and a heavy smattering of freckles. His china-blue eyes were bisected by a nose that had, at one time, been straight but was now bent from having been broken more than once. It saved him from being pretty. When he grinned, he displayed a Terry-Thomas gap in his front teeth, and he seemed to have a perpetual grin. Montgomery had grown up just outside of Albuquerque, and when he spoke, it was with a soft, southwestern drawl. Aside from a face that would be well placed on a box of cornflakes, he was a prototype Navy SEAL who at this stage of the war had spent more time in combat than any soldier, sailor, airman or Marine in any previous conflict. His body armor and Rhodesian vest, stuffed with extra magazines, grenades, radio, and assault hardware, did not entirely mask the wide shoulders and firm torso of his breed of special operators.

Montgomery was on his eighth combat rotation—more than some of his teammates, yet not as many as others. And like the others on this mission, he was emotionally exhausted from pre-mission prep and the flight into the target. This was not from the anticipation of going into action, but from the anxiety that this very special mission might be aborted. This was a mission that every SEAL and every special operator worthy of the name wanted to be a part of. It could be aborted for weather, a compromise in security, adverse last-minute intelligence, or most likely, for political reasons. For the last several hours, Montgomery and his mates had lived in fear of a recall. Now that they were on the ground, moving from room to room through the compound, those fears had melted away. Now it was all violence of action and professional execution.

Montgomery moved forward aggressively, giving the door a vicious kick. It exploded inward. He quickly followed the shattered door inside, moving into the center of the room—his pre-assigned sector. Behind him, two other SEALs crisscrossed the room to his left and right, visually digging their corners and sweeping the area with their M4s. The fourth SEAL held security on the door.

The room was in shadows, with only moonlight slanting in through a single window. Yet the four special operators saw the room clearly in multiple shades of green from their night-vision goggles. Two women in burkas, huddled against the far wall, let out a dual-pitched shriek and charged at the intruders. To M-Squared's left, a rifle cracked and one of the women went down with a gunshot to the leg. The teammate on his right took the other woman down with a barrel stroke to her temple–possibly a fatal blow.

Montgomery himself was totally focused on the tall man in robes who rose from a seated position and stepped toward him. Instantly, he knew who he was and what had to be done. The green dot from his infrared LA5 targeting laser was already on the man's chest, and he had only to press the trigger. The first round was a center-of-mass shot and certain to be a kill shot unless the man was wearing some kind of body armor.

He was not.

Montgomery next lifted the laser to the man's bearded face. As the man half turned and began to fall, he pressed the trigger again— most definitely a kill shot. Special Operator First Class Michael Montgomery had just killed Osama bin Laden.

He stepped to the prostrate corpse and saw the dark cranial blood rapidly spreading from the exit wound in the back of OBL's head. Montgomery kept his weapon trained on him, as if expecting this larger-than-life figure to recover and possibly jump back to his feet.

But M-Squared had shot enough men to know when he had killed one. He toggled the encrypted tactical net of his AN/PRC 148 multi-band inter/intra team radio—M-BITR (em-biter for short).

"Boss, M-Squared here. We got him. Definitely Osama and a definite EKIA."

Lieutenant Commander Bill Gentry stood next to his radioman in the courtyard of the compound. Behind him and several yards down the wall of the compound lay the crumpled hulk of a crashed MH-60 stealth helicopter. Gentry's M4 rifle hung around his neck, available if needed, while he manned his primary weapon—his radios. In a special-operations raid, the raid leader, or ground-force commander, coordinates the action and serves as a communications link. His fire teams do the assault work and, as needed, the shooting and the killing. Gentry pressed the transmit button on the radio of his command tactical net.

"You sure, Mike? I mean, you gotta be sure."

"Hey, sir, he's double-tapped, down, and dead. I can shoot the fucker again if you want."

"Commander, this is Brooks here with Mike. It's the big guy all right, and he's toast—an EKIA for sure."

Gentry clicked off and took the handset from his radioman, who carried the PSC-5 satellite radio. The radioman also held a portable concentric antenna array. He manually held a lock on the communications satellite, which linked Gentry to their base in Jalalabad and no telling how many others up the chain of command.

"Home Plate, this is Delta Alpha One, over."

The response was immediate, "Delta Alpha One, this is Home Plate, over."

"Delta Alpha One Actual here. Geronimo. I say again, Geronimo. Primary target is a confirmed EKIA." The SATCOM link was encrypted and totally secure, but military communicators and special operators alike are conditioned to use cryptic responses and code words. In military speak, a KIA is one of your own killed in action; EKIA refers to an enemy killed in action.

"We copy primary target as EKIA. Is that affirm?"

"That's most affirmative. We got him."

Gentry then busied himself with the mechanics of directing the intelligence collection effort at the compound and getting his force off target with the backup helo assets. He also had to be mindful of his limited time on target and potentially his worst nightmare—the arrival of a company of Pakistani infantry.

Up the chain of command, to and including the White House, the news of the death of Osama bin Laden was traveling at the speed of heat. The "For God and Country" phrasing was added somewhere along the line—along with a great deal of other unneeded, superfluous, and often inaccurate information.

Gentry, a heavyset man who had waited patiently outside many an enemy compound while his teams worked the target, again wondered why he had elected to become an officer. As the SEAL chief petty officer he used to be, he would be inside directing traffic and making decisions—take this, leave that, get this computer or that person ready for travel. He sighed, dropped to one knee, and waited. That his team leaders worked better and more efficiently knowing a man like Gentry was outside running the big picture and managing the support efforts was not lost on him. Still, a part of him wanted to have been in on the compound assault and takedown—and working the site exploitation of the target. He sighed and told himself, not for the first time, *All of the responsibility and none of the fun.*

Up on the third floor, two more men entered the room as the two women, one subdued by her leg wound and one semiconscious from the rap on the head, were held off to one side and treated by a member of the clearance team. One of the men who had just entered the room was a special operations medic who would photograph the body of the al-Qaeda leader and prepare it for transport. The second man was a mystery. He was older, perhaps in his mid-forties, but he moved with a certain grace and purpose that said he was both ex-military and ex-special operations. There was a calmness about him that suggested this was not his first special operations rodeo.

5

This stranger had appeared just before they boarded the insertion helos—fitted out with body armor, helmet, night-vision equipment, a tactical radio, and an Uzi submachine gun. He had stayed off by himself and out of the way. Yet, the SEALs in the assault elements had noted that their senior enlisted leaders—the master chief petty officer and the two senior chiefs—greeted him warmly. In the world of Navy SEALs, this had told the younger SEALs that he was a made man.

Lieutenant Commander Gentry had introduced himself to this last-minute addition to his raiding force with measured respect. This deference had not meant that he was happy to now be meeting this guy, nor that he was comfortable having to take him along on this critical mission. In fact, he'd had no idea who he was or why he was on the operation. Yet it had been made clear to him that, subject to mission-essential tasks and responsibilities, he would accompany the raiding party. He would also be allowed all freedom of movement on target and extended all courtesies. This did not mean Gentry had to like it, but when these orders were given him by his task force commander, he had replied: "Aye, aye, sir," which meant he understood and he would obey.

Garrett Walker was, in fact, a former Navy SEAL, a medically-retired SEAL master chief and well known to senior special operators in the tight-knit SEAL community. At one time, he had held sway as one of the elite SEAL special operators, like those who were conducting this very special mission. Walker was still a powerfully built man—six-two with a close cap of brown hair that was cut almost within military specs. He had regular, even features and a weathered complexion that stood in contrast to his deep, almost-iridescent green eyes. His mouth was a fixed, serious straight line that gave away nothing, and he spoke with great economy, as if he were a practiced ventriloquist. He exuded confidence, yet with no trace of arrogance.

Upon closer inspection as he now moved about the room, his load was assault-team light. His radio was a 148 M-BITR, but a state-of-the-art Iridium satellite radio rode in a Velcro carrier next to the tactical radio. He had only two additional magazines for his Uzi machine pistol. His helmet was a close-fitting, modified combat free-fall parachutist's model that mounted the same state-of-the-art night vision goggles as the other SEALs. Under his vest and body armor, he wore a safari shirt that was tucked into cargo pants and clinched to his slim hips by a nylon web belt. All special operators wear foot gear of their own choosing. Walker had low-top olive-drab Merrell hiking shoes. He gave the impression of strength while seeming to sacrifice nothing in speed and efficiency.

The woman who had been struck in the head now began crying loudly and resisting those who tried to remove her from the room. At one point, she broke away from her minders and threw herself onto bin Laden's corpse. Walker took her by the arm and spoke a few sentences to her in Arabic. She quickly quieted down and allowed herself to be taken from the room. Then he turned to the body. There was a centeredness about the ex-SEAL, as well as a quiet composure that said he was someone to be taken seriously. Yet when he knelt next to the body, he spoke to the SEAL medic in an affable, conversational voice.

"Help me turn him over. I need to get a look at his back." The combat medic started to protest, but there was also an unmistakable authority that accompanied Walker's soft tone. Both had turned on the IR floodlights of their night-vision goggles and worked in the near-daylight of the phosphorescent green of the floods.

Bin Laden was a tall man, and it took both of them to roll him from his back, where he had fallen, onto his stomach. The expanding circle of blood seeped from the exit wound on the back of his head, matting his hair and beard. Now on his stomach, the dark red blood bathed one side of his face and continued to pool on

7

the floor. Walker drew a sharp knife from his combat vest and parted the dead man's garment from the neck to his waist.

The frangible .556 round that had entered the front of his chest had not exited his back. The bullet had shattered his sternum and been deflected down into his bowel, where it had come to rest. But his back was not unmarked. There on the lower portion of his abdomen were two long surgical scars that ran from the back portion of his rib cage to just above the tops of his buttocks. They were well-healed incisions and bore the handiwork of an excellent surgeon, but they were scars nonetheless.

The medic watched as Walker took out a small camera and photographed the scars. Then, Walker took his knife and moved to the small of bin Laden's back. For a long moment, he manipulated the area, carefully feeling along either side of his spine. Then, he looked up at the medic.

"What I'm about to do is not to be photographed. Nor are you to talk about it with anyone. If you have an issue with what takes place here, then take it up with your troop commander once we're off target. Understood?"

The medic could only shrug. "Roger that, sir." Then he added, "And I *will* take it up with my troop commander."

Garrett Walker nodded. Quickly and carefully, he again felt along the lower thoracic region of bin-Laden's back. Then, to one side of the spine, he made a deep four-inch incision next to the T-9, -10, and -11 vertebrae.

Next, he produced a large pair of forceps and began to probe into the fresh wound. There was very little bleeding as bin Laden's blood volume was slowly draining onto the floor by way of his shattered cranium and chest wound. Walker bent close, too close for the medic to see much of what he was doing, and found what he was looking for. He first took a small set of side cutters and clipped two thin nylon straps that were embedded in the incision. Then, with the jaws of the forceps, he clamped onto a small metal capsule, a half inch in diameter and no more than two inches long, and eased it from the split in the skin. A thin gold strand of wire trailed from the wound, which he nipped with the side cutters.

He examined the capsule only briefly, then secured it in a small case before slipping it into a pocket of his combat vest. He performed a similar operation from a second incision on the other side of the spine, producing a similar small cylinder, but with only a few inches of wire. He carefully stowed the second capsule as he had the first. Walker then slapped a single, specially-prepared, hemostatic battle dressing onto the wounds to seal them. Once in place, the plastic sheathing made the fresh wounds hardly visible. Garrett nodded to the medic, and they both turned the body back over. He snapped a close-up of the al-Qaeda leader's face and stepped away.

"Thank you," Walker said politely. "He's all yours."

The medic hesitated, wondering what the hell had just occurred, and then proceeded to begin his photograph inventory of the body and the preparation for its removal from the building. Now that the compound was secure, other members of the raiding party were conducting a meticulous search of the area.

Garrett Walker quietly made his way down to the courtyard and out to where Lieutenant Commander Gentry and his small command-and-control element had positioned themselves. Garrett was carrying his own tactical radio, so he could hear that Gentry was busy giving directions to his search teams. And, as Walker rightly guessed, Gentry was managing his assault elements while fielding a steady stream of requests for information from multiple layers of higher headquarters.

The crash of the lead insertion helo in the compound had made things complicated for him—complicated but manageable. Alternate, prepositioned extraction platforms were the norm, not the exception, and he had things well in hand. Like any number of competent, experienced SEAL team leaders, this was not Gentry's first compound takedown. He was busy, but in control. When Walker sensed there was a pause in the flow of radio traffic, he stepped to Gentry's side.

"My tasking is done here, Commander. Thank you for your patience." Gentry only glanced at him and nodded. "You and your people did some fine work here tonight. Congratulations." He moved away, taking up a position by the courtyard wall, well out of the way. Once there, he took out his Iridium satellite phone and keyed in a preprogramed number. It was answered on the first ring.

"Garrett, hello. How are you, and how are things there?"

"The insertion had its moments, but all is well. He's confirmed dead, killed in the assault, and I was on scene shortly afterward. I have the two items. We should be extracting shortly."

"That's good news. Be careful and we'll see you when you return."

"Until then, Garrett out."

Walker secured the phone and waited patiently as the raiding party completed their work and prepared to extract from the compound. As he waited, he followed the flow of tactical talk on his M-BITR radio. It was precise, measured, and professional— punctuated by the time hacks from Gentry's radioman, "thirty-seven minutes, sir." Then, "thirty-nine minutes."

Time on target was a serious consideration on any mission, but especially this one. They had just invaded a friendly foreign nation. The curious might be slow to venture out, but they would eventually move in for a closer look. And at some point, there would be an official presence on scene. It was best to be gone before that happened.

Walker was not just being kind when he congratulated Gentry on the operation. These SEAL operators *were* good, and so was their ground-force commander. They could be proud of this night's work. For them, it had been the result of several months of intense training and preparation. It was, after all, *the* operation—the one they would remember and savor, even if discouraged from openly talking about it, for the rest of their lives.

Yet it would be only a year before conflicting, unauthorized accounts of the killing of bin Laden would begin to emerge. The money offered by greedy publishers would simply be too good for a few of the SEALs in the assault element to refuse.

But Michael Montgomery would not be one of them. While he, in fact, had fired the two fatal shots, he would never speak of it out of school; he would never break faith with his SEAL brothers. When asked by those close to him why he remained silent when others had not, he would simply reply, "This was a team effort. My teammates and those closest to me know what I did, and that's enough. And c'mon," he would add with a boyish grin and that easy drawl, "it was the luck of the draw. We were the first team on scene, and I happened to be the first guy in the stack. How someone could take money for that, let alone lie about it, is something I could never live with. Maybe others; but not me."

For Garrett Walker and *his* team of specialists, this night was the final and closing chapter in an operation that had begun in late 2005. Walker couldn't help but think back to the genesis of this mission, but it was only a momentary reflection. A big MH-47 Chinook extraction helo set down just outside the compound, and amidst all the noise and dust, he followed the raiding party aboard.

CHAPTER TWO: JOSEPH

It was late afternoon when Joseph Simpson finally returned to his apartment in the Watergate. It had been a trying day and an exhausting one—physically and emotionally. The rain had held off, but the threat of rain had stalked everyone at the crowded grave site. The internment at Arlington National Cemetery had been something akin to a circus. Though invited mourners had been small in number, they included two former presidents and the incumbent, along with an assortment of secretaries of state and national security advisors, former and currently serving.

The attendant security and flocks of reporters made it seem more like the burial of a rock star than of a political appointee, even one of such importance, distinction, and longevity. Simpson would have avoided the service altogether but for the potential conspicuousness of his absence. The decedent, Armand Gustov Grummell, had personally ordered the front tier of mourners, an arrangement that placed Joseph Simpson between the president (George W. Bush) and his national security advisor (Condoleezza Rice). And Armand Grummell, in his long and productive life, seldom acted without purpose. This was apparently one of those acts—perhaps his final one—although with Armand Grummell, one never knew. Both George W. and Condi Rice seemed fully engaged with the person on either side of them, leaving Simpson alone with his thoughts about the former director.

Armand Grummell had served five administrations as the director of Central Intelligence. He had not lived to see the position of director of National Intelligence created. Simpson idly wondered what Grummell would have made of the new organization layered on top of his—probably not much. He had been to the CIA what J. Edgar Hoover had been to the FBI, but Grummell's intellect and integrity were in keeping with his long tenure. He was totally apolitical and served his country and each succeeding administration with deference, candor, courage, and a great deal of administrative skill. The man was, in a word, a patriot.

Since before the end of the Cold War, one of the first duties of a president elect was to summon Grummell to the White House and ask him to stay on as the DCI. The man himself had been a rare blend of political awareness and character; many had disagreed with him over the years, even bitterly disagreed, but no one in the White House or in Congress had doubted his loyalty or his honesty. He had carried out the wishes of the chief executive, those with whom he had agreed and those with whom he had disagreed, with professionalism and dispatch. He had never abused his position or the trust of others.

Personally, Grummell had been a predictable, fastidious man and a lifelong bachelor, always coming to work early and leaving late. Yet, he could be cross with others who had attempted to put in similarly long hours. He had lived simply, in a small but elegant brownstone in Georgetown. It was said that he had come from money, but if that were true, his wealth had been carefully sequestered in a blind trust.

Now he was gone, and there would never be another like him. His hand-picked successor was a highly capable intelligence professional who lacked the political savvy of his mentor and was, as was clear to all including the man himself, but an interim DCI.

As for close friends, Grummell had never had any. Men like Armand Grummell, and Joseph Simpson for that matter, did not

13

have close friends. They had associates whom they respected and with whom they enjoyed working, and that was what passed for friendship. Had either man been pressed to name a person with whom they had the most in common or whose company they valued, each would have been on the other's short list. Yet months had often gone by without either man so much as calling the other. When they had met, it had usually been professional, and the meetings had been cordial, candid, and brief. Yet on a rare social occasion, they had met for dinner or for a quiet drink, usually when Simpson had been in Washington on other business. For men like these, meaningful work had been everything, and meaningful work in concert with someone who shared your commitment and vision had been intimacy itself.

The Watergate apartment was elegantly and adequately furnished, yet with the cold, impersonal touch of a professional decorator. Simpson went to the side table and poured himself two fingers of a specially-aged Talisker whiskey, one of the few extravagances he permitted himself. Recalling that, on an infrequent occasion, he and Armand Grummell had shared a glass of this same rare scotch, he splashed in another dollop.

Loosening his tie, he slumped into an armchair and gazed out over the Potomac to Rosslyn. It was now a typical chilly November afternoon, with an impenetrable low overcast that refused to relinquish the prospect of a cold rain. The threatening conditions matched his mood.

Joseph Simpson was a tall man, close to six-four, lean, and with a thick mane of white hair. He had a ruddy complexion that spoke to his New England roots, and watery blue eyes that had known much struggle, success, and suffering. He would be seventy next year, and while most who knew him thought of him as vigorous and much younger, at times like these, when he was alone and contemplative, he looked his age and then some. To say Simpson was successful was an understatement; he was extraordinarily so—one of the wealthiest men in America.

Joseph Simpson grew up in Boston and attended Northwestern University. After two tours as a Marine infantry officer in Vietnam, he went to Harvard for an MBA and then into business for himself. His years at Northwestern had allowed him to spend time at the stockyards in Chicago. This had kindled an interest in the beef industry, and he studied the inefficiencies of the meat-packing business in great detail.

While at Harvard, he developed a business plan to address those inefficiencies. It took but fifteen years for Simpson and his Ameribeef Corporation to become in the meat-packing industry what Boeing was in commercial aviation.

Thanks to his Marine Corps training, he put a premium on finding and retaining good leaders—he never used the term manager. A solid core of young mid-level talent supervised the worldwide operations of Ameribeef. Direction and guidance came from the top, but like the Nordstrom Company, compensation and recognition resided with the bottom tier of leadership. Joe Simpson listened to his front-line leaders, gave them great latitude and authority, and they produced for him. While Bill Gates was looking for and recruiting the smartest young intellects in America, Joseph Simpson recruited the best leaders, a good many of them former military officers and non-commissioned officers.

Ameribeef all but ran itself and continued on a path of incremental revenue growth and market-share capture. Thanks to Joe Simpson, beef and burgers from America found their way onto dinner tables in Kobe and Stuttgart. In the late 80s, he took

Ameribeef public while retaining a controlling interest. In the process, he became a multi-billionaire.

In 1996, President Bill Clinton made him Ambassador to Russia. His picture was on the cover of *Time Magazine*; his counsel was sought by business and political leaders alike. He stepped down from his ambassadorial post during Clinton's second term. Joe Simpson had enjoyed Moscow and had become fluent in Russian, but the social demands of the position and his wife's aversion to the Moscow social scene brought him home.

He settled back into a semi-corporate life, chairing the board of his company, but allowing the company to continue under the CEO he had trained to head the organization. He held a limited number of advisory positions, and lectured a few hours each week at the Harvard Business School.

Simpson and his wife, Prudence, owned a comfortable home with acreage on Martha's Vineyard, and he commuted by helicopter and private jet to wherever his business took him. Some men who have enjoyed prominence and notoriety find it difficult to step into the background. Joseph Simpson was not one of them. He easily moved from one period of his life to the next. He was more than content; he was happy.

Then, his life began to unravel.

In 2000, while he was on a business trip, Prudence Simpson was exercising her favorite mare on their Vineyard property. It was a cold winter evening, and she was heading for the stables when she was thrown. The fall was not fatal, but she was unconscious, and the cold took her. Her death also took something irreplaceable from Joe Simpson. They had met in college and been married for over thirty-five years. She was his lover, his confident, and his only true friend.

His grief was overwhelming, and her loss left a void that Joe knew could never be filled. Yet, the tragedy did not end there.

On the night Prudence had fallen from her horse, Joe Simpson's daughter, assuming her mother had simply retired early, didn't realize she was missing. She would not find Prudence until the following day, which made the incident all the more traumatic.

It proved a double tragedy, for Simpson's daughter blamed her mother's death on yet another of her father's frequent absences. Their relationship quickly became strained, then distant, and finally nonexistent. Joe Simpson missed his wife terribly; each day he woke up dreading yet another day without her. And his daughter became a constant reminder of how lonely he was.

For the better part of a year, he did his best to immerse himself in work and teaching. Then came 9/11. His son, Joe Jr., was working at the Ameribeef corporate headquarters in the first tower when it was struck. He had no chance to flee as he was in the floor just above where the airliner impacted. Two months later, Joe buried a small portion of the identifiable remains of his only son on Martha's Vineyard, next to his wife. His daughter was there but left quickly after the service. He was now utterly and completely alone. Following the funeral, he immersed himself in a short, intense period of unimaginable grief.

Yet, Joe Simpson was that breed of New England stock that could feel sorry for himself for only so long. He was a man of action and a man of service; personal comforts or considerations were of no particular concern to him and less so after these tragic events.

After several weeks of walking the deserted winter beaches near his Vineyard home, he made some decisions. One had to do with helping others; he vowed to do all in his power to help those in need on a global basis. The other decision was to do all in his power to seek out and destroy those responsible for the attacks of 9/11. Humanitarian relief and retribution; these were to become the focus of his life from that point forward.

His first order of business was to begin a careful divestiture of his business assets, which—for someone as wealthy as Joseph Simpson—was no small task. Once he had gone to cash, he then set about building a nonprofit organization whose goal was the elimination of hunger and suffering in developing nations. Because its founder was no stranger to building a strong and efficient enterprise, the Joseph Simpson Junior Foundation was jump-started with more than adequate capital and soon became a player in the fight against world hunger and getting aid to refugee populations.

The foundation specialized in timely response when prompt aid was needed to address an emerging humanitarian crisis. Simpson acquired a fleet of aircraft, from cargo jets to heavy-lift helicopters, and hired former military pilots to fly them. Whether it was a flood in Bangladesh, a drought in the Sudan, or fighting in Nigeria, he could get aid to the scene of suffering promptly. There was no board of directors to consult and no U.S. State Department objection that he could not overcome with a phone call. And if local officials had to be bribed to ease the delivery of needed aid, he could do that as well.

Within a very short time, the Joseph Simpson Junior Foundation became the go-to organization in rapid-response to disasters—both the natural kind and those of a political origin. Soon, old 707s, 737s, and Russian Mi-6 helicopters, with a Red Cross or a Red Crescent on the side and the white JSJF lettering on the tail, were a common sight on the airport aprons of places like Mogadishu or Sierra Leone.

Joe Simpson built his foundation with the same attention to detail and bottom-up management style he had used to build Ameribeef. A number of Ameribeef middle-management leaders, made rich through their stock options, left Ameribeef and came to work for the foundation. Within a year, the Joseph Simpson Junior Foundation was up, running, and under the direction of a corps of proven leadership that left Joe Simpson free to devote his energies elsewhere—to the second of his objectives.

Simpson had first met Armand Grummell back in 1996, during the course of his intelligence-briefing package before he took up his duties in Moscow. Over the course of his ambassadorship, he had visited Washington regularly and received subsequent intelligence briefings.

During those years, Simpson and Grummell had developed a professional, then a personal, respect for one another. This relationship had evolved to a point where, on each home visit, the two of them met for a quiet dinner at the Army/Navy Club in Washington. Simpson had admired the intelligence, wit, and character of the director; he genuinely liked the man.

For Grummell, it had begun as duty and the care-and-feeding of the ambassador of a key operational station. But, then, he had come to personally like Simpson as well. They were kindred, patriotic spirits, and their discussions had ranged from current matters of state to philosophy, history, and the health of the republic. More to the point, there had developed between them a deep bond of trust.

In Moscow, Simpson had also become close to the CIA station chief, Jim Watson. Some ambassadors wanted to know nothing about station activities so as to preserve an honest deniability of an intelligence operation gone wrong, or they were meddlesome and/or condescending to the point of hampering station operations. Simpson had treated Watson with respect but had remained constructively engaged in station activities. During their time in Moscow, they had worked well together.

Shortly after he established the Joseph Simpson Junior Foundation, Simpson called Jim Watson, who was then the assistant deputy director for operations at Langley. They met for a discrete lunch, where Simpson asked for the name of a competent, retired covert actions officer. Two days later, Watson returned the call with a name and a point of contact. He asked no questions, but both men knew that the request and the name had been vetted by Armand Grummell.

After that time, there was no formal or overt connection between Joe Simpson and the CIA—or any governmental entity for that matter. To his neighbors on Martha's Vineyard and business acquaintances, Joseph Simpson had seemingly emerged from his personal tragedies and was trying to get on with his life by immersing himself in the foundation named for his late son.

This was true, and the foundation—with its forward-looking rapid-response capabilities—had indeed saved a great number of lives and relieved a great deal of suffering. But the foundation was, in many ways, just window dressing for another venture that commanded most of Joseph Simpson's waking hours. This one had to do with retribution—retribution and justice.

In addition to generously funding the Joseph Simpson Junior Foundation, Joe senior began to deploy a portion of his extensive fortune to fund the development of a clandestine and highly capable organization to conduct small-scale covert and paramilitary operations on a global scale. He again applied the same organizational and managerial skill to this new and secret enterprise that had made him successful in business and with his foundation.

Since this new enterprise ostensibly did not exist, it had no formal name. Those on the inside of this small organization came to call it the IFOR, or the intervention force. In encrypted correspondence, it was referred to as I-4. It was tailored to intervene where the interests of the United States were deemed both critical and threatened, and where normal diplomatic, intelligence, or military options were considered inappropriate or ineffective.

I-4, by design and implementation, could quickly move into the seams of an emerging trouble spot and bring resolution before things got out of hand. As the organization matured and grew within this limited scope, they became increasingly engaged in situations where novelty, delicacy, and non-attribution were required. Yet, this was no rogue enterprise that operated at Simpson's whim.

Ever the bottom-up organizational man, Simpson established internal controls within I-4 to carefully assess issues of risk versus reward and the probabilities of operational success. As was his method, he gave considerable authority and autonomy to those whose integrity and professional competence he trusted. And, most importantly, I-4 never acted without the knowledge, consent, and—on occasion—support of the United States Government.

This official blessing came from or through Armand Grummell. Sometimes Grummell included the White House and key members of Congress with oversight responsibilities in this knowledge-and-consent process—and sometimes not. Simpson and Grummell shared the Jeffersonian ideal that they, if the conditions warranted or the risk to the republic was severe enough, could act independently for what they deemed to be in the interest of their client—the United States of America. Their wealth, commitment, vision and position gave them that right. They acted judiciously in this regard, but then they shared a deep love of country and were prepared to accept responsibility should their actions prove embarrassing, illegal, or even criminal. Both considered this the province of true patriots.

What Joseph Simpson had created, and Armand Grummell supported, was a modern, highly capable, and restrained version of the Impossible Mission Force, one that in some ways resembled that of the old television series and the modern movie sequel, without the inter-agency drama and personal heroics.

Just before his death, Armand Grummell summoned Simpson to his bedside at the Bethesda Naval Hospital. He and those around him, both care givers and senior administration officials alike, knew the director had little time left. He would have preferred to die at home, but in deference to those who had to see to his needs in these final hours, he had allowed himself to be admitted.

Per his instructions, he had asked for the dispensation of final life-prolonging measures, but insisted on a regimen of stimulants and only mild pain medications. He wished to be in command of his facilities for as long as possible.

When Simpson reached him, he found the old spymaster tired, relaxed, and resigned, but very alert. As he pulled a chair close to the bed, Simpson felt no need to ask how his longtime associate was feeling or proffer sympathy. Grummell would not have appreciated such words. Time was short. Both knew this, and Grummell would not have sent for him without reason. Men like Armand Grummell and Joe Simpson did not lead lives that required the mending of relationships or personal closure. They did what good judgment and love of country required, and moved on. This included their mortality. But in a rare display of intimacy, Grummell extended his hand, which Simpson immediately took.

"Old friend," Grummell began, "thank you for all that you have done in the service of our nation and what I know you will continue to do." Simpson only nodded his thanks and waited for the old man to continue. "Our association has been both professionally and personally pleasing to me. And on occasion, we've been able to confound and confuse those who might wish to do our nation harm."

This caused Simpson to smile in agreement. *That* they had. They had foiled an attempt by a Muslim sect to detonate a nuclear weapon along the Afghan-Iranian border in an attempt to create an al-Qaeda caliphate in Afghanistan. They had defeated a plot to introduce a deadly hemorrhagic fever virus into Saudi Arabia as a means to destabilize that oil-rich kingdom and put those resources in the hands of extremists. And there had been other successes. Few in or out of government had known what they had done. That the two of them had been able to orchestrate these covert victories was enough for them. Though they had done all this without any need of recognition, and certainly with no thought of reward, Simpson perceived that these important but unknown triumphs would be something of a catalyst to help this good man from this world to the next—not that either believed in a hereafter.

While he had no need to "let go," Grummell, like Simpson, had a need to serve, if only one last time. And Simpson sensed with some certainty that, even now and on his deathbed, Armand Grummell was not finished.

"Joseph," he said. As he spoke, Grummell raised his head from the pillow to make better eye contact.

Simpson noted that this simple act seemed to require an inordinate expenditure of effort from his old friend. For the first time since he had entered the room, Simpson was aware that Grummell was in some discomfort. This slight but painful movement on the old man's part somehow added dignity to his person.

"Joseph," Grummell repeated, swallowing with difficulty, "I have a request." He paused to gather himself before continuing. Even in this deathbed setting, he spoke with a sense of formality. "Within the constraints of good judgment, good tradecraft, the reasonable risk to your people, and of course, the national interest, I want you to get him." He paused again, swallowed, and then added, "Will you do that for me?"

It was a most serious request, and both men knew it. They also knew the extended implications and complexities of such a request. Simpson hesitated, but only for an instant. He put his other hand on top of Grummell's bony grasp, and took a deep and measured breath.

"Yes, sir, I will—for you, and for this nation we both love."

The spymaster was more than adept at masking his feelings and emotions, but Simpson could see the relief in his features.

"Thank you" Grummell murmured. And then with what Simpson perceived as something of a twinkle in his eye said, "This makes the journey I'm about to undertake just a little easier." He released Simpson's grip, and for several moments, they sat in companionable silence.

The younger man perceived that Grummell had drifted off to sleep. Simpson quietly made his way to the door, turning to once again look at the man he so respected and admired. Then, he slipped out.

Late that evening, when the charge nurse was on her rounds, she looked in and found that the director of Central Intelligence had died in his sleep.

———

The director was finally in the ground. Now, and not for the first time, Joe Simpson contemplated the mission he had been given. He understood that, within the bounds Grummell had laid out, he had to "get him."

Grummell had not mentioned Osama bin Laden by name. He had not needed to. Nor was it required to define the full meaning of the word "get." They had, at various times since 9/11, known the precise location of bin Laden, but it had always been politically, operationally, or for humanitarian reasons, unwise to kill him with an air strike or by sending in a special operations team. There were compelling and rational reasons to want OBL dead, but his death had always been measured against the cost—a costing or calculus that involved issues of martyrdom, relations with Pakistan, tribal relations in Waziristan, or even the benefit of leaving him in place to prevent the ascendancy of a more capable subordinate. The list went on.

Grummell and Simpson had talked about this on occasion and had, by and large, agreed that the benefit of OBL's death had to outweigh the risks of killing him. Or why kill him? There was always the notion that if bin Laden were to be killed, it would be much better to have him die at the hands of a Muslim organization or government. And if not by a Muslim entity, then overtly by the United States—the nation he had attacked directly. That he more than deserved a bullet was, at best, only a tiebreaker in whether to kill him.

But now Simpson had told a dying Armand Grummell that, within reason, he would get bin Laden. And Simpson now knew why he had been so strategically placed between the president and his national security advisor at the funeral that morning. Did either of them know the mission Grummell had laid upon his shoulders? Probably not. What else, Simpson wondered, had the director done to make it possible for him to now undertake this delicate mission?

"Getting bin Laden" did not mean just killing him. That would have been relatively easy and would not necessarily have to involve the special skills and talents of the I-4.

No, by promising to get him, Simpson had agreed that he would find him, turn him—or in some other way fashion the use of the al-Qaeda leader against his own cause—and then dispose of him in a manner favorable to the U.S. government's own interests.

It was no small request, and it would be no small undertaking. Grummell knew this in the asking, and Simpson knew this in his acceptance. And both Simpson and Grummell knew that it would be done only if it *could* be done and, as in other I-4 taskings, done in the national interest.

In the days following the director's death and prior to his interment, Simpson had toyed with some general idea or notion of just how this might be done. The only inkling that he might not be alone in this undertaking was a discrete phone call from Jim Watson at CIA, ostensibly to see how he was doing and to exchange condolences over the director's passing. Yes, they would have to find some convenient future time for a quiet drink and to properly reminisce about this remarkable man.

In his role as the deputy director for operations, Watson was one of the few at CIA read into the existence and function of I-4.

On Armand Grummell's recommendation, he had been appointed temporary director of Central Intelligence, with an interim term of six months.

During the phone conversation, Watson had also hinted to Simpson that Director Grummell had asked him to be prepared to assist Simpson in the near future, should Simpson need Agency assistance with a project they had discussed. Simpson had to smile at Watson's mention of this "project." The old fox was still calling the shots.

With vague notions of what could or could not be done to fulfill his promise, Simpson reached a decision, one that he knew was both right and necessary—and, above all, professional. He picked up the phone and dialed a number from memory.

"Hallow," came the accented greeting after the third ring.

"Hello, Lon. This is Joe Simpson calling. How are you?"

"I am fine, Mister Ambassador. Very good to hear your voice. I think maybe you wish to speak to Steven, correct?"

"If it's not too much trouble."

"It's no trouble; he's right here."

A moment later, another voice came on the line. "Good afternoon, Mister Ambassador, and my condolences, sir, on the loss of your friend."

"Thank you, Steven. He was a great American, and he will be missed."

"Indeed, sir. How may I be of service?"

Simpson paused to frame his words. Even as he was agreeing to Grummell's deathbed request, he had known it could only be done with the help of Steven Fagan, the former CIA covert-operations officer whose name Jim Watson had given him right after 9/11. Since that time, Fagan had been the key planner and strategist for I-4. Only last year, he had told Simpson that he would like to take a less active role in what they called "the business," but that he would be available should something important or unusual arise. Simpson had agreed and, until now, had refrained from calling him.

"Thank you, Steven. I know this is rather short notice, but with respect to your inactive status, I find myself in need of your advice. I'd like to meet with you as soon as it might be convenient."

"As you think best, sir. Would you like me to come there?" Steven knew from the caller ID that Simpson was in Washington.

"I think not. If you don't mind, and Lon can spare you for a few days, let's meet at the Vineyard. I'll send a plane for you. Could you leave, say, tomorrow—midmorning?"

Steven Fagan paused as he sensed the urgency in Simpson's voice. "That'll be fine, sir."

After they had rung off, Simpson returned to his drink and watched the encroaching dusk swallow up the dark ribbon of the Potomac in exchange for the moving reflections of car lights along the George Washington Parkway. He thought of many things that he and Armand Grummell had done together—and of what, he mused, they were still doing.

Chapter Three: Steven

As Steven wrapped up his phone conversation with Joseph Simpson, he and his wife were sitting on the veranda of their Larkspur, California, home. It was a glass and screen enclosure with tall ceilings that served as a sitting porch, a greenhouse, and an indoor/outdoor garden. The setting enjoyed by Steven and Lon Fagan could not have been more different from Joseph Simpson's Watergate suite overlooking the Potomac.

The sun hung low in the sky and burnished the buildings of the city and the Golden Gate Bridge in soft afternoon light. It was quite warm for this time in November, but both wore fleece pullovers to ward off the coming evening chill. Lon had strategically placed candles about, some free standing, others floating amid gardenias in shallow glass dishes. In a few hours, she would light the candles, and those floating in the dishes would take on the appearance of small lighted fishing boats. It was an area where Lon nurtured plants and gently orchestrated the mood of their time together on evenings like the one that was approaching.

Each had their own hobbies, and both served as volunteers in and around their community of Larkspur. And both read voraciously—Lon on eastern religion while Steven liked history and national security affairs. But late afternoons, they usually managed to find each other on the veranda. Sometimes it was with incense and native Lao delicacies wrapped in banana leaves. Other times, like on this occasion, it was artfully placed candles, a clay pot of a hyper-aromatic chai, and a dish of nuts and dates. Steven never knew what it might be, but it was always something he looked forward to—something that ended the day with a warm and desirable conclusion.

In this fashion, the woman was an artist. Lon was one of the reasons Steven had told Joseph Simpson that he wished to step back from his duties with the intervention force. He had spent much of his life fighting wars for his country. Now he just wanted to be home—to do what most men do who have the luxury of a comfortable retirement. He wanted to spend his evenings immersed in the ever-changing, yet gently exotic constructions this marvelous woman seemed to engineer with such little effort.

Even as he was hanging up the phone, Steven reminisced about the day, forty years ago, when (as a young Special Forces Sergeant) he had first laid eyes on her.

A battalion of North Vietnamese regulars was hotly pursuing them. Steven Fagan was with a company of Montagnard tribesmen on the Plaine des Jarres, in Laos. It was a close-run engagement, and they were managing to stay a step ahead of their pursuers with skillful rearguard holding tactics. They were making their way through a rubber plantation with little idea how they were going to break contact and get to a secure location where an Air America CH-47 could lift them to safety.

And suddenly, there she was—a young Lao girl in a tattered dress, showing absolutely no fear. She was but a teenager, reed thin with quick, bird-like movements. Yet she had the face of an angel, with large eyes like in a Goya painting. That day, she was both an angel and their savior.

"Where do you wish to go?" she asked in flawless French.

"An open area or a hilltop where a helicopter can land," he replied, as much with hand gestures as with his schoolboy French.

"Follow me, but we must move quickly," she said and took off at a run.

She led them to a shallow rise with a clearing for a landing zone, where Sergeant Fagan, his Montagnards, and the girl who had led them to safety scrambled aboard the extraction helo just ahead of the North Vietnamese. The big Chinook took ground fire as they lifted off, but they made it—just barely. When they landed in Savannakhet, she disappeared as soon as the rear boarding ramp was let down.

That was the last Steven saw of her—in Laos.

Three years later, as a contract employee with the CIA, he was on assignment in Phnom Penh when he passed a flower cart in the central market district, near Quatre Bras. There she was again—taller, still thin, but with that same angelic face and those same enormous dark eyes.

"It is you," he said in his now-passable Cambodian.

"Yes," she said simply. "It is I."

"What happened?" he managed. "Where have you been?"

"I have been waiting for you to return," she said quietly.

From that moment on, they were together. They were married a few months later in a Buddhist ceremony; something frowned on by his CIA superiors, even for their contract paramilitary case officers. The fact that Lon's father had been French and that he and her mother, a highborn Laotian, had been killed by the Pathet Lao made no difference.

The following year, she and Steven were repatriated from Cambodia. He was granted staff status at Langley and enrolled in the Basic Operations Course to prepare him for duty as a foreign intelligence case officer. It was during this training that one of his trainers at The Farm, the CIA's remote training facility in southern Virginia, saw in Steven the makings of a covert operator.

The term covert operations is often used as a general term for secret operations. This is inaccurate. Covert operations are highly sophisticated, nuanced, quasi-intelligence undertakings—and often controversial ones. The job of the CIA is to gather intelligence using open sources, technical collectors, and on occasion, undercover methods. Their customer is the U.S. Government, specifically the executive branch. Traditionally, only the "spooks" in the Operations Directorate conduct clandestine operations, which means using secret collection methods that may involve foreign agents.

A covert operation is not a means of collecting intelligence; it is a means of changing the course of events in a foreign country to produce an outcome favorable to the United States. It often involves the illegal meddling in the affairs of another sovereign nation, perhaps even an allied nation. When done poorly, as in the toppling of Salvador Allende and his communist government in Chile, or Daniel Ortega and his Sandinista Liberation Front in Nicaragua, it can become messy and public. When done properly, as in helping the early political career of Alvaro Uribe in Colombia, it is cheap and effective, leaving no one aware that events have been manipulated, unless of course, the strategy calls for one or more parties to receive the credit or to get the blame. Sometimes the blame or attribution is laid at the doorstep of another nation or government, one who did not participate in (or even know about) the events.

Covert actions are nearly always preceded by a great deal of research and target analysis. Those who prove to be good covert operators are usually naturally good at crossword puzzles and chess. Success is in the details. It is an intellectual exercise that often requires just the right amount of flair and daring, and on occasion, the judicious application of lethal force.

Steven Fagan possessed that rare blend of patience, intelligence, organizational skill, and judgment that made for a superb covert operator. He became one of the CIA's best. Following the end of the Cold War, the Agency, under the Clinton Administration, stepped back from covert operations and Fagan was offered early retirement. He was living quietly in Larkspur and doing quite well as a corporate security consultant when Joseph Simpson came calling. Fagan's corporate work was lucrative, but mundane for a covert-operations specialist. Simpson told him what he had in mind, and Steven Fagan, after talking it over with Lon, became the architect of the I-4.

Fagan immediately grasped what Simpson had in mind and began building the organization. He quietly hired the team of analysts, planners, area specialists, logisticians, and former special operators and configured the operating divisions along regional lines. Soon I-4 had the ability to put people on the ground in Africa, South America, Southwest Asia, and the Middle East to conduct a wide range of operations, to include classic intelligence collection, paramilitary operations, and covert operations. For the most part, they avoided the active military theaters of Iraq and Afghanistan, working instead in those nations that might harbor terrorists but where the U.S. was not actively or overtly engaged. With discreet and highly compartmented liaison with the CIA, they began to entertain and conduct small, secret ventures—operations that were outside the capability of normal intelligence or military capabilities—especially where non-U.S. attribution was essential.

This was all made possible by the financial backing of Joseph Simpson and, on occasion, under the cover of the Joseph Simpson Junior Foundation. Foundation assets and aircraft made it possible to move men and materials around the world and to position them to support the activities of the I-4. With the focus on al-Qaeda and their franchises, as well as emerging threats like ISIS, much of I-4's work was paramilitary in nature or in the current lexicon, "kinetic."

The force was, in essence, a highly decentralized and sophisticated mercenary organization. While Steven Fagan was at the helm, they maintained and deployed a robust covert-action capability.

But that was all in the past. Today, he was enjoying his retirement from all that, in as much as an intelligence operative can ever retire. And now, out of the blue, this call from Joseph Simpson.

The call had intervened on their quiet evening on the veranda. Fagan pressed the disconnect button but did not immediately relinquish the portable phone. He glanced at Lon, who held him in a measured gaze.

"Another mysterious phone call?" she asked gently.

He smiled. "Another mysterious phone call."

He did not speak for several minutes, and she would not prompt him until he was ready. Over the years, it often began like this. The organization maintained a number of safe houses and secure skeletal training facilities around the world. When a mission came to the I-4, trained specialists and retainers were assembled for the task. They met at one of the isolated training locations to plan and rehearse. Then, they deployed to conduct the mission.

Steven was able to work from his home in Larkspur a great deal of the time. He had a home office with a state-of-the-art, secure communications suite. Most of what needed his attention in managing I-4 could be done without leaving Larkspur. Only when he was on an operation did he leave home for extended periods of time.

And much like Joseph Simpson and his Ameribeef organization, Fagan had a team of dedicated and well-paid subordinate leaders who attended to the day-to-day, non-operational functions of the I-4. They could mobilize and be on an operational footing in a matter of hours. Since his retirement six months ago, they had attended to operational matters in his absence, leaving him to other pursuits.

Now, apparently, something important had come up or Simpson would not be calling him.

"Did Ambassador Simpson say what he wanted?" Lon finally asked.

"No, but I sensed a certain anxiety in his voice. He's asked me to come east to meet with him." He reflected a moment and then continued. "It would appear that something has come up—

something that he feels is very important or something out of the ordinary."

"And when would you be leaving to go back east, my husband?"

"Sometime tomorrow morning."

"What will you need for your trip?"

Steven did not answer.

After a long moment of silence, she gently continued. "Is there something I might need to make ready for your journey? A suit or a sports coat?"

"Oh, forgive me," he said. "I was just thinking ahead to what the ambassador might want. No, there is nothing to get ready. This will be informal and at his home on Martha's Vineyard. Just a change of clothes—a pair of corduroys, a sweater, and maybe a winter coat. Nothing we can't take care of in the morning."

She poured them each a cup of tea, then moved closer to him. He put his arm around her and they watched as a late-afternoon fog bank rolled in from the Pacific, claiming everything but the upper spires of the Golden Gate.

A discreet car service collected Fagan just before 0930 and delivered him to the Oakland Airport just after 1030. The aircraft, a Gulfstream G5, was waiting on the tarmac outside the private aviation terminal. A small burgundy carpet was unfurled at the base of the boarding stairs, and one of the pilots stood by to receive his passenger. This version of the G5 could carry up to fifteen passengers in first-class comfort; today there would be only one, and an unpresupposing one at that.

Steven Fagan was not a large man, perhaps five-nine and a hundred sixty pounds. He had been a wrestler in high school and remained fit, as he was always careful with his weight and exercised regularly. He retained the heavy muscles in his neck and a slight slope to his shoulders that marked many wrestlers, at least those who had not run to fat.

His wiry brown hair was thinning in front and on top, and only recently had begun to show traces of gray on the side. Once a week, Lon took to him with her barbering tools, and he was always neatly trimmed. Soft pleasant hazel eyes and a slightly rounded face suggested that he might have been an actuary rather than a man of action. He was a man that you would pass on the street and never look at twice. But there was a particular intensity about him when he turned his attention on someone. Fagan's eyes seemed to darken and become quite focused. He at once became a man who people seldom forgot once they had met him.

More than a few workers at the Oakland corporate terminal were keeping an eye on the sleek Gulfstream, thinking it might have landed to collect a celebrity. They were disappointed when a distinctly average-looking man in a mackinaw, carrying a briefcase and a small overnight bag, made his way from the terminal to the aircraft. He was, perhaps at best, some large corporation's chief financial officer. As Fagan reached the boarding stairs, the pilot stepped forward to take his bag.

"Good morning, Mister Fagan. Good to see you again."

"Nice to see you, Curtis." Fagan offered his hand. "How's the family and those two lovely twin daughters?"

"All are well, and those daughters are now thirteen going on twenty-one and making their parents crazy."

"I can imagine. Just me?" Fagan asked, thinking there might be someone else in one of Simpson's organizations who would be making the jump from the Bay Area to the East Coast.

"Just you today, sir, and we're ready to depart when you are aboard and comfortable."

The G5 quickly reached its cruise altitude of 49,000 feet, well above commercial traffic and just under the aircraft's service ceiling of 51,000. With a strong tail wind, the flight took just under four and a half hours, more than enough time for Fagan to read his daily papers and enjoy an excellent lunch of poached Dover sole, wild Jasmine rice, fresh asparagus, and a small glass of Oregon pinot. A thin slice of New York cheesecake and a cup of freshly brewed Kona coffee followed.

After the meal, Fagan went forward to visit with the pilots. It had been a while, but both men in the cockpit remembered Steven Fagan well. He sat in the jump seat between them. In a very short time, in response to his queries, he had them both talking about themselves. That was Steven Fagan's gift. His interest in others was genuine, and people naturally wanted to tell him things.

The 5,000-foot runway at Martha's Vineyard Airport was more than ample to land the Gulfstream and just long enough for it to take off. They came down through several thousand feet of overcast and set down neatly in a light dusting of snow. When they taxied up to the private aviation terminal, there was a single vehicle there to meet them.

Joseph Simpson, dressed in wool slacks, flannel shirt, down vest, and hiking shoes, was leaning against an old Land Rover. He wore no coat or hat, and the cold ocean breeze riffled his thick gray hair. As Steven stepped from the boarding stair, he was there to greet him. When the pilot brought Fagan's bag down, Simpson took it himself and put it in the back of the vehicle.

Fagan thanked both pilots and the flight attendant, and joined his host in the Land Rover. They quickly left the airport for Simpson's estate, which was but a ten-minute drive, as was just about everything else on Martha's Vineyard—but only in the winter, when there were few tourists about. It appeared that they had landed just in time, as the weather closed in quickly. It began to snow harder, and it came at an angle.

The Martha's Vineyard property belonging to Joseph Simpson occupied a large piece of ground near Chilmark. Considering the size of the property it sat on and the size of the Vineyard homes that belonged to many of the Boston Brahmins, the quaint, turn-of-the-previous-century Cape-Cod saltbox was modest. The home was served by a barn and stables, and several smaller outbuildings.

Simpson pressed the electronic opener and the eight-foot wrought-iron gate slid back to admit them. From there it was but a short drive up the circular drive to the house. The residence itself enjoyed a sweeping view of South Beach and the Atlantic.

"Steven," Simpson said as they braked to a stop in front of the home, "I know I'm repeating myself, but I appreciate you making this trip on such short notice. As you might imagine, a project has come our way and I wanted to discuss it with you. But before we get into that, let's have a bite to eat."

Simpson took Fagan's bag from the rear of the Rover, and led him up the front steps and into the house. He dropped the bag in the foyer and they proceeded into the large country kitchen. The housekeeper had left a beef casserole in the oven for them, and there was clam chowder simmering on the stove—basic fare, but it was hearty and delicious.

There was nothing basic about Simpson's choice of wine, a vintage Bordeaux from his private stock.

The two men ate in the living room, before a crackling fire and periods of comfortable silence. When they did speak, it was of politics and the recent books both had read—biographies about Teddy Roosevelt, FDR, and Steve Jobs. Both agreed that it was a full-time job to keep up with the numerous and scholarly historical biographical works that seemed to be crowding the market.

Fagan moved to help Simpson with the clearing of the dishes, but the older man waved him to his seat. Several minutes later, he returned with a tray service bearing a thermos of coffee and a carafe of thirty-year-old port. Fagan took a mug of black coffee and only a small measure of port in a delicate snifter. His host followed suit.

"Steven," Joe Simpson began, "a matter was brought up to me by Armand Grummell just before he died. Actually, it was in the form of a request. The director asked me to do something, but only if it could be done within the established guidelines of the I-4 and the associated operational parameters that have always guided our organization. It was a very special request. Now, before I tell you about it, I want to be clear on one issue. I understand and respect your retired status, and it will be totally your decision as to whether you wish any involvement with this, or no involvement at all. As with all projects considered by I-4, it has to begin with a feasibility study and a careful risk/reward analysis. After I've told you of the request, I'm going to ask you to do the study and the analysis—if, and only if, you're willing to undertake the study. Past that, it will be your decision, and yours alone, if you wish to be a part of the operational phase—should it ever get to that."

Simpson paused to warm up their coffees. Neither had touched their port.

"You have been a long and valued asset to the I-4. Some would say you *are* the I-4. Or at least you were." Simpson smiled easily. "The men who now have your job are doing superb work, but as I said earlier, this is a special situation. I need your perspective and judgment—and again, only if you're willing. Our business has always been done on a choose-to basis, and you know I will respect whatever you decide in that regard. So, with that understanding, I'd like to tell you about Armand's last request. Fair enough?"

Steven Fagan did not answer immediately. He had always been treated well by Joe Simpson, who had afforded him great latitude when he'd served as the chief executive officer and then the chief operations officer for the intervention force. Operations were Fagan's forte, and as the I-4 had grown to a sufficient size, he had hired a CEO to manage the organization. Their work was important, and the last several years had provided Fagan with a sense of professional accomplishment and fulfillment that he had never known during his years at CIA or in the military. He had gone into retirement for personal reasons, but also to allow for the younger men in the organization to blossom. They had recruited some excellent talent, and that talent needed room to grow. And there was another issue. Now into his sixties, he feared that he might be losing a step. Lives and matters of national security and statecraft were involved in their work, and Steven Fagan was keenly aware that nothing less than his best effort would do. He had watched too many intelligence professionals and covert operatives stay in the game past their prime. He was not going to be one of those.

Yet, here he was with another project in the offing, with Joe Simpson asking him to take a look at it—just a peek. He was under no illusion regarding the dangers of "just taking a look." The project, whatever it was, would no doubt offer him a chance to do what he had loved doing for so many years. Like most career intelligence professionals, he believed there was good and evil in this world. He also believed that those like himself stood for what was good, and that, if left unchecked, evil would overtake them. Though he was a most understated individual, he believed that he was, or had been, one of those rough men that George Orwell was said to have spoken of—men who stood ready to do violence on evil-doers so others could sleep peacefully in their beds at night.

More than that, Steven Fagan was proud that he had been privileged to serve in that role. While Joseph Simpson might say that he only wanted a consulting opinion, both men knew that there was more than an even chance that Fagan would do a great deal more than that, *if* this particular project met the criteria regarding national security, national imperative, and operational risk. And both men knew that once Steven Fagan did become involved, there likely would be no turning back.

Fagan was silent for several moments, staring across his coffee into the fire. Then he turned to Simpson. "Very well, Mister Ambassador. Please fill me in—from the beginning."

Simpson held back a smile, not for the fact that he had managed to enlist Fagan's involvement, but for the fact that after all these years, and even after he had gone into semi-retirement, he had yet been able to get Steven Fagan to call him Joe, or even Joseph. It was always Mister Ambassador. He took a sip of port and a deep breath, and began.

Simpson omitted nothing. When he had finished, Fagan said nothing for several minutes. Respecting the silence, Simpson did not intrude on his thoughts.

Steven Fagan had listened carefully and had not moved during Simpson's monologue. Now he regarded the older man. "Are Director Watson and the Agency prepared to lend support for an operation that would accomplish this?"

"That is my understanding," Simpson replied, "but that obviously would depend on the concept of the operations. Director Grummell said as much before he died, and Jim Watson confirmed as much, if somewhat obliquely, when we last spoke by phone."

Fagan nodded. "And what about State and NSA? Their assistance would probably not be needed, but their non-intervention would need to be assured. Which means that while they would not have to be read into such an undertaking, they would only have to be advised of the operation in general terms." Fagan did not have to add, "which would mean involving national command authority— the president."

Simpson had thought about this and was glad Fagan had brought it up. "I don't know this with any certainty, but I cannot imagine that this requirement would have escaped Armand Grummell's attention. There is only one person who can guarantee that kind of cooperation, or at least the neutrality, of State and NSA. I believe the president has been prepped on this. And while the late director did not say as much, I think he may have laid the groundwork for such an authorization before he died."

Steven was again silent for a while. Then he smiled to himself and gently rubbed his hands together. "It would certainly be a credit to the former director if we could bring this about."

Simpson nodded slowly. "*If* we could. Do you think it can be done?"

This time Steven Fagan answered quickly. "I really don't know. Perhaps; perhaps not. As you well know, these things take research and study. And if we come up with a workable plan, the risks may be too great to move to the operational phase." Now he spoke with care. "So if I understand what you are asking, you want me to develop a concept of operations that would 'get' bin Laden in keeping with Director Grummell's wishes and in a manner that would serve the interests of the United States. Furthermore, you want me to vet the plan with regard to the rewards for success and the potential blowback for failure."

"Exactly."

Again, the silence hung between them.

Then, Steven Fagan cleared his throat and looked straight at Simpson. "Mister Ambassador, given our long and productive relationship, I would like to undertake this project. The only caveat is that I must discuss it with Lon. Not the specifics, of course, but that it will take me away from our life together and that it will mean a certain amount of isolation as I close myself off to carry out the study. And it might involve some travel to gather information and perform site surveys. For a project like this, I have no idea how long that might take—perhaps a month, perhaps three or more. And that's just a study of feasibility. As you can imagine, it's a tall order, and the operational details, if it comes to that, may be an order of magnitude greater than any of our previous operations."

"I understand," Simpson replied. "Take as much time as you feel you need."

"And as with previous projects," Fagan continued, "if I run into major difficulties or a serious non-starter—like the man's already dead—then of course, I'll break it off and let you know. Otherwise, you'll hear from me when I've done the feasibility study and developed an initial outline for the operational requirements."

Simpson set down his drink and offered his hand, which Fagan took. "Thank your Steven. I sincerely appreciate your engagement with this and will await whatever comes from your study." He paused and then continued, "And when you've finished, and if there is an operational plan, it will be at your discretion as to whether you wish to see it through or hand it off to the I-4 for execution. Agreed?"

Steven Fagan hesitated, but only for an instant. "Agreed." His relationship with Joseph Simpson had always been one of cordiality and trust. The only real issue between them had been one of compensation.

When Simpson had first hired him, it had been strictly fee-for-service. That "service" had been the development of the first operational plan for what was to become the I-4 and hiring the people to execute it. They had agreed on a price, Fagan had done the work, and Simpson had paid him for it.

Since then, their relationship had always been on the basis of a handshake, but Simpson always wanted to pay more than what Fagan felt was fair compensation. He was comfortable being paid twice what he had been paid at the CIA for roughly the same kind of work; Simpson always felt that it should be three or four times that amount. This time, they did not discuss money. Fagan knew from experience that it would be more than generous.

The next day, the G5 delivered him back to Oakland International Airport and the same car service returned him to Marin County. On the flight back, Fagan enjoyed a wonderful breakfast and thought about the project Simpson had in mind. As he thought the project through, he made notes on a legal pad. It was mid-afternoon when he arrived, so he and Lon decided to take a walk in Muir Woods, among the giant redwoods. He often did this when he needed to turn a matter over in his mind and reach a conclusion. He told Lon what Simpson wanted; and, while not divulging the specifics, he hinted at the enormity of the enterprise.

"It is my sense," she said as they walked hand-in-hand down the shaded path, "that this is something you need to do, my husband. And if it comes to it, see it to a successful conclusion. Only you can determine if it can be done or it cannot be done. If it cannot be done, you will know this. If it can, then your spirit will not be able to rest until you see it through. Is that not so?"

Fagan smiled, pulling her closer so that they now walked with his arm around her shoulders and hers around his waist. "Once again, you seem to know me better than I know myself."

"No, my husband. I just know that you will always do the right thing. And I will be here for you while you do that which only you can do."

For seven weeks, Steven Fagan worked around the clock, made two trips to Europe, one to Lahore, Pakistan, and three to South America. He then returned to Martha's Vineyard with the fruits of his labor in a thick file in his briefcase.

The evening was not unlike their previous meeting. Fagan laid his research on the coffee table between them, but neither man looked at the file. For the next hour and a half, Steven Fagan told Joseph Simpson exactly how he proposed to get Osama bin Laden.

CHAPTER FOUR: YOSEFF

Jim Watson rapped quietly on the door of room 318 of the New York Plaza Hotel. A moment later, it was opened by a very relieved security man. Even as an interim director, Watson was afforded a personal security detail, a precaution he felt unnecessary but with which he nonetheless complied. However, for the last three hours, he had had to shed his security detail—but not his surveillance. During that time, he had window shopped, stopped for coffee, ridden in taxis, and taken subway rides.

All the while, he was under surveillance. The team of watchers who shadowed him on his journey were from the CIA's counterintelligence division and normally followed foreign UN diplomats of interest and an occasional CIA case officer who had to be deloused for a meeting with one of those diplomats. Not since Richard Helms was the director had they surveilled a sitting director of Central Intelligence for an agent meeting. But then, with the exception of the reclusive Bill Colby, not since Richard Helms headed CIA had a career intelligence case officer held the directorship.

"Good to see you, sir." The relief in the man's voice was evident.

"Thank you, Tom. Everything in order?"

"Yes, sir. The surveillance team just called in and you're clean. And," he added with a grin, "they said you worked the street very well indeed."

Watson smiled. Defeating hostile surveillance was like riding a bicycle—you never forgot. And if tradecraft were bike riding, Watson was a multiple Tour de France veteran. For twenty years he had worked denied-area operations, ending his tenure in the field as Moscow Chief of Station. Under Armand Grummell, he had served as the DDO (deputy director of operations)—the head spook at Langley. Now, again at Grummell's request, his dying request at that, he was made director of Central Intelligence, albeit an interim director. The DCI was now an administrative position as well as a political one, and politics was not Jim Watson's strong suit. But he could still work the street, and he could still handle agents. But that was not his purpose here today, or not entirely.

"Tell the watchers to stand down once our guest arrives. I should be no more than fifteen minutes once he gets here."

"Understood, sir." The security man slipped out through the door and stepped into the next room, to where the other member of the director's detail waited with the communications specialist who was with the surveillance teams. Until the business in the adjoining room was completed, the surveillance in and around the hotel would continue. After the meeting, the surveillance teams would then track those leaving to make sure they were not followed. All standard.

After the security man left, Watson turned to the two men standing by a settee and an arrangement of comfortable armchairs surrounding an elegant coffee service. He greeted the shorter man first. "Steven, how are you?"

"Very well, Mister Director. And yourself?"

Watson had taken Fagan's hand, but had not relinquished it. "It's Jim, Steven—just Jim." Jim Watson and Steven Fagan went back a long way. They had at one time been colleagues, fellow case officers, and little had happened at I-4 that Watson had not been read into.

But the years had been kinder to Fagan than to Watson. The professional, political, and social strain associated with the life of an expat member of one embassy legation after another had taken its toll. The Spencer Tracy-like white hair was still thick and full, but the watery-blue eyes now hid under tired brows that fell to either side like the loose sides of a canvas pup tent. He was thicker at the waist now, and the broad, handsome face was more lined than Fagan remembered. Yet there was the same confidence and sense of purpose that good intelligence professionals acquired and never seemed to relinquish.

Watson now turned to the other man.

He was taller than Fagan, almost painfully thin, and with something of an academic slouch—noticeable for someone in his mid-thirties. He wore glasses, and his dark, straight hair and olive skin suggested a Mediterranean heritage. His teeth were yellow from tobacco. A large coroneted nose dropped from dark, brooding eyes. The slight one-sided upturn of a smile suggested he might be something of a cynic.

The man offered a bony, delicate hand with a surprisingly strong grip. "Pleased to finally meet you, sir. You'll not mind," he said with a slight twinkle in his eye, "if I'm allowed to call you Mister Director?" He spoke with just a hint of an accent.

"Not at all," Watson replied warmly, "if you don't mind me calling you Andre. And I'm happy to finally meet you as well. I've followed your work, and it has been superb." The phrase "following your work" meant that Watson had read the operational message traffic and studied the man's 201 file.

Andre Messinger was born to a Syrian father and Algerian mother. His father was a diplomat posted to Washington at the time of his birth, so he held American citizenship. He had lived all over Europe and was attending Amherst College when his parents were killed in a car accident in Lebanon.

When Andre learned that the accident had been precipitated by Hafiz al-Assad, the Syrian dictator, he immediately contacted the CIA. Once the recruiters at Langley learned of his background, he was kept away from headquarters and brought along the NOC track. "Nonofficial cover" officers were highly screened and vetted, and then trained at secure locations for undercover work. They typically handled secure assets and, for the most part, flew below the radar of foreign security services.

Messinger's legend (cover identity) was that of a freelance travel writer/journalist. His work was featured in airline magazines and vacation journals that earned him a salary that exceeded his GS-14 pay scale. Only recently had NOC officers been allowed to retain the overage between their cover position salary and that paid by their real employer, the U.S. Government. Over the past thirteen years, Messinger had worked for the Agency's Near East Division, handling secure assets. The one asset that brought them together this day was Yossef Khalil.

Yossef Khalil was a rarity among his fellow Arabs, in that he was a devout Muslim and a staunch opponent of Islamic fundamentalism. He was secular in his beliefs and felt that Muslims and Muslim culture were at risk if the faithful handed over all governance to the radical clerics who advocated *Sharia* law. He had held these beliefs long before a fundamentalist offshoot called ISIS metastasized in Syria.

Khalil was Lebanese by birth and had been born into wealth. His family was in the shipping business, which—for a Lebanese— equates to smuggling with legitimate shipping as a cover. As the oldest son, he was Oxford educated and, with the guidance of his many uncles, had run the family business after the death of his father.

Following the Lebanese civil war, his father had moved the main offices of the family business to Rio de Janeiro. Now under Khalil's guidance, the family had offices in New York, London,

Beirut, and Rio, but Rio was increasingly the center of their activity. The city welcomed Arab expatriates, and there were close to eight million Lebanese in Brazil, half again as many as lived in Lebanon itself. While Khalil traveled a great deal, he felt most comfortable in Rio.

At one time, Yossef Khalil had been a pan-Arab nationalist and contributed heavily to the charities that funded *jihadist* activity throughout the Middle East. And it had been good for business; he supported the cause.

But, with experience, he came to see the strangling effect that the fundamentalist factions had in Lebanon, Syria, Jordan, and Egypt. All were at risk and vulnerable, from oil-rich Saudi Arabia or oil-poor Yemen. Then, there was the emergence of the many al-Qaeda franchises that sought theocratic control of the people. What Osama bin Laden had started was bad for the Muslims and bad for business.

It was through a business associate in New York that Khalil had been introduced to an intermediary who recruited him to work for American intelligence. CIA was never mentioned, at least not at first, but Khalil was no fool. He had never been paid; he was not in this for money. Yet, on occasion, he had been provided with information or an introduction had been made that paved the way for a lucrative shipping contract.

After being vetted and trained, and after proving himself a reliable agent, Khalil had been turned over to Andre Messinger, who—as his case officer—had run him for the last seven years. In running him, Messinger had made Yossef Khalil spy on no one. Nor had Khalil elicited secrets on al-Qaeda or any other militant Muslim group. With CIA backing and direction, he had simply made contributions to an array of Muslim charities in such a manner that those at CIA and NSA could mark and track the funds as the charities sought to launder them and get them to the end users—al-Qaeda Central and the various al-Qaeda affiliates. In doing so, the CIA had been able to carefully chart the financial underpinning of al-Qaeda, and Khalil had acquired a subtle notoriety and stature among the enemies of America.

When Khalil arrived at the Plaza Hotel and knocked on the door to the room where the meeting was being held, it was Messinger who welcomed him. Yossef Khalil was a short, stocky man in a conservative Seville Row suit, starched white shirt, and guards tie. He was in his mid-sixties but looked much younger due to a well-tailored toupee. Dark intelligent eyes, a regular nose, and full—almost feminine—lips graced his nearly unlined face. He gave the impression of precision, authority, and a touch of warmth. Messinger embraced him heartily and then introduced him to the director of Central Intelligence.

Khalil's eyes widened. "You—you are the director at CIA? Yes, yes—I have read about you. I am honored to meet you. I do not know what to say. Forgive me; I am speechless."

Watson needed no coaching to play his role in this. He greeted Khalil cordially and respectfully—and with the accepted Arab courtesies. Only after seated over coffee and carefully working through the ritual inquiries about family, sons, health, and business, did Jim Watson turn to the business at hand.

"Mister Khalil, I wanted to meet you to personally thank you for all that you have done for America in the fight against those of your religion who use the Koran and the words of the Prophet to misguided and extreme ends. We are in your debt. For this, I sincerely thank you."

Yossef Khalil lowered his head in humble obeisance to the compliment.

Watson continued. "Now, on behalf of the United States of America, I would like to ask your assistance in another endeavor. It is but an extension of the help you have given us to date, but it involves a larger sum of money. And..." Watson paused for effect. "...it involves a plan that will blunt the influence of Osama bin

Laden and his al-Qaeda organization." Watson again paused. "I must be honest with you, there will be some risk. Manageable risk, but risk nonetheless. Would you consider such a tasking?"

Watson saw the Lebanese straighten his back and sit a little taller. There was little personal risk in this for Khalil, but often in the case of a committed agent, the mention of risk and the unspoken admiration for the risk taker helped to cement the relationship.

"Why, yes, of course. I wish to help in any way I can." Yet behind this willingness to help, there was hesitation in his voice. Yossef Khalil did not get to where he was by being impetuous or incautious. "Perhaps, if I know more of the details of what you have in mind, I will be able to better assist you in this matter."

Watson nodded solemnly in apparent understanding and satisfaction. "Naturally, this matter will have to be thoroughly reviewed and reviewed to your satisfaction before we can ask for your assistance." This was not new territory for Watson; recruited agents periodically had to be re-recruited. "My meeting with you today, other than to offer my thanks for your past work, was to seek your consideration in this new venture. The details of it I will leave to Mister Messinger and Mister Fagan. They will convey what it is we have in mind and how you may be of great help in this matter."

Though he had been there the whole time, Yossef Khalil now seemingly noticed Steven Fagan for the first time. Fagan was like a chameleon in that way.

Watson motioned toward Fagan as he continued speaking to Khalil. "You know Mister Messinger, but I'd like you to meet my associate, Mister Fagan. He will be in charge of this project going forward."

Steven Fagan greeted Khalil formally and deferentially. He exuded candor and trust. "It is a great pleasure to meet you, Mister Khalil. I have been briefed on your past contributions, and I look forward to working with you in the future."

Having set the table for the meeting, Jim Watson now departed, leaving the three men to talk about the future and the key role that Yossef Khalil would be asked to play.

Steven Fagan did most of the talking. His tone and voice were measured and respectful. As Khalil listened, he felt increasingly at ease—as if he had known Fagan for a long time. So, when the details of the project—Fagan was careful never to use the word operation—were revealed to the Arab shipping owner, he reacted favorably. In as much as it was a staggering undertaking, the soothing manner in which Fagan had laid out the venture and attended to the details allowed Khalil to signal his willingness to help.

After a plate of sandwiches was delivered, Andre Messinger quietly left the room. Steven Fagan continued to expand on Yossef Khalil's role in the plan in his polite, unhurried way. Fagan then moved from operational matters to the details of future communication, meetings, and contingency plans. Khalil would be told much about the mechanics of the proposed operation, but not the sensitive details or the ultimate goal.

Past that, Fagan took a sincere interest in Khalil's business activities and the welfare of his family. Fagan offered snippets of his own life, but for the most part, he listened while Khalil talked. In this manner, the handover was made to the new case officer.

———

It had been six weeks since the meeting where Yossef Khalil had agreed to participate in the project about which he knew only enough details to fulfill his role. He was making his way through the lobby of yet another hotel, this one far more palatial than that of the New York Plaza.

The Doha Four Seasons was truly one of the more elegant hotels in the Persian Gulf region, or anywhere else for that matter.

And because of the relative ease with which persons of all nationalities could move in and out of Qatar, it was a hub for business transactions that were both legal and illegal in nature. Yet Doha was a safe city, with a robust, yet unobtrusive, security service that allowed all to travel freely, so long as both residents and visitors were unarmed and broke no laws.

The U.S. Navy enjoyed a secure naval base, a rarity in the Arab world, but no off-base revelry took place. Members of both the underworld and the terrorist world were allowed to come and go as they pleased. So long as they conducted no illicit activity within the borders of Qatar, they could move about uninhibited. All parties knew and respected this.

Khalil had come straight from the airport to the Four Seasons. The five-hour first-class flight from London had left him somewhat refreshed and eager to engage in what he had come here to do. He had booked a room for himself for a single night. Having registered at the desk, and with his overnight bag sent ahead to his room, he boarded the express elevator for the penthouse suites.

Reaching the penthouse, he stood before the recessed double doors that glistened with a new coat of paint. He tugged at the sleeves of this coat, took a deep breath, and knocked three times.

The door was immediately opened by a swarthy Arab in an ill-fitting suit. He motioned for Khalil to enter, and then quickly and professionally searched him. While he was being patted down, Khalil looked past the gatekeeper to a second security man who stood beside a seated individual in traditional Arab dress—white robes and checkered *keffiyeh* head scarf.

The man was Jordanian by birth but had lived in Egypt and Palestine. He was a lean man, with aquiline features and deep-set dark, serious eyes. There was a cruel set to his mouth that was complemented by a scar that carried from his lower lip to the bottom of his chin.

The imposing figure rose from the armchair and seemed to glide across the room toward Khalil. He was a full head taller than the shorter Lebanese and had to stoop as he greeted Khalil in the traditional Bedouin greeting of shaking hands while bussing cheek-to-cheek on one side, then the other. He respectfully escorted Khalil to an armchair next to his own and made him welcome. The man smiled as they exchanged the ritual greetings, but there was no warmth to it. Coffee and flat breads were delivered and the security men disappeared into the further reaches of the suite.

"Again, I bid you welcome, my brother, and let me again give thanks to Allah for your generosity and support of our cause."

Khalil lowered his head in acknowledgment and tried to compose himself. Several weeks earlier, he had wired funds to a Muslim charity front that supported *jihadist* causes. The amount was for ten million dollars. The money had been well traveled and laundered many times before and after the transfer from Khalil to the charity. The funds had come from Joseph Simpson and had ended up in the coffers of Osama bin Laden's al-Qaeda Central organization.

Khalil had made it known that, along with the donation, he would like to speak with a senior member of bin Laden's inner circle—that he wished to do more for the cause than just contribute money. He had been contacted and given instructions that brought him to Qatar and this hotel at this time and date.

Yossef Khalil had been provided CIA dossiers on al-Qaeda senior leadership, but he had not expected this.

The man before him was Atiyaht Abd al-Rahman, who served as bin Laden's chief of staff for al-Qaeda Central. Al-Rahman had escaped with bin Laden from Tora Bora in Afghanistan after the routing of the Taliban in 2002 and made his way to the Federally Administrated Tribal Area in Pakistan. Like bin Laden himself, as well as many in his inner circle, al-Rahman was educated, cultured, wealthy, and committed to the cause.

The western security agencies knew he was still active but had lost track of his whereabouts. Now, here he was in Doha, brought out of hiding by al-Qaeda's ongoing need for money.

Khalil responded to al-Rahman's expression of gratitude. "I am but a poor business man whom Allah has seen fit to bless with much good fortune. My family and I no longer live in the Middle East, but that does not relieve me of my duty to assist with the struggle. I am not in a position to take an active part in the fight, but it is my privilege to support this effort as I am able."

The man in robes, who had introduced himself as Abdul, set his cup and saucer aside and leaned forward. "You made it known to one of our associates that you wished to be of further assistance in the *jihad*. Your past generosity has been noted by the *imam* himself, but may I know of how you wish to help in the future?"

Khalil was silent for a moment, searching for the words he had rehearsed for the past several weeks. "It is a matter of some delicacy, but let me first tell you of my observations in what is now my permanent home in Rio de Janeiro. Rio, as we call it, has extended hospitality to a great many of my former countrymen. A great many good Lebanese Muslims live in the city. And a great many other Arab expatriates have made their way there as well. Yet it is a sinful city in which many decadent Western customs and excesses have been allowed to take root. There is crime and criminal activity for which the authorities have been paid to look the other way." Khalil lowered his head and looked at his hands. "My own interests have, I confess, taken advantage of this permissive environment."

"Please don't trouble yourself with this, my friend," the man called Abdul said soothingly. "You are a businessman and the head of your family. You must act accordingly."

"It is more than just business. My father, may his soul rest in peace, has a younger brother who developed a defective heart, and was facing a greatly shortened life due to this ailment. He is my father's only surviving brother and a favored uncle to my brothers and myself. We took him to the best clinics in America and Europe, but they were unable to help. He was indeed a candidate for a heart transplant, but due to his age and condition, he was given low priority for a new organ. I also suspect," Khalil said with some distaste, "that it was because he was Muslim that these Western medical centers rejected him. Yet, he is my father's brother and, in many ways, a father to me. What was I to do?"

"Indeed, what?" al-Rahman offered, watching Yossef Khalil very closely.

"So, I took matters into my own hands. Fortunately, I am a man who is not without resources. Rio is one of the world's leading markets for sale of transplant organs. And there are none of the restrictions and priority protocols found in North America and Europe. There are world-class private clinics and European-trained physicians available to those who can pay. In addition to state-of-the-art medical facilities, the clinics have access to organs, both from those recently deceased and those who, for a fee, will donate one of their redundant organs. For a fee, someone who needs an organ can receive an organ transplant under optimal conditions and performed by some of the best surgeons in the world. This was my experience. My favorite uncle is now my children's favorite great-uncle. For this I thank Allah daily."

Al-Rahman knew where this was going, but he wished to hear it from the Lebanese smuggler. "And how, dear friend, is this of interest to us?"

"If I may be so bold, does the *imam* not suffer from a kidney disorder? It was my understanding from reading the Western press that he is ailing—that his kidneys are not functioning properly and may, in fact, be failing him."

Khalil paused to take a deep breath, then continued. "Much of this is beyond my grasp, and there is no need for me to understand it, but this I do know. Only once in a great while does a leader of the caliber and stature as Osama bin Laden come along. He is vital to our struggle against the West; he is himself the *jihad.* Does his health not mirror the health of our struggle? I come here to offer my services and my resources. If the *imam's* life is indeed dependent on organs that may be failing him, should we not do all in our power to prolong and enhance his life? If it is a question of who to contact, I may be able to help. If it is a question of money, I would be honored to underwrite the cost."

Al-Rahman was silent for several moments. Then, "Yossef Khalil, on behalf of the *imam* himself, I want to thank you for your past support and your gracious offer of future support. What you have proposed is interesting. *Fi complimentary Allah.* [Go in God's protection.] I will think on what you have told me."

That evening, Yossef dined alone and permitted himself a single glass of wine. He played the brief meeting with al-Rahman over and over in is mind, hoping that he had shown the right amount of sincerity and conviction. And he hoped that the story about his uncle was as fully backstopped as Steven Fagan assured him it would be. He felt he had played his role well, yet he instinctively knew that this was a high-stakes game—that these were dangerous men he was dealing with.

Yossef Khalil was on a return flight to London the next day. The morning following his return, he was in a cramped Chelsea flat, on loan from MI6, where he was debriefed by Steven Fagan. There, Fagan heard him out and thanked him for his service.

By the time Khalil left the meeting, the American had made him feel very comfortable, even noble, about the role he was playing. Yossef Khalil knew only that the plan was to get Osama bin Laden to agree to consider a kidney transplant operation and that he, Khalil, would pay for it. Past that, he could only speculate what the CIA and Steven Fagan had in store for the al-Qaeda leader.

CHAPTER FIVE: HOSNI

Dr. Hosni Hasani had two passions in his life—or at least two public passions: medicine and politics. Regarding the former, he was well-trained, well-compensated, and arguably one of the best surgeons to be found outside the United States or Western Europe. He would have been a welcomed addition to the Cleveland or Mayo Clinics or just about anywhere else, including Johns Hopkins, where he completed his residency.

He was a gifted surgeon who specialized in organ transplant operations and practiced this specialty at an exclusive private clinic just outside Cairo—a clinic in which he owned a controlling interest. His clientele was composed primarily of wealthy Arabs from all over the Middle East and Southwest Asia, so he was indeed well compensated. He operated with the oversight and consent of the Egyptian government and the governing medical board, but was often able to sidestep some of the regulations that governed organ donors.

This meant that his activities were closely monitored to ensure those government regulators received a kickback on each operation that was in keeping with the exorbitant fees Doctor Hasani was able to charge.

Regarding his passion for politics, the good doctor was an avowed Islamist, which made him, in the eyes of his Western colleagues, an extremist, as well as something of a racist and a sexist. In his professional life, he was careful, measured, and precise; in his political leanings, he was strident and emotional. He had chafed under the regime of President Hosni Mubarak, but aside from sharing the same given name of the Egyptian strongman, he had performed a liver transplant for the president's sister-in-law, and that afforded him protection for his unwelcome politics and his membership in the Muslim Brotherhood.

Years later, Hasani would welcome the Arab Spring, the Egyptian Revolution, and the election of Mohamed Morsi. A month later, he would protest the ouster of Morsi by the military in favor of a more secular and conservative government.

But while he was not one to hide his Islamist leanings, he stopped just short of allowing it to interfere with his surgery schedule. His heart may have been with the Prophet, but his tastes and lifestyle were what most Muslims would term as Western and decadent. This particularly extended to his appetite for women, which bordered on the insatiable. He was known to keep at least one mistress in a conveniently located apartment.

Hasani was tall and urbane, and carried himself in a self-important and imperial manner. He had wide-set eyes, a Nasser-like nose, and a generous mouth with lips that one might have thought to be the result of Botox treatments. Hasani could seldom pass a mirror without checking his appearance or smoothing his jet-black hair with a manicured hand. He could be pleasant and charming when it served his interests, but universally impatient with those who had to work for him.

Around the hospital and the few outlying clinics where he sometimes practiced, few female staffers were exempt from his unwanted attentions, and those who were not compliant suffered professionally. Dr. Hasani was consistently brilliant in the operating room, and universally disliked outside the OR. His wife and three daughters were pampered, cloistered, and seldom seen in public.

Hasani was returning to his office early in the afternoon, following a successful transplant operation. It was yet another liver transplant, this one for a member of the Sabah clan, the Kuwaiti royal family. The operation had gone without complication, and the fee had been enormous. It was his final procedure of the day, and Hasani was looking forward to a late afternoon rendezvous with one of the new surgical nurses.

When he entered the office, he found three men waiting for him. One man was seated in front of his desk, while the other two stood along the wall. Hasani started to protest, but the sinister expression of the face of the man seated, along with the cruel look of the other two, held him in check.

"Who are you?" he asked evenly in what he hoped was a commanding voice, but it was without force. "And what are you doing here in my office? You have no appointment. What is the meaning of this?"

"If you will please sit down, Doctor, I will be more than happy to explain why we are here, and how you might be of service to Islam and our cause, one to which you are known to be sympathetic."

His speech was precise and polite, but neither the man nor his tone were any less threatening. He was not a large man, but he emanated strength and power. A neatly trimmed goatee and thick black hair, combed straight back, said he gave close attention to his appearance. Only a large mole on his chin marred his regular features. He wore a tailored gray suit with a dark shirt and tie.

Hasani made his way around his desk and slipped into the padded swivel. He glanced quickly to the two men posted along the wall by the door, then turned his attention to the man seated across from him.

"Doctor, my name is Amir Ra, and I am an Egyptian, like yourself. I represent a client who may be in need of your medical expertise. Our principal is a man of much influence and stature. I must also tell you that there are a great many nonbelievers who would like to do him harm, so your confidence in this matter is essential. That is why he sent me on his behalf to meet with you and to arrange for you to examine him personally. Your medical expertise and excellent reputation have brought us here. Naturally, we understand there is a fee for your services, which will not be an issue—for an examination or for any procedure that may be recommended after you have made your examination."

Hasani began to relax; this was familiar territory. Quite often, influential politicians or members of a royal family needed both medical attention and discretion. It was with these *special* patients that Hasani was able to double or even triple his obscene fees. These engagements usually began with a meeting like this, followed by an examination at a local private clinic and a procedure done in the private wing of a medical facility with only limited public access. Many of these special patients wanted their medical needs met at an offshore, remote location.

Hasani reached for his appointment book. "Very well, Mister ah, Ra, let me see what I might have available in the next few…"

Ra's hand moved like a snake. He snatched the desk calendar from Hasani's grasp and gently laid it on the desk. Hasani was struck speechless with the man's quickness and the careful manner in which he returned the object to the desk.

"Doctor Hasani, this particular patient will take priority over all others. Now, we have a private corporate aircraft at Cairo International Airport standing by to fly us to Islamabad, where we will journey by car so you can examine our principal. He is waiting at a well-equipped private clinic. We can be there before first light tomorrow, but only if we leave now."

"You can't be serious," Hasani protested. "I have a surgery schedule; I have no travel documents, no clothes, no medical kit prepared. I'm sorry, but there is just no way . . ."

The man rose and leaned across the desk. "Doctor, your operating schedule will have to be canceled," he said in a low voice that brooked no dissent. "You will need no travel documents, and all else of a personal or medical nature will be provided for you."

Then he bent closer and whispered, "Our principal and your patient is Osama bin Laden."

An hour and a half later, they were airborne and over the Sinai Peninsula, en route to Pakistan. The aircraft, a Gulfstream G4 charter made available by Yossef Khalil, had reached its cruising altitude of 47,000 feet in a matter of minutes. Ra and his two Arab minders were seated forward, near the cockpit, drinking espresso. Hasani was sitting back toward the rear of the aircraft in a well-appointed leather settee.

He was studying a file that contained bin Laden's medical history, although his name was nowhere to be found in the material. It was a classic case of degenerative kidney function, a condition that normally could be managed without replacement surgery, but only up to a point. Because the degeneration was slow, there was no immediate threat to life. But there was no question that the quality of life, and the patient's ability to live an active functioning life, would degrade over time. In its progressive stages, the condition could be treated with dialysis, but those treatments would need to be increasingly frequent and would only delay the inevitable. The patient would grow less vigorous and weaker over time; and, in the end, he would be listless and bedridden.

It was a classic case with classic symptoms. Of course, Hasani would have to examine the patient, but there was usually only one cure; bin Laden needed a replacement kidney to have a normal life. He closed the file and rubbed his weary eyes.

"May I get you something to eat, sir?" the flight attendant asked. "We can offer you poached fish with an assortment of steamed vegetables or breast of chicken with curried rice."

She was Indonesian, with a gracious manner and a nice round bottom. Perhaps on the return trip, Hasani thought. What he really wanted was a double shot of a premium Johnny Walker scotch. Given the patient he was to examine and that the three hard men in the front of the Gulfstream were drinking bottled water, that may have been too much to hope for.

"I'll have the chicken," he replied with a warm smile as he looked up at her. She kept her eyes politely averted as she returned to the galley. He glanced around the lavish interior of the Gulfstream and wished he had not volunteered to wave his fee when he learned the identity of the patient. There was money here. Hasani sighed and went back to the file.

The flight from Cairo to Benazir Bhutto International Airport in Islamabad was just over 3,000 miles and took a little more than five hours. Hasani was able to sleep for the last half of the journey. The Gulfstream was vectored to a strip of hardstand well away from the main passenger terminal and a short distance from the corporate aviation facility.

Two Mercedes SUVs were waiting for them. Hasani was directed to the second vehicle and climbed in the rear seat with Amir Ra; the other two men boarded the first SUV and led the two-car convoy out of the airport.

The journey proved far longer than Hasani would have imagined—as long as their flight time. The first half of the journey was on paved roads. Each time Hasani asked how much longer it would be, Ra curtly informed him only that it would be yet a while to their destination. Hasani was dozing fitfully when the vehicle finally stopped at the gates of a walled compound.

Before Hasani was fully awake, a dark covering was pulled over his head, and they drove on for a short distance. Then, he was helped from the SUV and into a building. The surgeon could only rightly conclude they were somewhere in the mountains of northwest Pakistan, perhaps even eastern Waziristan.

When the hood was removed, Hasani found himself in a white clinical setting with Ra, one of the two security men who had accompanied them from Cairo, and a woman in dark Muslim dress, complete with burka.

"You will wait here, Doctor," Ra said. "Your patient will arrive shortly." Then he and the other man left.

Hasani ignored the woman and made a slow circuit of the room, inspecting the facility. It was a medical exam room with seemingly everything he would need for a complete physical examination.

Despite his inattention to her, the woman in the burka began speaking to Hasani. "My name is Aabidah, Doctor." The woman spoke in perfect modern standard Arabic, with an accent that Hasani couldn't place. "I trained at the Arif Memorial Teaching Hospital in Lahore, and I am a qualified surgical nurse. I am here to assist you as you may direct."

All Hasani could see of her was a quick flash of dark, intelligent eyes.

"Within this compound," she continued, "there is a fully equipped and staffed laboratory to support your examination. We can do urinalysis and blood work on site."

Hasani knew the value of good lab work but left those issues to the technicians. He was a doctor and a surgeon. Hasani found a freshly starched white lab coat and slipped into it.

The nurse pulled on rubber surgical gloves and began to remove instruments from a small sterilization unit and lay them out in a professional manner.

Fifteen minutes later, a second door opened, and a tall man in traditional Arab dress filled the doorway. Hasani drew a sharp breath as the *imam* himself stepped into the room.

Osama bin Laden was a physically imposing figure, close to six foot five inches; and now, after 9/11, he was a mystical one as well. Perhaps the most recognizable figure in the world, certainly in the Muslim world, his presence evoked power and respect. He was also the most wanted man on the planet. Bin Laden was well aware of the effect he had on those he met for the first time, and he used it to good advantage.

He paused for a long moment to allow his personage to be fully appreciated. Then he stepped further into the room as if he were stepping onto a stage. *"As-salamu alaykum,"* [Peace to you.] he said formally, inclining his head in the direction of Hasani. He too ignored the nurse.

For all his experience, training, and polish, Hosni Hasani was totally unprepared to be in the presence of this man. Early on, he had resolved to himself that this was just another patient, and he would treat him accordingly. And subconsciously, he had assumed bin Laden would treat him with the respect and deference that patients normally held for a practitioner of his stature. All this evaporated when bin Laden stepped into the room. Hasani was intimidated and uncharacteristically humble in the al-Qaeda leader's presence—an altogether new and unsettling experience for him. He was at a near-total loss on what to say or do.

Hasani finally managed to speak. "Peace be with you as well, *Imam.*"

For his part, bin Laden found this supplication, especially among educated professionals, somewhat tedious. Yet, he was not without ego and allowed himself a moment to bask in the physician's esteem. Hasani remained rooted in place until bin Laden moved to his side and placed a hand on the shorter man's shoulder.

"Doctor, thank you for making this journey to see me. Now I think we must get on with this as quickly as possible."

Bin Laden was almost as nervous as Hasani, for he was deathly afraid of needles, and he knew full well that blood would have to be drawn. Both the *imam* and the doctor worked to stay in character. Bin Laden tried to appear aloof and reserved, and Hasani tried to carry on in a businesslike and professional manner—especially during his physical examination of bin Laden.

The al-Qaeda leader succeeded better than the doctor. Following the examination, an exhausted Hasani was shown to a motel-like room with a cot and side table, where he slept for six hours.

When he awoke, he was provided a simple breakfast of fruit, flat bread, and labneh—a strained Arab-style yogurt that Hasani would never have touched had he not been so ravenous. He was then led to a small, well-furnished office. A single file folder was resting on the otherwise empty desktop—the lab results and a complete blood panel of his patient.

There was no name on the file. Nor was there a need for one. The report was detailed and well organized, just like the reports he saw daily at his clinic in Cairo. He flicked through the findings with a practiced eye. The tests verified much of what Hasani already knew of this patient and confirmed another issue, one with which he was not unfamiliar, but a complication nonetheless.

"May we interrupt?" Without waiting for an answer, Amir Ra led another man into the room, and they seated themselves across the desk from Hasani. "Doctor Hasani," Ra said formally, addressing the physician, "may I present my colleague, Shakir. He is a close advisor and confidant of the *imam*. He has come to hear from your own lips what you may have learned during your examination of our esteemed leader."

The man Shakir was in fact Abd al-Rahman. Al-Rahman, together with Amir Ra, bin Laden's personal security advisor, were two of bin-Laden's closest and most trusted advisors.

For a moment, Hasani entertained the issue of patient-doctor confidentiality and thought of asking to again meet with bin Laden to discuss his findings, but a glance from one grim face to the other quickly put that notion from his mind. These were two very serious and intimidating men. And Hasani rightly assumed that these two men had a great deal of influence on what bin Laden may or may not elect to do regarding any medical procedure. Yet Hosni Hasani was in his element; he was the doctor.

"The results of my examination and the tests are quite clear. On one hand, the tests confirmed a condition I had anticipated, but the tests also raised another issue." Hasani tapped the folder. "First of all, the *imam* is suffering from kidney disease. His kidneys are only partially functioning. With proper rest, good nutrition, and a modest work schedule, he can function normally—for now. But the condition is progressive. There is no medical cure, and the condition is likely to deteriorate with time. There will be the need for periodic dialysis treatment in the very near future. Over time, he will be less and less able to maintain even a restrictive lifestyle. If not now, certainly in the future, he will be a candidate for an organ transplant operation. Under these conditions, and these only, I might recommend that he be treated with a carefully-monitored dietary regime and some of the new drug therapies that are now available. But there is another issue.

"The *imam* is also suffering from advanced stages of Marfan disease. Marfan disease, or syndrome, is a potentially fatal disorder that is not well understood. It was thought that the American president Abraham Lincoln suffered from Marfan."

Hasani folded his hands on the file and assumed a professorial demeanor before continuing. "Marfan is a genetic disorder that affects the connective tissue. Its most visible signs are skeletal. Those with Marfan are taller than average, with elongated limbs and fingers. It can attack the lungs, heart valves, eyes, and central nervous system. Marfan alone can be combated with drug therapy, and its symptoms can be addressed as they arise. And while there is no known linkage between Marfan and kidney disease, the presence of both puts the *imam* at far greater risk than with either of these maladies alone."

"So, what is the prognosis, Doctor?" al-Rahman interrupted. "And what is your opinion and recommendation?" He knew these self-important doctors could go on forever. He wanted to know what was ahead for their leader and what might be done for him.

"The *imam* can continue on as he is for a short while, maybe even a few years. But, ultimately, one or both of these conditions will cut his life short. Together, they compound the issue. There is no cure for Marfan, but it is treatable. The only cure for kidney disease is a new organ or organs. With a good tissue match and a successful transplant, the health issues that come about from Marfan syndrome can be addressed aggressively, and—with Allah's blessing—there is every chance he will live a long and productive life. Without the transplant, his time is limited—perhaps even severely limited. And his quality of life will not be good. In fact, it will be debilitating and painful."

Hasani paused and, for the first time, spoke from his heart. "For what this great man represents, what he has accomplished, and what he means to his followers, he does not deserve the fate that awaits him if these conditions are left untreated. I strongly recommend that he consider a transplant operation. The sooner the better, while his health is relatively good."

For several moments, no one spoke.

"Very well," al-Rahman said at last. "On behalf of the *imam*, let me thank you for your work and for your medical opinion. But let me ask you one or two further questions. If the decision were made to undergo an organ transplant operation, is that something that is within your medical expertise?" Al-Rahman knew it was, but he wanted to gauge Hasani's response.

"It is well within my medical specialty. Furthermore, I would be more than honored to provide such a service."

Al-Rahman nodded. "And if you were called upon to do this, where would such an operation take place?"

"That is not so easy a question," Hasani hedged. He knew the answer but was hesitant as to how to phrase it for these two men. "It's a matter of the facility, the surgical team, and the donor. Modern drug therapy now allows for a wider range of tissue matching, which increases the donor pool. Finding a suitable donor-tissue match for the *imam* should not be too difficult. If I am to be involved, I would wish to have an assisting physician of my choosing, competent surgical nurses, and an experienced anesthesiologist.

"As for the facility, there are few options outside North America or Europe that I can recommend. The major medical centers in our region that have the equipment and operating theaters, like those in Cairo, Karachi, Kuala Lumpur, or even Tehran, are closely monitored by the government, and both privacy and security may be an issue. Such an important personage would not go unnoticed. You see, it is not just the operation, but I would want to see the *imam* fully on his way to recovery before he is moved from a hospital environment. That means at least a week, perhaps."

"And do you have a more discrete option?" prompted Amir Ra. He leaned forward as he spoke. For him, it was all about the security.

CHAPTER SIX: JANET

Joseph Simpson was seldom in residence, so his suite at the Watergate Apartments was available for planning meetings like this. As much as those assembled this day disliked meetings, sessions of this type were inevitable. When a covert operation moved from concept to the operational planning phase, those involved had to clearly understand their roles and responsibilities. Schedules and timelines had to be developed, site surveys had to be planned, and support technologies had to be developed.

It was now all about the planning and the details. This was not a CIA operation, but it could not be carried out without CIA support. This was the first meeting of the I-4 team and their CIA support cadre. Present at the Watergate from the I-4 were Steven Fagan, Garrett Walker, Janet Brisco, and Bill Owen.

Owen was a rumpled, anemic-looking man who, like Janet Brisco, was in perpetual need of a cigarette. He was average in most ways—medium height, nondescript features, and brown hair that defied the efforts of comb and brush. His movements were furtive and ferret-like, and he often had difficulty making eye contact. He had a hint of a sparse mustache that served only to dirty the space between his nose and his upper lip. His blue oxford dress shirt was on its third day and his suit, which was off the rack, had not seen the dry cleaners in months. The yellow tie looked as if it doubled on occasion as a napkin. Janet Brisco had tried to better assemble him on more than one occasion, but with only temporary success. He always reverted.

Yet he was loyal, hard-working, and versatile. Bill Owen had spent two decades in the backwater of the CIA Science and Technology Directorate, and he was one of the best documents men in the business. Owen joined the I-4 team when some objectionable material was found on his workplace computer—material that his superiors at Langley could not overlook but that Steven Fagan did. He was a master forger, could pick any lock, crack just about any safe, and gain access to almost any building. He could quickly create a security system—or defeat one. And he was a master at the art of facilities management as it applied to covert operations.

A great deal of the mechanics of what Steven Fagan envisioned would be executed by Bill Owen, often without Fagan's having to ask. Owen would be running ahead of the group, solving problems. Both Owen and Fagan knew that I-4 offered Owen a chance, perhaps his only chance, to semi-legally practice his many skills, and this in no small way contributed to Owen's loyalty and work ethic. Bill Owen was the I-4's utility infielder, and a valued member of the team.

The CIA was represented by Malcolm Grey and a communications technician named Brad Gregory, who looked more like a professional football player than a signals-capture expert.

Gregory was six-five and close to three-hundred pounds. He had a bullet head that featured a Marine-style high-and-tight haircut. He wore clear plastic glasses that housed thick lenses, and his clothes seemed to fit him just a might too snugly, as if he wished to be smaller than he was. Gregory had narrow-set eyes, a button nose, and a slight over-bite that combined to give him an unremitting puzzled expression.

But in his field, the transmission and reception of data built on nano-technology architecture and micro-circuitry, he was the best there was in any intelligence service. This big man built small bugs. His great passion in life was making highly capable electronic listening devices in very tiny packages. Brad Gregory had advanced degrees in electrical engineering from Georgia Tech, loved professional wrestling on TV, and hated Edward Snowden.

One of Steven Fagan's overarching concerns in this venture was the integration of I-4 and the CIA. Steven knew he needed both CIA technical support and CIA station support. This support had to be measured and, in as much as possible, be overtly deniable should things come apart. Men like Malcolm Grey and Brad Gregory would be told only what they needed to know to facilitate CIA support. They had both direction and top cover from Jim Watson, at least while he remained the current interim director.

But these were intelligent and perceptive people; they would know what was on the table and the full scope of the intentions of the operation. If, and it was certainly an "if," the initial phases of the operations were successful, then there would be an ongoing need for CIA involvement in data recovery and information analysis.

But for now, the job of Fagan's team and their Langley augmentees was to plan and prepare. And the bulk of that preparation would be in the hands of Janet Brisco.

"Where are we with our survey of Rio?" Fagan asked. He already knew the answer, but the man overseeing this operation wanted everyone to hear it from Janet Brisco so they would all be on the same sheet of music.

"Rio de Janeiro seems to be the perfect city for what we have in mind. It's an ethnically diverse city of more than six million and home to decadence and affluence as well as crime and poverty. It's a reasonably civilized city where most of the residents live well and just about anything can be bought. The corruption is less than in Moscow, but more than might be found in London—probably what you might expect in Chicago or Marseilles.

"I don't want to sound like a travelogue, but it's a charming city, with high rises alongside old-world architecture and some of the world's best beaches. The two signature landmarks—Sugarloaf

Peak overlooking Guanabara Bay and the Christ the Redeemer statue standing atop Corcovado—make it one of the most picturesque urban settings in the world. It's a major tourist destination, for the average vacationer as well as the wealthy, which makes it ideal for both our people and our patient.

"It's one of the easiest major cities to move in and out of with only cursory customs requirements. There are large ethnic communities that live reasonably peaceably beside one another. Among the largest and most successful of these are the Lebanese. There are close to eight million Brazilians of Lebanese descent, with perhaps four hundred thousand of those in Rio alone. Many of them are Christian, but there are sizeable Shia and Sunni populations.

"As for the business of organ transplant procedures, Rio is one of the hubs of the illegal trade. It goes on all over the world, but Rio is where a great many of those who can pay the price go for their organs. They do them all there—heart, lung, kidney, liver, and pancreas. Along with a supply of illegal organs, there is the medical infrastructure to support the trade. Some ten to fifteen thousand illegal transplant operations take place each year worldwide, and about half of them are performed in Rio.

"Our helpful Egyptian doctor goes there three to four times a year. On each of these trips he will perform two to four such operations. He travels there on a tourist visa, and he keeps a small apartment there—as well as a mistress. He operates by day and enjoys the Rio nightlife when he's not in the OR."

Brisco opened a file folder and consulted her notes. "He might be a playboy, but he's a first-class surgeon. In his legal practice, he's recognized as one of the best in the world. As for his illegal operations, he must be just as good. His fee for service is a respectable five-figure number."

"Tell us about the clinic," Steven Fagan prompted.

Brisco opened a second file folder. "The clinic is an interesting setup and probably the key to this operation—no pun intended. It's called the Bonsucesso Private Clinic. It's located in the Bonsucesso neighborhood, a few blocks from the *Hospital Federal de Bonsucesso*, or the Bonsucesso Hospital. This hospital is a fully equipped medical center but, more importantly, is served by nearby laboratories and medical support facilities that also provide services to our clinic.

"It's convenient to Rio International Airport and well away from the other major hospitals clustered around the downtown area. The clinic serves a high-end, highly restricted clientele that can pay for restricted procedures and who want the best care available. Past that, we don't know all that much about them. But it stands to reason that since they deal with special patients in need of nonstandard—sometimes illegal—medical attention, they must be operating with some form of kickback to the local authorities. We need to know a great deal more about them before we can go much further."

"And this is the only clinic that Hosni Hasani uses, correct?"

"That is correct. He has operated at the Bonsucesso Hospital on occasion for legal transplant procedures, but uses this clinic for the more lucrative, illegal transplant operations."

Steven Fagan was silent for a long moment, then, "Janet, how's your Portuguese?"

"Nonexistent," she replied, "but as you know, I'm fluent in Spanish."

"Close enough. I think that we had best take a closer look at this clinic." Fagan then turned to Garrett Walker. "How are you with all this?"

His reasoning for seeking Walker's opinion on this was twofold. Garrett Walker would be tasked with both operational and security responsibilities associated with this venture and would assist Janet Brisco in the planning. Walker also had more than a passing understanding of organ transplant procedures. He himself was an organ donor, having given one of his own kidneys to his twin brother. In fact, it was Fagan's awareness of Walker's ordeal as a donor that had sparked the concept for this bold plan.

"I have no issues with the concept," Walker replied, "but the devil is in the details. We need to know a great deal more about this clinic and their operations."

Two days later, Steven Fagan, Janet Brisco, Garrett Walker, and Bill Owen were aboard a Gulfstream bound for Rio. The aircraft was on permanent charter to the Joseph Simpson Junior Foundation. Fagan was credentialed as John Foster, the personal representative of Joseph Simpson. The others had documents prepared by Bill Owen as foundation staffers who were touring foundation-sponsored free clinics that served the outlying slum areas of Rio de Janeiro. Their legends were fully backstopped within the internal workings of the Joseph Simpson Junior Foundation.

Once airborne out of Miami, each studied a comprehensive file on the Bonsucesso Private Clinic. The clinic took its name from this suburb of Rio, which loosely translated means "good luck." The clinic itself, with nominal Brazilian ownership and staffing, was in fact owned and controlled by a South African consortium that operated similar clinics in Durban and Cape Town, as well as facilities in Bucharest, Beijing, Ho Chi Minh City, and Tel Aviv.

The consortium was a group of transplant surgeons, but the money behind them came from organized crime. The clinics, as in the case of the Bonsucesso Private Clinic, dealt in a range of high-end care for the wealthy, but the organ-transplant component of the business was the one with the biggest profit margin. Interestingly, the activities of these clinics were illegal in all the cities where they operated but Tel Aviv. The universal Israeli national healthcare system pays for organ transplants—legal or illegal.

The foundation Gulfstream landed at Rio de Janeiro International just before 1800. After a bored nod from a Brazilian customs officer, the team piled into a stretch limo and made for the JW Marriott Hotel Rio de Janeiro on the Avenue Atlantica. They were booked into adjoining suites and ordered dinner in.

They gathered in Steven Fagan's suite for the meals, and after the dinner service was removed, they sat around a low table for coffee.

"This is not bad—not bad at all," said Garrett Walker as he gazed out at the sweeping view of the South Atlantic. "But isn't this a little over the top for employees of a nonprofit foundation?"

"It's more for me than for you," Fagan replied matter-of-factly. "More specifically, it's for my status as Joseph Simpson's personal representative. I have business with some folks who need to think I have connections to wealth. But since it's only for a few days, I thought you might as well all enjoy the nice accommodations at the ambassador's expense. Are we straight on our foundation tasks? You comfortable with this, Bill?"

This was Bill Owen's first outing in the field; he would normally be working documents in a laboratory. "I think so. I'll be meeting with some lower functionaries at the Ministry of Health and some customs guys to talk about expediting visas for transient facility and staff that serve in the foundation's clinics. There's also the issue of the handling of drugs for our clinics in the back country. It's being held up on arrival, and not all of it gets to the assigned facilities."

Fagan nodded. The Joseph Simpson Junior Foundation operated free clinics and schools in remote areas of the Amazon Basin. Both Simpson and Fagan were careful to use the Foundation as a cover organization only when necessary or when a pending operation was time critical. And, Fagan reasoned, what better way to maintain a cover legend than to attend to some needed work.

"Garrett?"

"I'll be meeting with an army colonel tasked with internal security and a mid-level official with their Ministry of the Interior. The foundation has no real security issues, as the work of the foundation seems to transcend politics, so I'm just here to press the flesh and see that the ongoing local security arrangements remain in place. The meeting's scheduled for 0900 tomorrow at the municipal building, so I'll be finished late morning."

"And you have the envelopes?" Fagan looked from one to the other. Bill Owen and Garrett Walker both nodded. The cooperation of the Brazilian government had been excellent, yet the only way to ensure that continued support was to make sure the right officials were tipped for their service. Fagan had arranged for those stipends to be delivered by Walker and Owen.

"I'll be taking a cab over to the Bonsucesso area and be on the streets," Janet Brisco said without prompting from Fagan. "Since I'm on a tourist visa, I'll pay a call at the Hospital Federal with a migraine and get a feel for the place. And I'll be looking for an apartment building in the neighborhood that will suit our needs."

Fagan again nodded, taking in all three. They were pros, and there was little to be said. "Very well. You know what we need, so let's get as much information as we can, but don't force an issue. We can always come back or send someone else back. Questions?" There were none. "Okay, we'll convene here tomorrow evening and see where we go from there."

Garrett Walker and Bill Owen rose and headed for their separate quarters. Advance work and the surveys of the primary and support site were both tedious and tiring. Yet the more unknowns that could be resolved ahead of time, the greater the chances were for success. Brisco remained behind in the main salon.

Fagan, sensing she might have something on her mind, saw the others out and closed the door. He was not really a drinker, yet he poured them both a finger of Macallan's and they settled back into a set of plush armchairs. As always, Janet Brisco came right to the point.

"Steven, do you really think we can pull this off? I mean it seems so…so farfetched. I've been a special-operations planner for a lot of years, but I never undertook anything like this. Excuse the expression, but this is some real James Bond shit."

Fagan smiled. "Yes, Janet, I think we can do this. It will be dangerous, though—not physically dangerous, of course, but there are any number of things that can spoil the operation or bring it to a halt. Not all, but a great deal of the risk can be mitigated by careful planning. And that's where you come in. I'm preaching to the choir here, but this will depend not only on good planning, but also on detailed contingency planning—things you're very good at. Our big advantage is that we have the ability and the means to give the opposition what they so desperately want—an extended life for their leader. If we keep that in focus and play to that strength, then it will serve to carry the day. And if we do fail in our primary objective, well, there's always the fallback position."

"Like killing him?"

"Like killing him. And I think we all agree that he deserves to be killed. But that's not what we really want, is it?"

She smiled. "After what he did, killing him is too good for him. But no, Steven. That's not what we want."

―――――――

At 1000 the following morning, Steven Fagan found himself in a palatial office at the Bonsucesso Private Clinic for a scheduled meeting. He was dressed in a lightweight business suit, a short-sleeved linen shirt, and a floral tie. He carried, but did not wear, a straw Panama hat and looked every bit the part he played—the emissary of a wealthy man with a medical issue.

He had introduced himself as Mr. Richards, but in keeping with a deeper cover he would use for this meeting, that was not the name on the passport with which he entered the country. Fagan smiled politely and pushed a business card across the table. It contained only his name, a cell phone, and a post office box in Arlington, Virginia.

The man seated across and behind a substantial mahogany desk took the card and studied it deferentially. He had connections in the Brazilian customs service, so he knew this American by the name on the passport he carried. Such information was made available to him with but a phone call. He also had no issue with addressing him as Mr. Richards or any other name he chose to use for this meeting. For Fernando Almeida, this was a commonplace occurrence.

Almeida was the Bonsucesso Private Clinic's director. He was a polished article, with smoothed-back dark hair and a Boston-Blackie mustache. His muted pinstripe suit would have been suitable at a coronation, the shirt and tie fashionable save for the dated tie-pin bar set in the rounded collar points. At one time, he had been handsome, but he was now rounding poorly into late-middle age, and his jowls had reached a point of no return. Yet he had presence, one of authority more than power. He also had the air of a man who was very careful. Almeida knew how this Richards fellow arrived in Rio and where he had spent the night. It appeared that he was a friend or an associate of Joseph Simpson, who was known to be a very wealthy American. But Almeida had yet to learn his business. Was he here at Joseph Simpson's behest, or was it something else? The passport he traveled under was that of John Foster, and he now called himself Richards. This suggested it was something else. Introductions were made, the two men shook hands, and Fagan was offered a seat.

"First of all, Mister Almeida," Fagan began in a quiet voice, "let me thank you for seeing me on such short notice." This was also expected; people who could pay for the services of Almeida and his clinic did not book appointments too far in advance. "And let me apologize for not speaking your language in your country. May we proceed in English?"

"Of course," Almeida replied with a British public school clip. "A great many of our patients are from English-speaking countries. And all our staff here at the clinic are conversant in English. Now, how may I be of service?"

"I represent a principal who has just been diagnosed with kidney disease, and it appears that he may be a candidate for a transplant operation."

Fagan paused, as if to carefully frame his words.

"Due to his age and some other factors, he may not meet the criteria for a normal donor-recipient procedure in North America. Or, those criteria may not be met in the time remaining to him. That being the case, we are exploring other options."

Another pause.

"It may be inappropriate for me to go into who recommended you or how you came to our attention. Let me just say that we have it on good authority that you have a capable staff and have helped others with this or similar diagnoses. So, given this scant information, perhaps you would be kind enough to let me know if you can help and, if so, perhaps give me a general overview of your services."

"It would give me great pleasure," Almeida purred. "But first, may I offer you a refreshment—tea, coffee, water?"

"A cup of coffee would be fine."

"Excellent." Almeida keyed the intercom and spoke rapidly to someone in the outer office.

Fagan's Portuguese was far less proficient than his Spanish, but he managed to understand the request for coffee, as well as the order to "activate the machine." Fagan was mildly surprised they had not been recorded from the beginning, but his expression gave away nothing.

After the coffee service was delivered, Almeida launched into a practiced detailing of the Bonsucesso Private Clinic's capabilities, enviable medical track record, discretion, and privacy. There was no discussion of fees; it was understood that they would be commensurate with the service.

Steven Fagan listened dispassionately and made a few cryptic notes, not that he needed them, for he too was recording the meeting.

When Almeida was finished, the two men again shook hands. Fagan thanked him for his time and said that he would be in touch. This too was a pattern Fernando Almeida was familiar with. Steven Fagan would call in a few days to begin the preliminaries and to schedule the necessary medical exams, or he would never hear from him again. Almeida had given up trying to guess as to which ones would call and which ones would not. There was simply no way of telling. For those who could pay, there were other willing and capable facilities.

In keeping with his foundation legend, Garrett Walker was meeting with Brazilian military and civilian officials, thanking them for courtesies extended to the Foundation. While the under-the-table gratuities were both welcome and low key, the work of the Joseph Simpson Junior Foundation was well supported on a number of levels. Those whom the Foundation clinics served were appreciative, and the local governments saw the work of the foundation as a service they did not have to provide. So, there was always a police or military presence outside foundation facilities for physical security.

But this support only went so far.

Walker had made it a practice to quietly pass an envelope with cash to the senior policeman he encountered at the front portico of each clinic he visited. At the third of the four clinics on Walker's list, the local police *jefe* somehow knew he was coming and was there to receive his gratuity. Garrett bore them no ill will; that's just how things worked in some parts of the world.

When Walker left the clinic, a quiet man in a shabby business suit followed him up the street and asked if he might have a word with him. The man proffered a police credential, which identified him only as a member of the organized-crimes division of the *policia federal*, but he did not give his name. His attire did not hide from Walker that he was a policeman. He struck Walker as a serious man with a serious agenda. They stepped into a nearby café and found a seat.

"First of all, *senor,* I wish to thank you for the work of the Simpson Foundation. Some of my relatives have been to your clinics, and they have been treated well and responsibly. Your work here is appreciated. But I must warn you of a danger to your facilities here in Rio and indeed all of Brazil. It is the gangs. They respect no one and no enterprise, not even one so worthy as yours. I wish it were in our power to keep them from preying on you; but they are very powerful, and we simply lack the resources to deal with them."

The man gave Walker a card with the name *Alehandro* and a phone number—nothing else. "Please call me if I can be of any service to you, but I must confess that we have had little success in dealing with these gangs. And if they know you are speaking with us, it will go that much harder for you. We will do what we can, but any help we might provide must be very discreet."

He looked down with some embarrassment. "I am sorry that we cannot do more, but in all honesty, we must balance our limited capabilities to deal with these vermin and your safety. I hope you will not take offense at my warning you like this."

"No, not at all, uh…" Walker looked at the card. "…Alehandro. In fact, I appreciate your candor, and I may indeed call you for guidance. I have just a few questions, if I may."

"Of course."

"I understand that, as in many of our North American cities, there are rival gangs. Of the gangs here in Rio, who might be the ones that would prey on our facilities?"

Alehandro did not hesitate. "The *Comando Vermelho*. They are, by far, the most organized and the most vicious—and our most serious problem. Their organization is very decentralized, so it's a neighborhood-by-neighborhood problem. We might be successful in penetrating the *Comando* in one neighborhood and curtailing their operations, only to see another faction in the next neighborhood move into the vacuum. Trust me, *senor*; they are a serious and growing problem."

"So, what do other facilities like ours—the other clinics—do about this?"

The man again looked down. "They pay, *senor*. The more prosperous the clinic, the more they pay. Those that have attempted to negotiate a preferential arrangement or refused to pay have had their facilities burned or had staff kidnaped and held for ransom— or simply murdered."

Walker thanked the policeman, pocketed his card, and left the café. On the way to his next clinic, he thought about the man he had just met. In the best of departments and safest of cities, there were crooked cops. And in the most crime-ridden metropolitan areas, there were good cops. Garrett Walker was an excellent judge of people, and he would wager that Alehandro was one of the good guys.

At about the same time Garrett Walker was greasing the palms of key local officials, Janet Brisco was beginning her site survey in the neighborhood surrounding the Bonsucesso Private Clinic. As she climbed into a cab in front of the Marriott, Janet looked very different from the stylish black woman who had checked into the hotel. Having removed most of her jewelry, she was dressed in a loose skirt, peasant blouse, and sensible sandals. She did not exactly blend in, but a tall, attractive woman of color was not an infrequent sight on the streets of Rio.

She exited the cab a block away from the clinic and casually strolled past the entrance, stopping at a coffee shop across the street and a few doors down. She sat at a sidewalk table, drinking her espresso as she monitored the traffic in and out of the facility. Most of those who came and went did so by car, and a great many of those cars were of the larger, luxury variety rather than the mid- and smaller-size flex-fuel vehicles that could use the ethanol-laden gasoline produced in Brazil. It seemed, she noted, that many of the staff and patrons of the Bonsucesso Clinic could pay up for real gasoline.

After she had finished her coffee, Janet began walking the streets near the clinic, window shopping and stepping into small stores to look at the wares as only a woman can do. When a shop keeper approached, she guardedly offered that a relative was a patient at the clinic and she was waiting for her to complete a minor procedure. She immediately noticed that once it was known she had an association with the clinic, she was treated differently, more deferentially. She was treated like someone who had money.

Later that morning, she stopped by the Bonsucesso Federal Hospital, a full-service medical facility that served the Bonsucesso neighborhood and surrounding area. She complained of a gastroenteritis issue and asked to see a doctor. When she stated that she was an American citizen on a tourist visa and could pay cash, she was seen by a female Cuban-trained doctor after only a short wait.

After a cursory but thorough examination, the doctor recommended the equivalent of Gatorade and told her to only eat hotel food until the symptoms passed. If she suspected that this tall, exceedingly healthy black American woman was faking her condition, she was either too overworked or too polite to comment.

Brisco paid her bill in cash and left the hospital.

The afternoon was spent looking for a nearby furnished apartment, one in a building that had more than one apartment to let. The application of makeup and jewelry had transformed Janet Brisco from a common attractiveness to understated affluence. She was now a commanding presence, one which conveyed the impression of wealth.

Heads turned when she stepped into the rental agency. When she mentioned that a close relative would be coming to the Bonsucesso Clinic for tests and possibly a procedure over the next few months, the rental agent on duty became immediately responsive. The third apartment they visited was a spacious three-bedroom top-floor furnished flat that was a five-minute walk from the clinic. Citing the need for additional rooms for possible visits from extended family, she leased the apartment for three months and paid cash in advance.

When she returned to the Marriott, the team was just assembling for debriefing. As the projected on-scene team leader, Brisco conducted the meeting and kept the meeting notes.

The following day, while Garrett Walker and Bill Owen tracked some additional agenda items for Janet Brisco, she and Steven Fagan visited the American Consulate on President Wilson Avenue. The consulate facility and staff were much bigger than the embassy in Brasilia and conducted the majority of the business of the United States Diplomatic Mission to Brazil.

Once admitted by the Marine guard, they were received by two consular staffers, who immediately escorted them to a sterile room—one that was swept on a periodic basis for audio surveillance. The two visitors were a study in contrast. The tall black woman, who had lost little to middle age, could pass for a model, while the shorter white man looked more like a high school science teacher than an operative on a cloak-and-dagger mission.

Neither of the staffers, both CIA, knew the nature of the business at hand, but they knew to treat these visitors with respect. Jim Watson had seen to that. They said little until they were in the safe room.

"I'm Dell Maxwell," the older of the two men began, "Chief of Station in Brasilia, but I spend most of my time here in Rio—when I'm not in Sao Paulo, that is. This is Tom Gardina, who will be your station liaison while you're here."

Fagan made the introductions for himself and Brisco. While Steven Fagan was a former CIA staffer himself, and known by reputation to both men, they understood that he now headed up a clandestine organization that operated in the shadows. Even as Fagan spoke, the two staffers had a hard time keeping their eyes off Janet Brisco. It was her presence as much as her beauty.

When Fagan had finished his introductions, Maxwell continued. "Steven, we have not met, but you and your work are still talked about at Langley. I have no inkling as to why you are here, but we understand that your business is to be at arms-length from the station and from the U.S. government. That said, Director Watson has told me to give you any and all the help we can, to include technical assistance and physical security should you require it."

As Maxwell spoke, Fagan studied him carefully. The good offices of the CIA station in Brazil had been afforded him at the direction of Jim Watson. That was probably done without prior consultation or discussion with this station chief. As chief of station, Maxwell would comply. Fagan now wished to know if this compliance had Maxwell's personal backing. CIA stations were little fiefdoms, and the chiefs of station had great latitude, or very little latitude, depending on the personality of the COS and the constraints imposed on him by the ambassador.

As if reading Fagan's mind, Maxwell put this issue to rest. "Again, I have no idea why you're here and really don't need to know—or want to know. But understand this: I served two overseas rotations with Jim Watson, and I consider him a mentor and friend. You'll get any support my people here can give you. Tom here is my most experienced case officer, and he will be available twenty-four seven until your business here is concluded. Fair enough?"

"That's more than fair, Dell—and much appreciated. How is your relationship with your chief of mission?" Fagan was now asking how Maxwell and the station got on with the ambassador. CIA station activity was conducted under the sufferance of the American Ambassador. Some ambassadors kept their spooks on a tight leash, while others wanted to know nothing to preserve their ability to deny knowledge. The Brazilian Ambassador was a political appointee, which meant he'd opened his wallet for the sitting president's campaign. He was not a career diplomat; which, in itself, meant little. Yet, all mission personnel, military attaches, and State and CIA staffers all reported to him. And career State Department staffers could be just as obstructive as those with friends in high office.

"My direction from the mission is that all station operations must be cleared with the ambassador's deputy—and anything major with the ambassador herself. But Director Watson has assured me that this is not a station operation, so you are under the radar on his one. So, do your best not to get caught or get me into trouble. I get on fairly well with the ambassador, and I'd like that not to change."

Fagan considered this, as he knew Maxwell was on the spot. Technically, the ambassador was Maxwell's boss and ultimately responsible for all intelligence activity in the country. If something went wrong and the operation blew up causing an embarrassing incident, Maxwell and anyone else involved could be sacked. Jim Watson could give him some top cover, but the influence of an interim director only went so far. Both Maxwell and Gardina, his case officer, were out on a limb. The two CIA staffers knew this, and they knew Steven Fagan knew they knew this. Fagan looked from one man to the other and saw nothing but sincerity and professionalism.

"Dell, I know this puts you at some risk; and, believe me, I appreciate that. And while I can't share the details of this operation, I *can* tell you that it has national strategic implications. We are in your debt."

Maxwell managed a grin. "That's why they pay us the big bucks, right? So tell us what you need and we'll do our best. But again, don't get caught."

Dell Maxwell walked Steven Fagan to the consulate entrance, while Janet Brisco remained behind to confer with Tom Gardina. She had a list of requirements for him in support of the operation. The first of those requirements was a detailed report on the Bonsucesso Private Clinic—its history, its finances, its ownership, and its staff, including anything the station might be able to come up with on one Fernando Almeida.

―――――――――

That evening, Fagan and Brisco had yet another meeting, this time with Yossef Khalil. Khalil had made his way on foot, as instructed, to Fagan's suite at the Marriott.

There was no reason to suspect that Khalil was under surveillance by al-Qaeda operatives, but Bill Owen and Garrett

Walker observed his movements to ensure he wasn't followed. Fagan had been in periodic contact with Khalil and had carefully followed the money trail that, through Yossef Khalil, had funded the Egyptian doctor's trip to Pakistan.

But Khalil himself was not in contact with Hosni Hasani. Nor was he privy to the details of Hasani's diagnosis of Osama bin Laden. But with Hasani's office and cell phone tapped, they knew the doctor was in periodic contact with al-Qaeda Central. They knew that Hasani had been told to prepare for a transplant procedure, but until he was told when, there was little he could do. And the team could only hope that Hasani's choice of Rio would be respected.

Once Khalil had made the offer to fund all costs associated with the procedure, he too could only wait until he was contacted by the man who called himself Abdul. All transportation arrangements, if there were to be any, would be made through him. All this he had relayed to Steven Fagan, which Fagan was able confirm from other sources.

Now, it was a waiting game. Based on al-Rahman's call to Hasani, the decision had been made. But when?

"So," Khalil began as Fagan and Brisco listened intently, "the man Abdul said that I was to await his call, and that if and when a decision was made, he would let me know. I have told him that, while I stand ready and am honored to fund this worthy enterprise, I will need a few days to ensure the funds are available for wire transfer."

"Then there is nothing to be done but await the call," Fagan told Khalil. "Meanwhile, if you need anything or you are contacted, Ms. Brisco here will be your contact here in Rio. She will be remaining here for an indefinite period and managing things on this end. And let's hope the call does not come too soon. We have a great deal of preparation to do if this is to work as we envision it. Do you have any questions for me—for us?"

"I understand the need for restrictions on information. But this man Abdul, or whatever his name is, he is the individual who will make the final decision, yes?"

This was information Khalil did not need for the role he was to play in the venture, but sometimes the sharing of information is a basis for trust. As this was a small piece of information, Fagan felt this was one of those times.

"The man you know as Abdul is Atiyaht Abd al-Rahman, al-Qaeda Central's chief of staff and perhaps the most trusted personal confidant of bin Laden. He makes a great many of the decisions for al-Qaeda. For something of this nature, all arrangements will be made by him or through him. He is key as to whether bin Laden does or does not agree to undergo this procedure. If the al-Qaeda leader is to submit himself to this procedure, you will be hearing from al-Rahman. He uses many names, but for you he will continue to be Abdul."

Khalil did not yet to know what the Americans and Steven Fagan had in store for bin Laden. He assumed they were trying to lure him out of hiding so they could kill or capture him.

CHAPTER SEVEN: ROBERTO

Over the course of the next two weeks, the Bonsucesso Private Clinic came under the quiet scrutiny of the I-4 team, the not inconsiderable research capabilities at the CIA's Langley headquarters, and the CIA station team in Rio de Janeiro. All this information was formatted and sent to Steven Fagan at his home office in Larkspur and to Janet Brisco at her apartment in Rio. While the equipment in Brisco's more portable communications suite was not as capable as that in Fagan's office, it was just as secure. Their shared data file of the target clinic was made safe by highly secure password protocols. They were able to talk over an encrypted Zoom-type link that provided a secure video teleconferencing capability, which they used almost daily.

Until the end of the operation, Brisco's apartment would serve as their command post and headquarters. While they awaited a decision from bin Laden and his personal advisors, they considered how best to penetrate the clinic.

There was discussion of simply buying the clinic by way of making the clinic owners a cash offer they couldn't refuse, but this might alert the clinic staff and those like Doctor Hosni Hasani who used the clinic. New and unknown ownership might not be in keeping with the permissive environment allowed by the current owners.

The key to a good covert operation was to give everyone concerned the impression that all was in order. This applied to before, during, and following the undertaking. While there would be actions taken to accomplish the mission, the least disruption in the day-to-day operation of the facility, the better. And when they were finished, it was essential that the clinic be left undisturbed in their practice, however unsavory or illegal that might be.

The Bonsucesso Private Clinic had to be penetrated, but that needed to be done carefully and unobtrusively. When Fagan and Brisco talked that evening, it was all about how to orchestrate that penetration.

"We'll have to have someone on the inside to facilitate our plan, and the higher they are in the clinic staffing, the better," Brisco began. "Given that we may have to move rather quickly on this, I don't think we have the option of bringing someone in at a senior level. Which leaves us working with someone who's already there, or would have reason to be there for the procedure."

"Or who will be there in some medical capacity when the operation is conducted," Fagan added. "Tell me what we know about our clinic manager, Mister Almeida." Janet Brisco's face filled his plasma screen, life-size and in high definition. Fagan himself was quite clear, but smaller, on her desktop presentation.

"Well, like most men in this city, he's a chauvinist and a pig. He lives in a coastal villa with his second wife, who's fifteen years his junior, and her two children. He had three kids from a previous marriage, but they don't seem to be in the picture. Wife number two was a model, who quickly went to seed after she married Almeida. They now have what seems to be a distant but cordial relationship. He doesn't keep a mistress per se, but he does have an apartment in a high-rise in the city center, where he contracts for companionship with an escort service on a pay-as-you-go basis. He might see one girl for several months, then move on to another. He usually overnights at his apartment once a week, but never more than twice–usually midweek. If the wife knows of this arrangement, she doesn't seem to mind. They are together and are out socially most weekends.

"Financially," Brisco continued, "the guy's got some bucks. He has close to a million dollars U.S. in offshore accounts, and while he has a big mortgage on the trophy house, he makes a very good living. It would seem that his salary is just enough to cover his fixed costs and living expenses, but not enough to feed the offshore funds. Since he doesn't gamble and he has no business interests outside the clinic, I'd say he's taking kickbacks from some of the more well-heeled clinic patients and that those kickbacks are off the books.

"He's not popular with the staff. I've made the acquaintance of a surgical nurse who works there, and we now see each other for coffee a couple of times a week. She says that while the medical staff there is first rate, there is no love lost between the medical staff and the administrative staff. It seems the admin staff, in general, and our Fernando, in particular, make a whole lot more money than the worker bees. And there's no love lost when it comes to the clinical staff and outsiders who contract for operating theaters for special procedures—people like Doctor Hasani. She says that when they come in and set up shop, they pay for the run of the clinic and often disrupt the flow of other clinic services. They're rude and condescending, but they generate a lot of money—very little of which flows down to the staff rank and file."

"So, there's some dissension in the staff," Fagan said, thinking aloud, "and Fernando Almeida might be bribed but not bought. And your nurse acquaintance—might she be recruited?"

Brisco considered this. "Perhaps. I know she's a single mom, and that the daycare service that allows her to work at the clinic takes a big chunk of her salary. She knows I'm down here looking at medical facilities, and I've told her I have a wealthy relative who may want a procedure done here in Rio if for some reason they don't move quickly enough up the donor list in the States. She's a source of information, but I doubt we could count on her to take an active role."

"Stay close to her for now," Fagan said, "and stay in character about your relative who may be coming there for a procedure. Learn what you can about the clinic contracts for services that fall outside the duties of the clinic medical staff. For this operation to work, we will definitely have to have a presence in the OR—and, for a short period of time, be in control of the procedure in question." He paused a moment in thought and then continued, "How are things working out with the station there?"

"Very well. As a matter of fact, I'm having dinner with Tom Gardina this evening. I've given him a list of requirements, and we'll see what he comes up with. We're going to a really posh place, so if he comes through, I might even pick up the tab."

"Do what you think is necessary," Fagan smiled, "about the tab I mean."

Tom Gardina was waiting at the table when Janet Brisco arrived. The L'Etoile was in the Sheraton, just off Av Niemeyer. The setting was elegant, the food passable, and the prices were well above what an embassy staffer might pay for a night out. It was late for an American evening meal, about 2100, but early for the upscale Brazilian dining crowd.

Gardina rose as the maître d' seated Brisco on the opposite side of the small private table. He was looking north and she south, but both had a splendid view of the South Atlantic. Every male head had followed her as she crossed the room to join him. Men in Rio don't simply stare—they leer. And they do so conspicuously.

"I hope I haven't kept you waiting," she said as the maître d' lingered at the table to drape a crisp white cloth napkin across her lap.

"Not at all," Gardina replied. "And you look spectacular, by the way."

She smiled. "And you clean up pretty well yourself."

Tom Gardina was thirty-six, and had been a working case officer at the CIA's Latin American division for the better part of the last twelve years. Following a tour at the large station in Mexico City, he escaped farther south, with previous postings in Bogota and Montevideo. After an ill-timed marriage to a State Department cultural attaché that lasted only a few years, he had lived the life of an expat bachelor and seldom took the Agency up on the annual six weeks of home leave that was his due.

Gardina was smallish in stature, with dark hair to match his dark eyes and an open, engaging smile. He had good shoulders, a quick wit, and the refined manners of an aristocrat—a carryover from his boarding school days.

As with many career intelligence officers, his father had been a spy—a denied-area operative who ran agents across Eastern Europe during the Cold War. For most of that time he was away at school in England. Gardina's grandfather had been a Jedburgh agent in the OSS and had parachuted into occupied France during World War II.

Intelligence work was in his blood. He spoke several languages, and he enjoyed his work, which he was very good at. And as an American living in Rio, he seldom wanted for female companionship. Tom Gardina, was not a womanizer, but he did love women. More than that, he appreciated and valued them.

Janet Brisco knew all this, as she had read excerpts from his agency 201 file, which Steven Fagan had somehow managed to pass along to her. For both Gardina and Brisco, this was business; but both enjoyed good food, good wine, and interesting company. Both knew not to mix business with the wrong kind of pleasure, and each could draw the line, sharply if need be. Instinctively, they both knew this of the other, so they were both companionable and relaxed.

Following a hearts-of-lettuce salad for two, escargot, trout Almondine for her and a poached Atlantic salmon for him, accompanied by a brisk Argentinian pinot gris, they took their sorbet with an excellent tawny port. With his permission, she lit a cigarette over coffee. To her surprise and approval, he produced a Cuban after-dinner Robusto. With some amusement, she watched as he carefully prepared, trimmed, and lit the cigar. They smoked in companionable silence for several minutes.

"God, do I ever miss a cigarette after a good meal. This must be the only place on the planet where you can smoke after you eat."

"It's one of the small compensations for being cast away in this remote part of the world." But there was laughter in his eyes as he spoke. Then he leaned forward, rolling the tip of his Cuban in the porcelain ash tray. A quiet but powerful ventilation system silently lifted the smoke toward the ceiling. "I have most of the information you requested," he said, touching the breast of his sports coat, "and the rest of it I can have to you by week's end. On the priority end of things, I was able to get a good workup of the physicians that assist our friend Hasani when he's in town.

"Both are employed or semi-employed at the Federal Bonsucesso Hospital. One is a staff anesthesiologist who does freelance at the clinic when Hasani's in Rio. He's a journeyman gas-passer who has a solid record at the hospital and is generally well thought of in his specialty. The other one is something of a wild card. He's a vascular surgeon with excellent credentials, having received his medical training at the University of Missouri. And he had a pretty good practice until he was sued for malpractice about ten years ago. He settled out of court, but his license was suspended for a year. It appears he has, or at least had, a cocaine problem."

Gardina took a moment to draw on his cigar, which burned with a pleasant aroma and a fine, even white ash. Brisco took out another cigarette, which he lit for her before continuing.

"I have a contact who's a hospital administrator and knows the guy. His name is Roberto de Silva. He now pretty much makes his living as a surgeon assistant. From what my friend says, he's a talented surgeon, but nobody really trusts him. The area hospitals won't let him operate as the primary surgeon. From what you've told me about our Doctor Hasani, this all makes sense. Hasani needs a good anesthesiologist; it's a job he can't do while he's operating. So, he'll pay up for the anesthesia work. But the assisting physician is really just a glorified surgical nurse and, under normal circumstances, will do little more than be an extra set of hands and maybe close the incisions. Since de Silva's competent and cheap, Hasani probably bills out for a front-line backup surgeon and pockets the difference. And our Egyptian doctor probably figures that there's no one in his league anyway. Guys like him think there's nothing they can't handle on their own. The backup is just for window dressing."

Brisco considered this. "All this is in the material you have for me?"

Gardina nodded as he took a fat envelope from his inside pocket and slid it quietly across the table.

"Thanks, Tom. And let me ask you something since you do this for a living. You think this de Silva might be turned or act under instruction?"

Gardina sent a perfect smoke ring skyward as he thought about it. "I'd say there might be a good chance of that. The good news might be that he may have an addiction—and that costs money, even in Brazil. And the bad news might be that he has an addiction, and addicts are unpredictable. But let me do some more work on him. Let's see how he's living, and what angle we might use. Or he might be straight. I have some feelers out, and whatever else I learn, I'll pass along."

They left together and parted in the parking lot, Brisco to her flat near the clinic and Gardina for a club and a nightcap. The maître de had watched them closely during the evening. He had taken the woman for an upscale call girl from one of the better escort services, and that was confirmed in his thinking when the man discreetly passed her a thick envelope. But then, it was she who took the bill from the table and paid in cash with a very generous tip. She must, he thought with an appreciative smile, work for a full-service service.

Within two days, those at CIA and at I-4 who were very good with computers had assembled an impressive file on Doctor Roberto de Silva.

And Tom Gardina continued to work the issue. De Silva was the only son of a Brazilian planter. His mother was German, and the family had lived well, sending Roberto to only the best schools. He had seldom lasted longer than a semester before he was kicked out for one infraction or another.

He was bright, lazy, and arrogant. The only thing at which he had excelled was playing polo and chasing women. He bore a striking resemblance to the actor Andy Garcia, which he had traded on in his dress and hair style. He had been both spoiled and indulged.

He might have continued in his ways—at best, marrying well or, at worst, becoming yet another Rio de Janeiro lounge lizard— but for a courageous stand by his parents. When they told him that they would no longer stand behind him when he got into trouble, Roberto didn't believe them.

He had just turned eighteen when he was picked up for drunk driving and found with a large quantity of marijuana. While sitting in a holding cell, waiting for his father to post his bail and take him home, he had been removed by two gendarmes and taken out back. After a through beating, he was chained to a line of large sweaty men, marched aboard an old school bus, and taken to the interior for six months of hard labor. When he asked for redress or complained, he was beaten again.

When his parents did come to claim him after his parole, they found him a changed boy—or rather a changed man. It was not until years later that Roberto learned that it was his father who had prevailed on a senior magistrate to have him sent away without a hearing or due process.

Roberto wanted no part of another trip to the work farm or the Brazilian justice system, so he had gone back to his studies with a will. Following two years at Federal University of Rio de Janeiro, where he had earned top marks, he was accepted into the pre-med program at the University of Missouri.

Following medical school at Missouri and a residency in vascular surgery at UCLA, he had returned to Sao Paulo, where he went into practice. The pay was exceptional for vascular surgeons in beauty-conscious Brazil, where he earned more for stripping out varicose veins than for the more medically demanding, internal circulatory work.

In Sao Paulo, he had quickly fallen in with the polo set, and had begun to attend anything-goes parties with an affluent crowd. And he had begun to use cocaine. Everyone did. De Silva didn't really have an addictive personality and was only a weekend user. But after a sleepover while he was on call, he had taken a line just to get himself straight—and then the hospital called. He had known he shouldn't take the case, but he had taken it anyway. It was a simple procedure, but the patient died. The inquiry found that he had not been at fault for the patient's death; it was the administration of the wrong drug on the part of the hospital pharmacy. But he had tested positive for cocaine, and was suspended from practice for a year.

Following the suspension, he had moved back to Rio de Janeiro where he was less well-known in the medical community. Since then, he had managed to find work as a contract physician, but he now made less than a quarter of what he had before the suspension. Doctor Roberto de Silva was flawed merchandise, and no hospital would hire him on staff or permit him to operate as the primary surgeon.

As the information on Roberto de Silva came in, Steven Fagan, Janet Brisco, and Tom Gardina digested it. It was learned that de Silva had developed a drinking problem, but following a traffic stop, he had been let off with a warning in exchange for a five-hundred-real note, about a hundred and twenty-five dollars U.S. As if remembering his penal-farm days, he had joined an Alcoholics Anonymous group in Rio, the English-speaking Ipanema Group.

Upon learning this, Brisco attended an Ipanema AA meeting and managed to catch Roberto's eye. A broad smile was all it took for him to seek her out following the meeting.

He was delighted when she suggested a cup of coffee. She found him charming, affable, and willing to talk about himself. When he asked about her and her reasons for being in Brazil, she told him a partial truth, that she worked for a wealthy individual and was in Brazil to explore the possibility of an organ transplant operation. At the mention of this, he offered nothing and his body language suggested it was a topic he had no interest in pursuing.

He asked to see her again, and they exchanged cell phone numbers. Brisco told him that she was fine with coffee, but that she was in a relationship back in the States. He seemed to accept this, and they parted on good terms. That night, she and Fagan talked about this at length over their secure Zoom connection.

"We have a good deal of background on de Silva," Fagan offered after they'd talked for a while. "We know he seems to have his demons under control, at least for now. Given what you've said, it would seem that he's our best hope for getting a surrogate into the operating room, and one involved with the procedure. What would make him want to work with us on this? What might we offer him that would elicit his cooperation?"

Brisco considered this. "He didn't say as much, but he didn't really want to talk about his work. We talked about everything else—soccer, polo, music, even politics. When he said he was a doctor and I told him why I was in Rio, he definitely became uncomfortable. When I asked about which hospitals were the best, he said they were all about the same. He did offer that, while the laws regarding organ transplants in Brazil were less strict than in the United States, it was still illegal to contract for a procedure outside the system.

"Still, he really didn't seem to want to talk about his work. And he didn't ask me any questions about the needs of my patient or what contacts I had made in the local medical community. I got almost the same negative reaction from him when I ask about his parents. He said he sees little of them. From what I understand about those in AA, there are certain topics that they wish not to discuss, so I said no more about it. When we moved on, he seemed relieved and became more comfortable. He's a nice guy, but there's something going on there—something I can't put my finger on."

Fagan thought about this for several moments. "Continue to go to AA meetings and keep his number handy. If we have to move quickly on this, Doctor de Silva may be our best avenue into the OR."

They talked for another half hour before they signed off.

Yossef Khalil was at his desk in his office in Rio, attending to some shipping manifests, when the call came in. The caller, who identified himself as Abdul, was cryptic and to the point, asking if he was still prepared to underwrite the procedure for their mutual acquaintance. Khalil told the voice at the other end of the phone that he was both honored and willing. The caller told him he would be in touch regarding details and arrangements. Following the call, he immediately texted Steven Fagan.

Then a caller, with the same voice print as Abdul, but who called himself Shakir, contacted Doctor Hosni Hasani and told him to schedule the procedure to take place some four to six weeks in the future. Shakier told Hasani to let him know once he had a firm date.

With this call, Atiyaht Abd al-Rahman had confirmed that bin Laden was prepared to undergo the transplant procedure. They now had a timeline window to work with.

When Hasani cryptically brought up the issue of a donor, he was informed that this had been arranged and he need not concern himself with that.

On this occasion, Steven Fagan took a circuitous route to get to Brazil. He left Larkspur early and caught a flight from San Francisco International for St. Louis. Following an overnight in University City, Missouri, and a two-day layover in Washington to meet with Malcolm Grey and Brad Gregory, he had time for a late dinner with Jim Watson.

The next day, he boarded a nonstop flight from Dulles International to Rio de Janeiro. On this trip, he traveled under the name of Clark Richards, a freelance security consultant with close ties to Lloyds of London. His credentials and legend had been created and fully backstopped by Bill Owen. He was met by Garrett Walker, who had taken an earlier flight to Rio. Walker tossed Steven's bags into the back of the rental car, and they set off for Janet Brisco's apartment in the Bonsucesso District.

Brisco had booked a couple of one-bedroom units in the same building for Fagan and Walker, plus a third for whoever might need it. After the two travelers dumped their bags in their rooms, they made their way to her more spacious apartment. She had a generous platter of pastel (a deep-fried pastry stuffed with cheese, chicken, and shredded pork) waiting for them. There was also an iced bucket of Eisenbahn Pale Ale. The three of them gathered around a small table in the kitchen of her flat.

"Since you may be down here for an extended period of time," she began, loading their plates, "I thought you might try some local fare."

The three of them tucked into the pastel, which tasted not unlike Chinese spring rolls, and savored one of the better Brazilian beers.

When they had finished, Brisco cleared the plates and leftovers, and served coffee. Then, she sat in the window casing, near the open screen, so she could smoke yet listen to what Fagan had to say. If this bothered him or Walker, neither said so.

"As you both know, we're now three to five weeks out from this taking place. Langley has the technical end of things well in hand and will be able to bring their support team down here when we need them, but we won't need them unless we can establish the kind of presence we need at the Bonsucesso Private Clinic. This means a presence in the form of security augmentation, which shouldn't present too much of an issue, and a presence in the operating theater, which is more problematic."

Fagan consulted his notes. "Our friend, the Egyptian doctor, has just booked space in the clinic, or I should say a wing of the clinic, for ten days—beginning twenty-five days from today. That means we have no more than three weeks to get our house in order if we're to pull this off.

"The first order of business is Roberto de Silva. We know from taps on Doctor Hasani's email server that Hasani has alerted de Silva that he wants him in attendance for this operation. Our medical consultants have told us that a patient will normally arrive two or three days in advance of this kind of procedure. Hasani will want to examine him prior to the operation and get some antibiotics into his system, as well as meds that will lower the chance of tissue rejection—antigens I think they call them."

"And what of the donor?" Walker asked. He knew all too well that this kind of procedure was, in many respects, more difficult for the organ donor than for the recipient. "We know our guy is not on any donor list, so I assume the kidney he needs is being procured locally on the black market. Might the issue of the donor be a local security consideration?"

Steven Fagan was silent a moment before answering. "It will not be a security issue, or at least not a local security issue. It seems that he's to bring his own donor with him."

"How's that?" Walker asked, a little louder than he had intended.

"According to our phone taps, a donor from Pakistan has already been to Hasani's office for type and tissue matching. The lab reports confirm that he is a suitable donor—that and the fact that he is a true believer. He will accompany bin Laden and provide him with not one—but two kidneys."

"What!"

"Yeah, what?" echoed Brisco. "Garrett's the expert here, but a guy can't get too far with no kidneys."

"No, he can't," Fagan said quietly, "but that decision is not up to us. Hasani raised the same issue with both the donor and al-Rhaman. The donor's willing to make the sacrifice and al-Rhaman made it clear that, given the risks associated with the journey and the procedure, and the value of the patient, two kidneys are better than one."

Garrett Walker sat back in silence; not Brisco. "Can we do this? Can we even be a part of it? I mean, we're essentially helping this 'true believer' end his life."

Fagan answered in a measured tone. "We can, and we will. If this guy didn't volunteer to surrender his kidneys for the cause, he'd probably walk into a crowded bazaar in downtown Lahore with explosives strapped to his body. Sorry, Janet—and you too Garrett; but there's just too much at stake here. If the organs are provided internally, then that's just one more consideration we don't have to contend with. What happens to the donor after he's done his job is not our concern."

They were all silent for a moment before Steven continued. "There are any number of things at issue here, and the role of the donor is just one of them. The other side seems to have solved that for us. Let's get back to the matter of de Silva. Where are we with him?"

"There's an AA meeting tomorrow, and I can only assume he'll be there. Or I can call him if need be. I have his contact number."

"Call him and arrange to meet him somewhere the three of us can have a private conversation—and the sooner the better. I think we have to go straight at de Silva and seek his help with this. Our ability to pull this off will depend on his cooperation. I've done some background work on him, and I think there may be a way to gain his cooperation. If not, we need to know that as soon as possible."

Fagan went on to tell them of his brief visit to the University of Missouri and of his meetings with Roberto de Silva's professors and his academic advisor. "We're certainly in no position to make him an offer he can't refuse, but we can certainly offer him something that he seems to desperately want."

"What if he turns us down?"

"Then we come up with another plan. Or the chartered jet that is to bring bin Laden to Brazil makes a stop at Guantanamo Bay, Cuba. But let's see what we can do to gain his cooperation of his own accord."

Janet Brisco had called Roberto de Silva and asked if he could meet her for coffee. He had been seemingly glad to hear from her, and they had agreed to meet at this outdoor bistro not far from the Bonsucesso Hospital. It was an open-air establishment, with a wide scattering of tables across a flagstone patio protected by a forest of colorful Ciao umbrellas.

The lunch crowd was still an hour away, and there were but a few lingering over a late breakfast. They both ordered espresso.

He was dressed in jeans, polo shirt, and a faded linen sports jacket. His dark eyes were bisected by a nose that was only a little too large for his face and saved from disproportion by generous lips and a wide smile. He sported a dense three-day-growth beard that was the fashion. There was a gentle din from the passing traffic, so they had to lean close to speak.

"You know," Brisco said as he sipped his coffee, "you really *do* look like Andy Garcia."

De Silva flashed an easy grin. He had even teeth that had seen orthodontic attention, but were now just starting to yellow. "So I've been told. I hope that's not a bad thing."

"No, it's not, Roberto." Brisco then turned serious. "But I have a confession to make. It seems I'm something of an actor myself."

He regarded her questioningly.

"It seems that I'm not exactly who I said I was. I have a friend who will be joining us, and I'll leave it to him to explain it to you."

At that moment, Steven Fagan approached the table and very politely asked to join them. De Silva started to rise, but Fagan placed a gentle hand on his shoulder to encourage him to remain seated.

He and Brisco had talked at length about how to approach the young doctor. Both agreed there was an element of chance to what Fagan had in mind, but that it was best to be straightforward with de Silva. Brisco was a little more than worried about how this was to turn out, but her apprehension was quickly dispelled as she watched Fagan work.

The Steven Fagan who approached the table and took his seat was not the same man who had briefed Brisco and Walker the previous evening, nor the same man they had met with that morning to go over plans for this meeting. He was dressed the same and had done nothing to alter his appearance; but, somehow, he *was* now different. He was more disheveled, more professorial, and more approachable. Brisco had seen this a time or two before, this re-emergence of the covert-action spymaster. It was like watching a concertmaster take the podium. She made brief introductions and then fell silent.

"Roberto," Fagan began, as he imperceptibly moved his chair a little closer to de Silva, "my apologies for this intrusion, and for this little subterfuge." He gave the young doctor a genuine, disarming smile. "Janet here has told me a little about you, but I wanted to meet you personally and present an idea. A few days ago, I met with Professor O'Gara and Doctor Kaplan in St. Louis, and they told me something about you. They spoke highly of you and of your time there at the University of Missouri, and of your considerable medical skills. Roberto, I need your help; we need your help. Both Janet and I work for a multinational organization that is dedicated to fighting terrorism on a global basis. Let me tell you about some of the things we have done, why we are here in Rio, and how you might be able to help us if, of course, you choose to do so."

For the next twenty minutes, Fagan outlined the parameters of what they were planning and the difficulties they faced if they were going to bring it to a successful conclusion. De Silva listened without interruption. Leaving out the donor issue and the security considerations, there was nothing unethical about the procedure, nor would he be asked to do anything he had not done previously during similar such procedures. It was tacitly illegal—but common practice. His role would change little under this arrangement; he would be assisting as necessary and helping with closing the incisions.

Brisco, while not in Fagan's league, was nonetheless very good at reading people. She watched de Silva carefully and saw him go from wariness and apprehension to relaxation and even understanding.

"For your assistance in this matter," Fagan continued, "I might be of service to you. I am aware of the circumstances that led to the suspension of your medical license and the restrictions that are still imposed on you. Janet has told me that you've worked very hard to put that behind you. And we think you deserve to have that behind you. If you would like to come to the United States to practice, we are in a position to help with that. You would be fully credentialed and board certified, so long as you continue with your twelve-step recovery program. You would also have the funds to set up a new life and the recommendations that would allow you to enter group practice as a fully accredited surgeon."

De Silva considered this for a long moment. "You can do all this?" he asked.

"We can," Fagan replied with great assurance. At this point, he knew he had him, but his demeanor remained unchanged. "And you would be helping to deal a blow against those who would bring terror to your country and mine."

"May I know the name of this person who will be coming here for an organ transplant?"

Fagan knew this was coming, as did Brisco. He looked to her and nodded gravely. It was then that Brisco leaned very close to de Silva.

"You will be assisting in a kidney transplant for Osama bin Laden."

De Silva's eyes widened, but he said nothing for several moments. Then, "And how is this to help in the fight against terrorism?"

Fagan gave him a concerned look. "We have trusted you by giving you his name. That seemed only fair. But now you will have to trust that we have plans for Mister bin Laden other than just this medical procedure."

There was another long pause. Then de Silva smiled and slowly nodded his head. Then to Janet Brisco, "I hope all this doesn't mean you won't have dinner with me tonight."

The following morning, Steven Fagan and Yossef Khalil presented themselves at the foyer of the Bonsucesso Private Clinic. They were expected, and it was Fernando Almeida himself who met and greeted them, then led them back to his office.

This time, rather than retreating behind his desk, he seated them around a comfortable sofa arrangement just across from it. An elegant coffee service was already in place.

The arrangements for the procedure of this yet-unknown important personage had been made by Doctor Hosni Hasani. They were much the same as those made for previous procedures; but, this time, an entire wing of the clinic had been set aside as an inpatient residence for the duration of the visit.

This was unprecedented—unprecedented and not inexpensive. Hasani had made it clear that the cost of this procedure would be the responsibility of Yossef Khalil, and indeed, Khalil had already wired a substantial sum of money to the clinic's offshore account. If Almeida was surprised to see the American Mr. Richards, aka John Foster, appear with Khalil for the meeting, he did not show it. People with money enough to pay for accommodation and anonymity often did things that were not to be questioned.

"We have Doctor Hasani's instructions and operating theater requirements in place," Almeida began, "and the space he requested for your patient will be made available. Is there any other way we may be of service?"

Fernando Almeida did not ask the identity of the patient, nor would he. Many of these clandestine, quasi-illegal procedures that were the life blood of this clinic involved patients arriving, receiving treatment, and leaving without their name being spoken aloud. The clinic senior medical and administrative staff quite often learned of their identity through clinic gossip or recognition, but respect for patient confidentiality was a prime directive of the clinic—for those special patients who could pay.

"There is," Khalil replied. "It is my foremost intention to secure the best medical care available for this very special client. I know your fine clinic, and Doctor Hasani's skill, can provide those services. My client, your patient, wishes to have an undisturbed visit to your city. By undisturbed, I mean quiet, uneventful, and secure. We have reserved a large space here at your facility for him and his security staff. In addition to that, I have retained Mister Richards here to provide additional security. We understand that this is a medical facility and not a fortress, so we will do our best to make these security arrangements as nonintrusive as possible."

Khalil then turned and handed the conversation over to Fagan. "Mister Richards?"

"Thank you," Fagan began. "Again, there will be two levels of security in place. The first is that which the patient will bring with him. These are trusted retainers from his regional origins and men with whom he is comfortable. The second level of security will be that which I and my small staff will provide. These redundant precautions may seem excessive, but they are what we feel is necessary.

"Those who will accompany the patient when he arrives will focus on his personal safety requirements while he is at your facility. My staff is familiar with the local security picture. While my responsibilities will be primarily external, I will ask that two of my people be attached to your staff. One is a fully qualified physician who will take no part in the operation, but who we want in the operating theater. The other is a man who, among other things, is a capable handyman and can be assigned duties on your maintenance staff. He will quietly oversee the duties of the patient's personal security detail."

Over the years, Almeida had been forced to indulge a great many security and privacy arrangements, but this taking on of additional staff, staff that he had not vetted, seemed excessive. He was about to say so, but Khalil intervened.

"*Senor*, I understand that these arrangements must seem a little extraordinary. They do to me as well. Yet, it is necessary. The services of Mister Richards here are at the behest of the company that insures the life of your patient—a policy that insures his life against those who would do him intentional physical harm. This policy does not extend to this medical procedure, a voluntary procedure that carries its own risks."

Khalil removed an envelope from his inside jacket pocket and laid it on the low table. "We understand that this creates inconveniences, but please understand that they will be minimal and will not interfere with the operation of your clinic."

Almeida nodded sagely in understanding; insurance considerations were something he knew about.

The three men then proceeded to discuss other details of the upcoming visit and the protocols that would accompany the procedure.

Almeida then took Fagan and Khalil on a tour of the clinic and the areas that would be reserved for their patient during his visit. After he saw them back to the clinic foyer and bid them good day, he made his way back to his office.

There was a trace of quickness to his step as he hurried to check the contents of the envelope Yossef Khalil had left behind.

———

A few days later, Garrett Walker presented himself to the Bonsucesso Clinic maintenance supervisor. When asked for his papers, he just shrugged and offered, in his broken Portuguese, that he had none.

Yet another Colombian expat looking for work, the supervisor assumed, and explained in Spanish the new man's duties. He did wonder why the clinic director insisted that he hire this man, a man who, except for his dress, looked very fit and capable—but he gave it only a quick second thought. Probably a relative of one of his mistresses, he thought. The new man seemed bright enough and picked up what was expected of him in short order.

At yet another private clinic just outside of Reston, Virginia, this one a very small clinic, a suite of rooms had been reserved by the deputy director of operations and fitted with sophisticated cyber-lock, complete with keypad and palm reader. The clinic itself had only nominal cover, and it was generally known, but not advertised, that it was a clinic owned and operated by the government—specifically the CIA.

The clinic primarily dealt with psychological disorders and drug and alcohol addictions among senior staff, conditions that those afflicted did not want to take to the ample medical facility at Langley on a walk-in basis. Alcohol claimed a lot more case officers during the Cold War than KGB assassins.

Behind the security door, in a room fully outfitted for surgery, Doctor Grace Davidson labored over the prostrate form on the operating table. She was gowned head to foot, and her face covered with a surgical mask. A sophisticated set of optics sat perched on her nose, with two long, narrow cylinders whose focal point was eighteen inches in front of her.

She straightened and took a deep breath while an attending nurse mopped her brow, then went back to work on the exposed spine before her. The flaps of epidermal tissue, exposing portions of the spine and the kidneys, were held back by clamps. The procedure had begun with the patient in much the same condition as he was now, save for the additional incisions she had made to either side of the spine. It was along these two incisions, one three inches and the other closer to four, where she worked. She worked from a schematic she had committed to memory, like a speaker who used a short outline of bullet points to stay in sequence.

The procedure was new to her, but the mechanics of movement were not. She was a skilled surgeon who specialized in spinal procedures. Grace Davidson knew her way around a backbone. She could move from one vertebra to the next like a UN translator from Spanish to English. Her hands flew over the prostrate spine for several more minutes before she again straightened, holding both hands in the air. They were slick with what appeared to be blood and tissue fragments.

"Done," she called. Then, "*Time?*"

"Twenty-one minutes," said the man with the clipboard and stopwatch.

"*Damn.* I thought sure we were under twenty. Let's try it again."

She pulled off her mask, cap, and gloves and slumped into a folding chair back along the far wall.

Meanwhile, the nurse, who in this case was Brad Gregory, and another technician inspected the surgical implants. After Gregory pronounced them properly in place, they began to remove the two dummy devices from the surgical manikin and prepare both the implants and the manikin for the next operation.

This would take a while.

Then, Gregory came over, handed her a cup of coffee, and lowered his considerable bulk on the folding chair next to her. "You're getting better," he offered. "I can see it as I watch you work, and your times are coming down."

"Yeah, but I'm not going to get much faster. I know the sequence and the movements, but the mechanics of what has to take place simply takes a certain amount of time. I can create a shortcut here and there, but shunting a nerve is shunting a nerve—it's a step in the process that, however refined, cannot be rushed past a certain point. I can probably get this under twenty minutes but not much more than that."

"Okay," Gregory replied, "what might we do to the devices that could speed up your time for getting them into position? After all, we designed them for size and operational capability, not necessarily around the requirements of a surgical implant."

For the next half hour, they talked about the mechanics of the medical procedure and the placement, wiring, and attachments associated with the two implants. Gregory began to think like a surgeon and Davidson began to think like an electronics technician. They finally agreed that there were a few things they could change, things they could not, and others that they could *try*, to see if they would work.

"Let me get back to the lab and make a few of these adjustments" Gregory said. " I'll make sure they will work real-time, then let's try again tomorrow."

They agreed and began to clean up the operating room. Except for the equipment that created sterile conditions, the anesthesia apparatus, and the life-support monitors, it was identical to the real thing.

The next morning, with only minor modification to the implants and their inter-connectivity, and some refinement to her surgical techniques, Grace Davidson did the procedure in sixteen and a half minutes—just a minute and a half over their goal of fifteen minutes.

Grace Davidson was a Harvard-trained neurosurgeon who specialized in spinal work. She was cleared and vetted by the CIA. Doctor Davidson was often sent referrals from the Agency, referrals whose fee-for-service arrangements were off the books and whose identity was never revealed to her.

Not that that mattered, as Davidson had a very lucrative practice as a partner in an upscale Bethesda medical group. They took no Medicare patients and operated a strictly private, concierge medical practice. Grace was forty-something, childless, attractive, and a committed patron of the arts. She lived in a small but fashionable home in Chevy Chase, one that had seemed all too large ever since her husband was killed in the north tower while he was there on business on 9/11.

One night a few weeks back, she had been visited by Steven Fagan, who quietly told her the story—the entire story. She immediately took a leave of absence from her practice to assist with the project. When he brought up the subject of a fee for her services, she looked at him as if he'd slapped her.

———

A week after Fagan's meeting with Yossef Khalil and Fernando Almeida, he received a call from Almeida. He was, at the time, in his quarters in Rio. Fagan immediately sensed the clinic director was in a state of anxiety.

"I think we need to meet," Almeida said over the phone, "as soon as possible."

"Very well," Fagan replied. "Would you like me to come to the clinic?"

"No, that might not be wise. We need to meet somewhere else." He gave Fagan the address of a sidewalk café, some distance from the clinic, and agreed to meet in an hour.

When Fagan arrived, purposely, about five minutes late, he found Almeida waiting impatiently. The nervous man rose to meet Fagan, but did not offer his hand.

Once they were both seated, a waitress approached, but Almeida waved her away. "Something has come up and I thought I should bring it to your attention, immediately. I had thought of calling Mister Khalil; but then, since it is a security matter, I decided to call you first."

Fagan nodded politely. "That seems reasonable and appropriate. Please continue."

"As you know, we have a gang problem here in Rio and few of us in business are immune from their attentions. In the past, we have paid them a fee, a generous fee, to be left alone. This is not uncommon, even for medical facilities.

"Then a few months back, I received a call from the local gang *jefe* seeking to know the name of one of our patients. Specifically, he wanted to know the names of patients coming to our clinic for treatment. Well, I flatly refused, which he seemed to accept, but he did insist that we increase the monthly cash fee we pay to him. I agreed to this."

Almeida was speaking rapidly now, and Fagan held up his hand. He signaled to the waitress to bring a bottle of water and some ice. This was a bad turn of events, but one not totally unexpected.

After the water arrived, Fagan carefully filled their glasses. "Please," he said in a reassuring tone, "continue."

"I thought that was the end of it. But this morning I took a call from the same man who wanted to know the name of the patient who had reserved an entire wing of our clinic. It seems he has an informant inside our facility. This gang member now knows we are expecting a wealthy patient. And he's demanding to know his identity. I told him that not even I know this person's identity, but he was most insistent."

Almeida looked away, unable to meet Fagan's soft gaze. "He's to call me tomorrow and I'm to give him the name—a name I myself do not even know. And if I did, how could I tell him? But these gangs have power—a great deal of power."

"Why do you think he wants to know the name of your patient?" Fagan was quite sure he knew the reason, but he wanted to hear it from Almeida.

Almeida lowered his voice, though no one was in earshot. "I've spoken with other clinic directors, and the gangs wish to know who is being treated for future blackmail. They feel that this information, and the nature of the procedure and its legality, might be worth money to them at some future time. I didn't know what to do, Mister Richards, other than to bring this matter to your attention."

"And what would you have me do?"

Almeida looked miserable. "I don't *know*! Others who have refused to comply have had their clinics vandalized—even set on fire. But the cornerstone of our service is confidentiality. If we lose that, we lose all."

Fagan was silent for a long moment. "Here's what you must do." For the next fifteen minutes he spoke and Fernando Almeida listened.

Moments later, Almeida left ahead of Fagan, not as disquieted as when he arrived, but still anxious.

That afternoon, Garrett Walker made a routine maintenance call to Almeida's office, and while the clinic director stepped away from his desk, he went to work on his phone. The multi-line console had already been bugged, but Walker installed some circuitry that would allow them to do much more than listen to the conversation.

The next morning, when Almeida took a call from a man who called himself Pietro, Almeida told him that he would know the name of the patient in three days' time. He also told him that he would provide a name this one time and one time only. Pietro accommodatingly told him this was indeed a one-time-only request, but that he must have the name in no more than the allotted three days.

After Fernando Almeida had hung up the phone, he called Steven Fagan. Fagan patiently listened to Almeida recount the conversation as if he had not just heard it.

CHAPTER EIGHT: RICARDO

Fagan and Walker met in Brisco's apartment to discuss just how to deal with this new threat. Earlier that afternoon, Walker—acting under the guise of his employment with the Joseph Simpson Jr. Foundation—had met with his acquaintance from the organized-crime division of the *Policia Federal*. The policeman, who he still knew only as Alehandro, had been helpful up to a point.

Walker shared the details of his meeting. "I told him only that one of our clinic managers had been threatened personally by a man named Pietro and that they were asking for more money than we could really afford. He said he knew nothing of anyone named Pietro, but that this was most certainly the work of one of the *Comando Vermelho* franchises. I gave him the name of one of the Simpson clinics, and he said he would alert the local police to keep an eye on the facility."

Walker thought for a few seconds, trying to frame his perception of Alehandro's response. "I'm not sure that he totally bought the personal threat to an employee of a Simpson clinic. The guy's pretty sharp. He did say that he hoped I wasn't going to try anything drastic or take matters into my own hands. Am I going to do anything like that?"

Walker looked from Fagan to Brisco, but it was Fagan who spoke. "It could just come to that, although we would like to settle this without taking measures that would draw the attention of the local constabulary. We have a few days to work this out but no more than that. If we can buy our way out of this, we will; but that might not be possible. Janet?

"I spoke with Tom Gardina earlier today and a part of the station work here in Brazil is to track the drug gangs. He was not too optimistic. The *Comando Vermelho* is probably the worst of the gangs, and they are very compartmented, so we're dealing with the local gang *jefe* in the Bonsucesso District. He pays a part of his extortion proceeds to the next level; but in his area, the neighborhood where our clinic is located, he is the absolute power. Whoever this Pietro is, he works for this gang boss and is speaking for him. Since we're dealing with a guy who's not too high on the food chain, he may not be all that smart—or reasonable."

"And can we find out who this guy is?" Fagan asked.

"Tom's working on that for us, but we do know that this fellow is both elusive and brutal. And that he may not be easy to deal with. He runs a tight organization, which is why Tom's having trouble even coming up with a name. And it's all about turf. He will want the name of our clinic patient for blackmail and for control. By knowing who the wealthy patients are at the Bonsucesso Clinic, he extends his control over the clinic. So, we may not be able to buy him off with cash; he may demand a name."

The three of them sat in silence for several minutes before Fagan spoke. "I think we have to be ready to deal with this issue on several levels. The first of those is to make every effort to pay these people off; and, as Janet says, this might not be easy. Then we have to look into some feint or misdirection regarding our patient; which, again, may not be that easy, as it seems these people have a source inside the clinic. Clinic gossip being what it is, keeping the identity of our patient under wraps may or may not work out in the long run. And, finally, we have to find out just who this local gang kingpin is and find some way to reason with him—*plomo o oro* as they say in Colombia, if you take my meaning."

They did. The gangs in Colombia, when they wanted the cooperation from someone outside the gang, offered them *plomo o oro* [lead or gold], meaning we will offer you payment, the gold, to do as we ask, or we will offer you lead in the form of a bullet.

"I think, Garrett, it might be time to get Akheem down here to help out with this."

Walker glanced at his watch. "He's been in the air for about an hour now. As this issue may eventually require some heavy lifting, I asked him to bring Bijay. They should be here just before midnight."

———

Raised by a British baron and his Irish wife, Akheem Kelly-Rogers was black and of indeterminate African parentage. His adoptive parents were Foreign Service careerists, so Akheem was raised in Africa, receiving his formal schooling at an exclusive boarding school near Hertfordshire. As a youth, his career in the confines of the tradition-bound institution was mixed, and he struggled with authority.

Then a chance meeting at a rural pub brought him into contact with a senior sergeant in the Special Air Service, also garrisoned nearby in Hertfordshire. From there, the young black preppy's life revolved around prospective service with the SAS. Bright, athletic, and handsome, Kelly-Rogers was accepted into Sandhurst, and served twelve years in the British Army, much of that time with the SAS.

His sudden resignation from the service on a point of honor left him unemployed and with a skill set that seemed suitable only for mercenary work.

Enter Steven Fagan.

As I-4 developed and expanded their interventionist portfolio, they also developed highly responsive, platoon-sized, direct-action components that could quickly and quietly intervene in regions of the world where the United States had interests. Fagan hired Akheem Kelly-Rogers to head up I-4's African response element. Yet he was an experienced and versatile special operator and could function just about anywhere.

———

Aboard a British Airways 747 from London to Rio de Janeiro, Kelly Rogers was comfortably seated in first class.

"May I get you another drink, sir?"

Kelly-Rogers was in his mid-forties but looked much younger. He was slim, fit, and stood close to six-three. He was handsome to the point of being conspicuous, and those who saw him often looked twice, taking him for a diplomat or a movie star. The Rio-based flight crew thought perhaps he might be a retired professional soccer star and treated him deferentially. He had just finished a premium Glenlivet scotch, neat, as he glanced at his watch. They were still two hours out of Rio.

"Yes, please, if it's not too much trouble."

The attractive young lady shook her head. "None at all, sir." As the senior attendant in first class, she had made it clear to her crewmates that she would attend to this gentleman. "And for you, sir?" she said to Glenlivet's seatmate.

"Another cup of tea would be most satisfactory."

She smiled and made her way to the galley. The two were clearly together, but the smaller man who accompanied the tall African had been initially overlooked in the wake of his handsome companion. But the attendant, who had been serving the beautiful and the ordinary for more than a few years, sensed there was something special about the man who drank tea and ate very little when British Airways offered the very best in first-class airborne food and drink. And there was something in the way the black man deferred to him. He was clearly oriental, probably Southwest Asian; but other than that, he was a nondescript, unprepossessing man.

Bijay Gurung had been with I-4 only a few years longer than Akheem Kelly-Rogers. One of the I-4's first interventions had called for a direct-action element that could move seamlessly in the urban cities of Lahore and Karachi, as well as the tribal lands of the Hindu Kush. Bijay Gurung had grown up in the foothills near Annapurna, and like all the strongest and most capable members of his tribe, the Gurungs, he had joined the Brigade of British Gurkhas. His great-great-grandfather had fought the Raj; Bijay had *served* the Raj.

He had just retired as a celebrated and respected Gurkha, living in Kathmandu, when he met Garrett Walker. I-4 had been contemplating an operation in northern Afghanistan and needed to recruit a small band of fighters who were both tough and discreet. Walker and Steven Fagan reasoned that the best way to do that was to hire a proven leader who could attract the kind of fighters needed.

Gurung had been comfortable in retirement, but had begun to become restless with inactivity. And there was something about the tall American who had so quickly mastered his Nepalese dialect when he spoke of I-4 and their work. With the prospect of getting back into harness with a highly professional contingent, Bijay Gurung had been coaxed from retirement.

The attendant returned with their drinks, and when she attempted to first serve the Glenlivet, Kelly-Rogers raised a hand in a simple gesture that indicated his friend was to be served ahead of him.

Gurung smiled and imperceptibly shook his head at this unneeded gesture on the part of his companion.

The attendant served first the tea, then the whiskey, and made her way back up the aisle, a puzzled expression on her face. She had no way of knowing that Bijay Gurung, formerly the command sergeant major in Her Majesty's 1st Gurkha Battalion, was also a holder of the Victoria Cross—England's highest award for gallantry. Had she, it would have made little difference to her, but it made a great deal of difference to the former British SAS major.

"I wonder what kind of mischief Steven Fagan is up to this time?" Kelly-Rogers mused as he sipped his scotch. "And why Garrett wanted just the two of us?" Kelly-Rogers and Gurung had worked together before, but their usual role with I-4 was at the head of a band of fighters—black Africans for Kelly-Rogers, Gurkhas or Southwest Asian fighters for Gurung. Kelly-Rogers spoke both Spanish and Portuguese—but why Gurung, who spoke neither?

"All in good time, my friend. All in good time." Gurung was a patient man and only anticipated future events out of operational necessity.

"Still," Kelly-Rogers replied, "it must be something special and very closely held for it to be just the two of us and none of our other retainers. Nonetheless, it should be interesting, and I understand the night life in Rio can be most entertaining."

Gurung simply smiled. He was a creature of the hills and mountains, but he could move well in a city when necessary. While he was infinitely more patient than Kelly-Rogers, he too wondered why only the two of them received the call from Garrett Walker.

But they would land soon, and all would be revealed.

———

Garrett Walker was waiting for them in a hired car and greeted them warmly as the comrades-in-arms they were. He took them to a small hotel in the Bonsucesso District, where there were rooms reserved for them. While Gurung carefully took in the sights and smells of a new city, Kelly-Rogers pressed Walker on the reason for their visit.

"It's an important undertaking," Walker told them, "and rather delicate. Let's get you settled in first. Steven has scheduled a meeting for all of us for later on this morning. I'll drop you off at your lodgings, and then I have to get to work."

"Work?" Kelly-Rogers asked with a grin, glancing at Walker's one-piece handyman's jumpsuit. "I'm so glad that you finally found yourself a job. And here I was concerned about your employability."

———

Later that morning, the I-4 team met in Brisco's apartment, all present but for Brisco. Walker was on his lunch break from the Bonsucesso Clinic. He and Bill Owen listened while Steven Fagan, in his patient and detailed manner, outlined the operation for the new arrivals. Like all quasi-military and intelligence-base entities, I-4 was a compartmented organization, so this was all new information for Kelly-Rogers and Gurung.

"As you might imagine," Fagan said, "this is an important and delicate undertaking. Since we may have to deal in a kinetic manner with the local gang presence, I wanted to have our best people available in case things go in that direction. Now, you must have some questions for me?"

Akheem Kelly-Rogers sat stunned by the sheer boldness of what they were trying to do. He was at a loss for words.

Bijay Gurung simply nodded and smiled before politely speaking. "What you are proposing is a most worthy undertaking, Mister Fagan. I am pleased to be a part of this venture. Thank you for bringing us here."

A lock turned in the door and Janet Brisco entered the apartment with a file clutched to her breast. She was flushed and smiling. After greeting Kelly-Rogers and Gurung, she dragged a chair into the small circle. "I just met with our station contact and we have an ID on our local warlord. His name, or at least his street name, is Ricardo Esteban. There's not a lot on him," she said, handing the slim file to Fagan, "but maybe enough, with a little luck, to get a location on him. It seems he's a vicious thug and enjoys the whole gang-violence, intimidation thing."

"Then we need to *be* lucky," Fagan said, "and track him down. This fellow Pietro is due to call the clinic tomorrow afternoon. We will offer him a sizeable sum of money to leave us alone. Perhaps, they will be reasonable and take the money and leave us to do our work. Otherwise, we may have to adopt more drastic measures."

Ricardo Esteban liked to cruise his turf just before taking his evening meal. It was a show of presence, if not a show of force, and a custom Esteban had adopted from his predecessor, a man whom he had killed to get where he was today. Many of Rio's gang chiefs followed this practice, but most of them did so in a more opulent manner, touring their territory in big Mercedes or BMWs. Esteban's ride was an older black Ford Excursion, with darkened windows and newer hubcaps that rotated independent of their wheels and sparkled as the night lights of the Bonsucesso District came on.

Ricardo Esteban, whose real name was Ricki Gonzales, was a Mexican expatriate who had grown up in Nogales before entering the United States illegally and making his way to Los Angeles. There, he had worked his way up in the illegal drug trade in East LA and had been poised to claim his own turf. He had put in the time, learned his trade, and had all the gang tats required to move up to a higher station in his chosen line of work. Then, fate had intervened. He was caught up in a routine traffic stop and deported. By the time he had worked his way back to his hood, an aspiring rival had taken over his territory—including those gang members he had groomed to be his lieutenants.

Gonzales was then faced with a choice; build a new organization that would lead to a turf war with an established gang power or simply move on. Having heard there was opportunity in Brazil, he had allowed himself to again be deported and had kept moving south.

As Ricardo Esteban, the skills he'd originally learned in East LA had adapted well into the drug culture of Rio de Janeiro. And the decentralized organization of the *Comando Vermelho* had served his interests as well. Once again, he had become a gang soldier, worked his way up to a senior position of trust, and then killed his boss.

He had claimed his turf and now guarded it with brutal attention to detail. He was determined to never again be pushed out of his hood.

About 2145 on their cruise, they passed the Bonsucesso Clinic, and he briefly surveyed the clinic and the grounds. The day before, Pietro, one of Ricardo's underlings, had called the clinic director to talk about fees and access to their client list. The director had been most generous about paying tribute, but not as forthcoming about the requested client information.

The money indeed was most tempting; but for Esteban, it was all about control. By having access to their clientele, he controlled not only the clinic—he also controlled those wealthy individuals who used the facility. Pietro had demanded both, and the clinic director had said he would see what he could do.

Pietro would call again tomorrow, and if the clinic did not comply? Well, in that case, Ricardo would have to pay a late-night call at the home of the clinic director. Pietro served as his intermediary in the negotiations, but Esteban himself would attend to any forceful physical confrontation himself.

This served several purposes. It let the "client" know that a good deal of personal discomfort awaited him for his failure to comply—and that discomfort could extend to his immediate family as well. Secondly, it let his subordinates know that the boss was not above getting his hands dirty. And finally—he liked it. Ricardo knew about intimidation and fear, and it gave him pleasure to instill it in others.

Pietro drove while Esteban sat in the front passenger's seat. "Where to now, boss?" In back was Arturo, a beefy enforcer who was reliable, loyal, and not terribly bright.

"Let's head over to Alvaro Way by that new car dealership. They're open late and it might be a good thing for them to see us pull through the lot."

"You got it, boss."

For the last three days, Steven Fagan, Walker, Kelly-Rogers, and Bijay Gurung had been working around the clock to implement a plan for this day at this exact time. When Pietro had rejected their offer of more money that afternoon, giving them but one more day to hand over the clinic client list, they accelerated their efforts to bring about what they now had to do.

As the Ford Excursion leisurely made its way through a deserted intersection, it was T-boned by a small moving van. The front air bags deployed pinning Esteban and Pietro to their seats. Arturo was thrown across the rear seat and into the door. None of them were wearing seatbelts. Garrett Walker, who was driving the van, was wearing a helmet and was restrained by a NASCAR-type racing harness.

When Walker stepped from the van, Kelly-Rogers, who had been on the sidewalk, was opening the passenger-side front door and dragging Esteban from the Excursion. Both front and rear driver-side windows were broken out. When a dazed Pietro and Arturo collected themselves enough to look to their left, they saw a man they took to be Asian peering at them over the top of a silenced automatic weapon. They did not have to be told what to do; they knew any resistance would bring instant death. Both men kept their hands where they were visible and did not move.

Kelly-Rogers dragged Esteban from the wrecked Ford to an open rear door of an old Peugeot and shoved him roughly toward the back seat. When Esteban put a hand to the roof of the car to resist, Kelly-Rogers brought a knee sharply into his crotch, pushed him headlong into the car, and followed him in. The last thing Esteban remembered, aside from the dull pain in his testicles, was the pinprick of a needle in the side of his neck.

Walker walked around the Ford to the Peugeot and got into the driver's seat. After he started the car, Gurung moved like a snake, treating Pietro and Arturo each to a barrel strike to the side of the head. He then calmly joined the others, and they drove away at a legal speed.

———————

They were on the top floor of a deserted warehouse on the outskirts of Rio, in an area where the predominant activity was the comings and goings of the homeless. Down in the street, a very nervous Bill Owen sat in the Peugeot with the doors locked and the windows only slightly cracked. If the few passersby thought the car and the man out of place, they didn't show it as they quickly averted their eyes and moved on. It was a neighborhood where no one asked questions or called attention to themselves.

In a large vacant room punctuated by I-beams that supported roof joists, Kelly-Rogers, Walker, and Gurung talked quietly, enjoying piping-hot coffee from Kelly-Rogers' thermos. They had just administered the counter-sedative and were waiting for Ricardo Esteban to come around. It was a quarter past three in the morning, and with any luck at all, they would be finished in less than an hour.

There were battery-served lanterns attached to some of the support columns that dimly lit the big space. A single lantern hanging from a nearby ceiling joist illuminated Esteban's face. It took but another five minutes for the gang *jefe* to clear his head and begin to look around.

Kelly-Rogers stepped into his vision and straddled a metal folding chair, its back to the captive and almost touching his knees.

Esteban too sat on a folding chair, but he was bound in duct tape—his waist and torso lashed to the back of the chair and his feet to the chair's front legs. His forearms were taped to his thighs and his thighs to the metal seat. He could only move his head. He was completely naked and aware that his penis was stuck to the tape that encircled his upper thighs. His mouth was dry, and he was not sure he could speak. For a full five minutes Kelly-Rogers just stared at him. Then he spoke.

"I know you speak Portuguese," he began, "but I also know you are more comfortable in Spanish, so we will do this in Spanish. I will speak, and you will listen. When I pause to ask if you understand what I've said, or if I ask a yes-or-no question, you will simply nod your head yes or shake your head no. Do you understand?"

Esteban simply stared at the soft-spoken black man. Kelly-Rogers' hand moved with a blur as he cracked the gang boss across the mouth. His head snapped back, and he wondered if it was his interrogator's quick hand that had hit him or something else. But the blow had authority. "Do you understand?"

Esteban nodded uncertainly.

"Good. Then let's get to the business at hand. You have a business relationship with the Bonsucesso Clinic, and we understand that you wish to expand on that relationship. Is that correct?"

Esteban again nodded in the affirmative.

"Very well. We understand your previous arrangement, and we wish not to come between you and your business with this clinic. *But,* we will not permit any expansion of that business that would reveal the names or identities of our client or any other client. Is that clear?"

This time Esteban shook his head no.

Kelly-Rogers sat back slightly as Esteban flinched, expecting another blow. After a moment of silence, he continued. "This one time, I will allow you to speak." He nodded to someone behind the captive and a cup of water was brought to his lips. Esteban gulped some of it down, the rest spilling across the upper part of his bare chest.

"It is a matter of honor and control," he managed. "I have made a demand of the clinic; and I cannot go back on that, or word would get around that those we deal with do not have to comply with our demands. It is simply business, and you ask what I cannot do." He swallowed hard and seemed to regain some of his composure. "So, you have me; but you see, there is nothing I can do to help you."

Kelly-Rogers stood and stepped away without another word.

Then, Bijay Gurung came into Esteban's view. He turned the empty chair around and took a seat. His expression was deceptively passive, and he gave Esteban a half-smile.

The drug lord had known hard and dangerous men all his life, and he immediately knew the man who now sat before him was both.

In a smooth motion, Gurung took a large sheathed knife from the small of his back and laid it on his knees, much as a surgeon would lay a scalpel on his operating station. As someone from behind Esteban slapped a strip of duct tape over his mouth, Gurung eased the curved blade from its scabbard.

"The man in front of you is a Gurkha," Kelly-Rogers said softly. He was now behind Esteban and bent low to speak into his ear. "And that is a *Kukri* knife he holds, a weapon that has very serious cultural and historical significance to the Gurkha people. It is said that once unsheathed, the knife cannot be returned to its scabbard without first drawing blood. That is, of course, but a myth. Yet in your case, it is also a fact."

The duct tape around Esteban's torso reached to just below his nipples. Gurung drew his blade from the top of one shoulder down to just below the opposite armpit, creating a long, half-inch-deep incision. Then, he made a similar cut, beginning at the top of the other shoulder.

Ricardo Esteban now had an "X" etched on the upper portion of his chest. He watched in horror as the grim Gurkha drew his blade across—first one way, then the other. Then, there was an audible hiss of an air-driven winch taking up slack on a cable winch. The cable was shackled into a bridle system that was married to the legs the folding chair. Both the chair and the man taped to it were snatched off the floor, inverted, and hoisted to the ceiling.

Blood from his chest flowed freely down Esteban's neck into his nose, eyes, and ears. Only the tape on his mouth kept him from tasting his own blood. But with the blood cascading into his nose, he was having a difficult time breathing. The air-driven winch was mounted on an I-beam trolley that allowed suspended loads to move easily along the beam—a beam that extended the length of the floor, out through a loft window.

The choking, inverted drug lord was traversed along the I-beam to a point outside the warehouse wall so he was looking down from four stories above the pavement.

"You have no control over what happens to you right now, Mister Esteban," Kelly-Rogers said to him. "And there is little honor in being found dead on the street in the condition you now find yourself."

Esteban moaned, struggled, and snorted blood from his plugged nostrils. He was upside down and effectively being water boarded in his own blood. Then, he fainted.

They pulled him back into the building and righted him. Then they cut away the tape that bound him to the chair, laid a towel across his crotch, and sponged the blood from his face. Blood still cascaded down his stomach. He sat in a pool of it, even as the wounds were beginning to clot. A crushed ampule of ammonia quickly brought him around.

Kelly-Rogers was back, seated in front of him, and the strong hands of Garrett Walker were on Esteban's shoulders, should he do anything but remain seated. Now resting on a small table between he and this menacing black man were two, heavy stainless-steel ankle bracelets.

Kelly-Rogers stared at him a long while. Then, "You will wear one of these ankle bracelets, Mister Esteban. Choose the one it will be."

Esteban's eyes roamed from one to the other, but he said nothing until Kelly-Rogers slapped him once more. "The left one," he heard himself say over the ringing in his ears from the blow. "The one on my left."

Without another word, Kelly-Rogers took the left bracelet and snapped it onto Esteban's left ankle. It made a heavy-metal sound, and once in place, there were no visible seams in the polished metal. He was made to stand, with Walker on one side of him and Gurung on the other.

They walked him to a vertical barrier constructed of half-inch steel with a heavy, armored window bolted into the protective plating to serve as a viewport. Kelly-Rogers walked behind the barrier and clamped the other bracelet to a four-inch-diameter oak dowel, held firmly in place by two workbench vises. He then joined the others.

Walker held up a small remote-control device with a glowing green light, a single rocker switch, and a button. With Esteban watching, he flipped the rocker switch that turned the green light to red, and pressed the button. The sound was deafening as wood and metal fragments splattered against the steel and glass.

Esteban watched in horror from behind the viewport. Only the blackened and splintered ends of the dowel still trapped in the two vises remained.

Back in the chair, Esteban was again looking into the cold eyes of Akheem Kelly-Rogers. "It's like this, Esteban. We know you are tough, and we know you have this don't-back-down honor thing going. And you might agree to cooperate if we let you go. But what's to stop you from taking extra security measures and going back to business as usual. Maybe you don't think we'll come for you again. But that device, the one that you chose, will be with you for a while. Try to remove the device—and it goes off, taking half your leg with it. Try to leave the city, and it goes off, taking half your leg with it. Refuse to cooperate and back off from the Bonsucesso Clinic, and it goes off. Now *that,* my *jefe* friend, is control."

Kelly-Rogers held up the controller and extended the telescoping antenna. He rocked the switch back and forth—red to green to red—several times.

Each time the red light came on, Esteban winced.

Kelly-Rogers handed Esteban a disposable cell phone. "Call your friends and tell them to come and get you. The address is on the back of the phone."

Esteban's three captors moved toward the door, and then Kelly-Rogers turned. "In a few weeks, and after we've left the area, that bracelet will drop away. But only if you keep away from the Bonsucesso Clinic—and their patients. And we'll be monitoring you. If our simple request is denied, we will take off your leg—and perhaps even a portion of your manhood in the process."

Then, they were gone.

Driving away from the warehouse, Bill Owen clicked on windshield wipers. "Got some red drippings on the windshield from that building," he said absently. "I wonder what it was?"

"In this neighborhood," Kelly-Rogers opined, "it could be just about anything."

The following day, Steven Fagan was in the office of Fernando Almeida when the director took a call from the man who called himself Pietro. Almeida put the call on speaker.

As the two men listened, they heard Pietro explain that access to the Bonsucesso Clinic's patient list was a misunderstanding, and that if they could continue on with their past arrangement, there would be no further demand put on the clinic. He even apologized for any inconvenience.

"How did you manage this?" Almeida asked after hanging up the phone. He was greatly relieved and had a new respect for this American security consultant. "Did you make them an offer they couldn't refuse?"

Fagan smiled. "I think, Mr. Almeida, that you've been watching too many American 'Godfather' movies."

CHAPTER NINE: GRACE

Doctor Grace Davidson arrived in Rio late afternoon on a direct flight from Dulles. Her passport was under her own name, but her entire legend—as constructed and fully backstopped by Bill Owen—documented her as a medical consultant for surgical procedures. Ostensibly, she was being retained by clinic insurance companies to observe treatment facilities that conducted complex procedures and to recommend ways to conduct these procedures more efficiently and cost-effectively. Her fees were paid by clinic insurers.

She was traveling separately, but on the same aircraft was Brad Gregory. As a CIA staffer and a Directorate of Science and Technology technician, he traveled on diplomatic credentials. Both boarded the shuttle for the Hyatt Regency and checked in at the elaborate registration desk—Gregory into a standard double, while Davidson was upgraded to a suite, in keeping with her role as a highly paid consultant.

That evening Grace Davidson was joined by Brad Gregory, Steven Fagan, and Garrett Walker in her suite. Room service delivered a platter of sandwiches and mineral water.

"Good flight down?" Fagan inquired as they settled around an oversized coffee table in the sitting room. They exchanged pleasantries and got down to business. "The clinic director will be expecting you and believes you are part of our security team, just like Garrett. He knows the nature of your cover story and that you will be visiting the clinic to observe procedures. You will have full access to all the facility's operating theaters, as well as the pre- and post-op rooms. The only thing that will be off-limits will be the clinic wing where the patient and his security detail will be housed.

Since your visit window should run no more than three to four days, we will be sending you to the clinic when we get word of the patient's arrival."

"Any idea when that might be?" Davidson asked.

"That's still up in the air, but it could be any day now. We know that the transplant surgeon has been put on standby and is no longer seeing other patients. When he leaves Cairo for Rio, we'll know it's about time. Once our Doctor Hasani arrives, we assume that our target will not be too far behind him. Hasani is holding an open ticket to Rio and the patient will be flying by private jet. We'll also be tracking his chartered aircraft. Once Hasani is here, we will get you into the facility so you can begin to familiarize yourself with the setup there. Garrett will be close by, but not in any of the medical procedure rooms. Yet, if for some unexpected reason you should need him, he'll not be far away."

Fagan turned to Gregory. "And the implants?"

"They were sent by diplomatic pouch yesterday, and I'll pick them up tomorrow. The station has a secure lab at the consulate where I can run the final diagnostics on the equipment. Then, they will be with me until I hand them over to Doctor Grace here for her part of the operation. They will be in a small one-by-three-by-five-inch sterile case. All she has to do is take them out and install them."

Fagan nodded his approval and asked gently. "So, Doctor, are you ready to do this procedure?"

Grace Davidson had not only carefully rehearsed her role in the transplant operation, but she had been briefed on the full scope of what they hoped to accomplish—that this transplant procedure was but one step, albeit a key element, in an extended covert operation. To willingly do what she was being asked required full disclosure.

Davidson smiled at Fagan. He reminded her of her father, also a skilled surgeon and her mentor. "I'm as ready as I can be, Steven. Honestly, standing next to this monster is going to be a trying and somewhat bizarre experience. But I know what's at stake, and I'll just have to do my level best to treat him like any other patient—get in, do my job, and get back out." She paused and seemed to collect herself. "Tell me again about the assisting physician."

Steven detailed once more the background of Roberto de Silva and the agreement that had been struck for his cooperation. The success of the venture all depended on timing, Davidson's skill immediately following the kidney transplant part of the plan, and de Silva's complicity.

"Is there a chance I might meet him ahead of time? It might be helpful."

Fagan considered this. De Silva's role in this, as Fagan envisioned it, was totally passive. Once she was in position, he had only to allow Davidson to do what she had to do, then attend to the relative routine work of closing the incisions. Fagan had not told him exactly what that "work" was to be, other than it would be nothing that would endanger the patient's life—at least not on the operating table. Once the operation was underway, the less de Silva knew about what was to transpire, the better for all concerned. He had been told the name of the patient, lest he learned of it at the last minute and back out.

Now Davidson wanted to meet him. This was not in the script, but since their initial meeting only a few weeks ago, Steven Fagan had developed a great deal of respect for and trust in Grace Davidson. And he was fully aware that the whole venture rested on her performance—and de Silva's compliance.

"Let me get with Janet and see what we can do about setting up a meeting with the two of you. Perhaps over lunch tomorrow."

The following morning, Brad Gregory made his way to the U.S. Consulate in Rio and to the small suite of rooms set aside for station personnel. There he recovered the package that had been delivered by courier in the diplomatic pouch from Langley. In the tiny room reserved for him there was only a table, a chair, and a round desktop device that looked like a small stainless-steel BBQ. It was a medical-instrument sterilizer that had been delivered a few days earlier.

Gregory carefully unpacked the metal case that housed the two devices. Each was about two inches long and three-quarters of an inch in diameter, with elliptical ends. They were not symmetrical but resembled elongated, slightly curved jelly beans. Both were of a titanium-alloy construction and a thin, three-inch umbilical joined the two. One had a thin gold wire of indeterminate length carefully wrapped around a small spool and bound to its parent cylinder with a piece of butterfly incision tape.

With gloved hands, the technician reverently laid the devices out on a clean cloth and proceeded to set up a portable suite of digital test equipment. After a series of tests proved that the devices were functioning properly, he placed them in yet another padded stainless-steel case and the open case into the sterilization machine. Once sterilized, he closed the case and fitted the case into a custom-made zip-lock bag.

That done, Gregory put the sanitized devices into his briefcase and left the consulate. They would not be out of his possession until he gave them to Doctor Grace Davidson.

At their first meeting, Davidson had asked Gregory about the implants. It was hard for Gregory to adequately explain their sophistication in layman's terms, even to a surgeon familiar with state-of-the-art medical technology. The two devices, he told her, represented a sensory array and transmission capability that, through cutting-edge advances in nano-technology and micro-circuitry, could achieve the discrimination of a sound studio and the burst-transmission capacity of a larger ground transmission station.

The devices also had what amounted to a sophisticated Wi-Fi capability that could use any nearby computer as an encrypted portal to the web.

In addition to audio surveillance, the array could sense and record the keystrokes of a nearby computer user. The system was powered by one of the most ingenious rechargeable power-cell prototypes in existence. It sustained itself with body heat.

Brad Gregory had himself designed and constructed the devices, and they represented the pinnacle of the master eavesdropper's art.

———

At a small sidewalk café in the Ipanema District, Janet Brisco and Grace Davidson were drinking iced tea as they waited for the arrival of Roberto de Silva. They made a striking pair—the tall, fashionable black woman and a petite and attractive blonde. In a city where appearances counted and middle-aged beauty in a woman was openly worshiped, more than a few heads turned as they were seated. Yet they soon merged into the panorama as one dazzling beauty after another made her way along the boulevard. It was like a parade of fashion models, many with platform shoes and a runway gait with one foot crossing in front of the other.

De Silva arrived five minutes late, out of breath and apologizing profusely. Brisco made introductions, and while de Silva smiled politely on meeting Davidson, he was clearly most happy to see Brisco. As she had told Davidson before de Silva arrived, they had gone out a few times, and she knew he was interested in her. But while wanting to hold his interest, she had not let the relationship go past a dinner date.

"I have an appointment so I'm going to leave you two doctors to get acquainted. I'll see you tonight, Roberto, and 'til then, I'm leaving you in good hands. *Ciao.*"

Davidson coolly appraised the younger physician and sensed his slight unease in suddenly being alone with her. She laid a hand on his forearm. It was a neutral, comforting gesture. Grace Davidson was on the wrong side of fifty, but looked much younger. The thick blond hair was natural, as were her piercing blue eyes and youthful countenance. She he gave him a wide, sincere smile that seemed to put him at ease. "Doctor, Janet has told me a great deal about you, and please understand that we both respect and appreciate your help with this. I myself wanted to meet you beforehand to get to know you and to answer any questions you might have—or any doubts for that matter."

De Silva looked back into the clear, steady eyes of this earnest woman colleague. "Well, first of all, it's Roberto, and yes, I do have some questions about all this." He started to continue but was halted by the hand that again found his arm.

"Let's do this, Roberto—and its Grace. Let me tell you why I'm here and why I believe this is a worthy undertaking. Then we can talk about the mechanics of our respective roles in this procedure. Would that be all right?"

De Silva nodded. She moved closer to him and began. First, she told him of her husband and of their life together. Then, in pragmatic but not unemotional terms, she explained what she had lost when he was killed on 9/11—of his last cell-phone call from the North Tower and what she and their two daughters experienced in the aftermath.

"I lost the love of my life," she quietly explained, "with no remains to bury and no father for our girls. Thank God I've had my work. I'm told you were suspended from your work for a period of time, so you understand how important work can be. If I didn't have my medical practice, I'm not sure how I'd have gotten through the loss of Donald."

As she spoke, he began to nod in understanding. This was her chance, she explained, and his, to save other families from similar heartache. It was the right thing to do. Then, she went on to expand on the medical dimension of what was going to take place during the upcoming operation. Instead of speaking of what *she* would do and what *he* would do, which was little more than to observe, she began to talk about what *they* would do and about *their* role in the procedure.

"Doctor David—, I mean Grace. Thank you. As you might imagine, this is a big step for me. I wish more than anything to have a normal practice again—and to be an honest and ethical practitioner." He hesitated before continuing. "I'm putting a great deal of faith in you and Mister Richards. I will do my part, but please don't let me down."

As she talked and—more importantly—listened, they slowly became collaborators. She hadn't the skills of persuasion that Steven Fagan had used with Roberto, but she was no less effective. When this was over and he got to America, she told him, he could call on her as a reference as he went into practice at his new home.

Later, when she relayed the conversation to Steven Fagan, he nodded in satisfaction. Recruiting a witting asset for a covert operation was sometimes the easy part, and a good operative ignored the re-recruitment process at his peril.

That afternoon, following a long walk, Roberto de Silva returned to his flat. He had almost convinced himself that this was the right course of action for him, that he could go through with this— almost. It was still a risky proposition. If something went wrong, these Americans would simply leave town and leave the whole mess behind them. He would likely go to prison and most definitely never practice medicine again. Yet if it all worked out, he would have a new start in America. Both the risk and the reward were great.

Once inside, he went to the kitchen and took a single bottle of vodka out of the freezer door. He kept it there, untouched, as a safety valve. If he ever needed a drink, it was now. He uncorked the bottle and was about to pour himself a shot when he noticed the blinking light on his answering machine. Setting the bottle on the counter, he stepped to the phone credenza and pushed the play button. "Doctor de Silva, where are you? I called your cell phone, but you did not answer. This is unacceptable."

The caller did not identify himself, but de Silva recognized the voice; it was dripping with contempt.

"I will require your services and wish you to hold yourself ready beginning tomorrow. I will arrive in Rio in the afternoon for an important procedure that will take place within a few days of my arrival. The exact date and time of the operation have yet to be determined, but I want you on call from tomorrow on. I am prepared to pay you my standard fee, but you must hold yourself in readiness until the patient arrives and I make my final examination of him. You are to return my call as soon as you get this to confirm your availability. And please be prompt about it."

De Silva listened to the message again before erasing it. So, there it was. If he did the bidding of the Americans, he would never again have to work for this Egyptian asshole, Hosni Hasani. Now *that*, de Silva told himself, was something to consider. He recorked the bottle and put it back in the fridge, where he hoped it would stay.

Then, he dialed Brisco's number. He told her of the call from Hasani and then called Hasani himself to confirm his availability.

The concierge at the Belmond Copacabana Hotel met Hosni Hasani as he stepped from the limo that had collected him at the airport.

The famous Egyptian physician was well known by the hotel staff as a player and a heavy tipper.

"Welcome back to Rio, *Senor* Doctor. I hope you had a pleasant flight." He snapped his fingers for a bellman to retrieve the luggage from the trunk.

"The flight? Oh, it was fine, thank you."

"Will you be with us long?" The concierge asked as he followed Hasani up the steps and through the opened double glass doors.

"That will depend on my work. Four or five days at least, perhaps longer."

"I see, and will you require your normal room services this evening?"

Hasani looked up from the check-in form at the reservation desk. "The what? No, no, of course not; not tonight and not for the next few nights." A look of irritation passed across his face. "Perhaps not this trip; I will let you know."

The concierge bowed slightly from the waist and withdrew, a puzzled expression on his face. For the last several years, the Egyptian doctor had booked himself into a suite of rooms at the hotel every other month or so. And always on the first night in, he had wanted an expensive bottle of champagne and a woman who was just a little on the plump side, with large melon-like breasts. Always. The hotel man shrugged to himself and went about his duties. Arabs could be unpredictable, even those with medical degrees and western tastes.

The next morning, Hasani had himself driven to the Bonsucesso Private Clinic, where Fernando Almeida met him at the front door of the clinic.

"Doctor Hasani. How nice to see you again, and welcome to Rio."

"Good day, Director." Then, without preamble, "Have the arrangements been made per my instructions? Is all in readiness for this medical procedure? If so, I would like to see everything without delay."

"They have, per your orders and with the approval of Mister Yossef Khalil, who honored us with a visit just a week ago." While Fernando Almeida was more than willing to allow this abrupt Egyptian surgeon to make demands, he wanted to let him know that he had met with and received the blessing of the individual who was paying for this patient visit. "If you would like to accompany me, we can begin your inspection immediately."

After a tour of both the medical facilities and the wing of the clinic reserved for the patient and his entourage, they found themselves back in Almeida's office over espresso. Hasani was somewhat mollified, having found nothing amiss, but was no less condescending.

Almeida had always found him demanding and rude, but there was something else present on this visit. Had he the perception of a Steven Fagan, the man he knew as Mr. Richards, he would have sensed that Doctor Hosni Hasani was very apprehensive, even afraid, but trying to hide it behind an overly brusque front. "May I ask, Doctor, when you expect your patient to arrive and when you might expect to conduct your procedure?"

"He is a very busy man," Hasani replied irritably, "and he will arrive when his schedule permits—perhaps within the next few days. Do not worry; you will be paid for the time your facilities await his arrival."

The clinic director, in fact, did not mind at all. The vacant clinic wing and the operating theater, with its pre- and post-op support facilities, could remain unused indefinitely. Their abeyance was being billed at $20,000 per day; and the attendant medical staff, which could be assigned other duties while they waited, was another $10,000. The margins for this standby status were quite acceptable to the clinic. They were prepared to wait as long as necessary.

But, in this regard, Fernando Almeida knew more about this waiting period than Dr. Hosni Hasani. It was all about security. The golden rule of personal security was that the schedule of a high-value individual—or a high-value target, as the case may be—was kept closely held. For the safety of the life being protected, knowing when was almost as important as knowing where. This told Almeida that it was not the busy schedule of this patient that was at issue; it was the identity of the patient himself. He was perhaps a well-known public personage, conceivably a head of state or a criminal—or both.

Fernando Almeida now thought he knew the reason for the private security precautions of the resourceful and helpful Mr. Richards.

———

Later that day, Steven Fagan—aka Mr. Richards—knew exactly when the patient would arrive. A chartered, extended-range Gulfstream G5 had just filed a flight plan from the Islamabad area to Rio. It was scheduled to lift off from a private airfield west of Islamabad in only a few hours.

Since the flight was paid for by Yossef Khalil, he was able to get a full manifest of those aboard. Although the count was right, most of the names were fictitious. The hourly cost of the well-appointed jet was well north of that of the idle facilities at the Bonsucesso Private Clinic.

Their special patient was inbound.

———

On learning that bin Laden would soon be in the air, Steven Fagan and his team shifted their focus from planning to execution. Fagan himself made straight for the Bonsucesso Clinic. As Fernando

Almeida was leaving the clinic that evening, the quiet American suddenly appeared as he was about to get into his car.

"Mister Richards," he managed after a start, "what brings you here at this hour?"

"Your and Doctor Hasani's patient will be here late tomorrow morning. He will come straight from the Galeao private terminal to the clinic, and he will not leave until the operation and the post-operative procedures are complete. He will be accompanied by his nurse and a personal security team of six individuals. They speak little English, if any, and will confine themselves to the residence wing of your clinic."

"I see," Almeida replied. "And does Doctor Hasani know about this?"

"He will be notified at the proper time. I wanted to give you some advanced warning of this—along with a caution."

"A caution?"

"Yes. The identity of this patient will hopefully remain unknown to you and the rest of the clinic staff. However, he is a man with an international reputation. The knowledge of who he is and that he is here could be worth a lot of money. Let me say, without seeming too dramatic, that no amount of money is worth anyone's life, and that's what we are talking about here. It's in both our interests to see that this man's identity remains anonymous while he is here at your clinic. Trust me on this. If all goes smoothly, there will be an impressive gratuity for you when he leaves. Are we clear on this?"

Almeida hesitated, but only for a second. "We are."

Late that evening, the team met in Janet Brisco's apartment for a collective meal and a final briefing. All were present, to include Bill Owen and Brad Gregory. Seemingly a courtesy, Tom Gardina had been invited, yet it was more than that. The resources of the CIA station team might still be needed as events unfolded. Brisco, who could cook when she wanted to, had prepared sausage lasagna and a Caesar salad.

After the dishes had been cleared away, Fagan addressed them. "Tomorrow, it begins. I know when we started this, it seemed something of a 'Mission Impossible;' but with a little luck and Grace's skill, we might just pull it off. The day of the actual operation could be as early as the day after tomorrow but, in all probability, the day after that. Whenever it takes place, we will have to be ready; so as of right now, we will be on full alert. We assume and hope it will go off as planned and without a hitch. But we have to be flexible; hope for the best but plan for the worst.

"Garrett will be the closest to the operating theater, and Bijay and Akheem will be in a parked car across the street. I myself will be in the director's office on the pretext of having to be on site when the procedure takes place. If there is some kind of issue, Grace will activate her transponder that she is in danger, and that will put us into motion. Garrett and I will go to the operating room for Grace, and Bijay and Akheem will seal off the reserved clinic wing and the patient's other security guards. We'll all be armed— but, needless to say, we shoot only if necessary and as little as necessary. All of us, but for Grace, will have silenced weapons. Good so far?"

Grace Davidson raised her hand. "If things do come undone during the procedure," she said in a quiet, restrained voice, "you want me to kill him?"

The room fell silent. Brisco, who was passing out dollops of sorbet in paper cups, paused in mid-delivery.

Fagan gave her a soft smile. "That really won't be necessary, Doctor, but thanks for offering. Our plan is to let him get back to the aircraft, where a squad of Navy SEALs will be waiting. They will engage his security guards and will take him down—alive if possible. Then we will fly him to Guantanamo Bay under guard. We'll deal with him there, dead or alive. As a precaution, all their rented vehicles will be tagged with GPS trackers and an FBI team of street watchers will be standing by in case there is a diversion between the clinic and the airport.

"As of this time, no one but us knows who the patient is. But let's hope these precautions and contingencies are not needed. We have better things planned for Mister bin Laden." As a matter of tradecraft, they seldom spoke his name, but Fagan felt it necessary to do so now. "And no matter how this turns out, thank you all for your dedication and your professionalism. That said, let's do this and do it right."

They made a short evening of it, with a certain amount of gaiety and forced laughter. Past that, it was time to go to work. Steven Fagan was naturally a quiet and reserved man, and perhaps a little more so this evening. More than once, his mind's eye flashed back to Joseph Simpson's account of the dying Armand Grummell and the promise Simpson had made to the old spymaster.

———

The following morning, Dr. Grace Davidson presented herself at the reception desk of the Bonsucesso Private Clinic and was immediately shown to the office of the clinic director. If Fernando Almeida expected something other than this diminutive, middle-aged and attractive woman, he was careful not to show it.

On Steven Fagan's instructions, Davidson was to be given a staff badge and allowed free access to all medical spaces in the clinic. As for the clinic staff, they were told that as a part of their malpractice insurance, a thorough review of their operating procedures was a routine part of the policy coverage.

"This credential will allow you access to any part of the clinic," Almeida said as he handed her the lanyard and badge. "As you know, the north wing of the clinic is reserved for our special patient and his staff, and that is off limits. Will you be requiring anything else?"

"I don't think so," she replied with an engaging smile. "I will make my way around your beautiful facility, beginning with your records department. And I will keep out of the way of your staff as much as possible. In addition to working with Mister Richards and his security team on this project, I'm also a board-certified neurosurgeon, and I know my way around an operating room. For the next few days, I will need to be scrubbed and gowned for any OR procedures and be admitted to the operating theaters as an observer."

"Will that also be the case for our special patient?"

"The one that is due here," she consulted her watch, "in about two hours. I will definitely need to be in there to observe that procedure. But make no mention of my plan to be there. I'll handle that at the time."

Almeida was suddenly uncomfortable. "I know all this from Mister Richards' instructions, but I'm not sure this will be possible. The transplant surgeon can be very…well…very demanding."

Grace Davidson leaned forward to speak. The warm smile was still there, but her eyes had taken on a cold and deadly character.

"Your job, Director, is to see that I'm admitted to the theater." Then she dropped the smile. "After all, what's one more woman in attendance, and an observer at that? It's not like I'm performing the surgery."

Following two hours of going over the clinic's records, she made for the small cafeteria for a light lunch. Grace Davidson was a naturally outgoing and cheerful person, and more so today on Steven Fagan's instructions. She was invited to sit with some of the other medical staff, who were always fascinated with Americans. There, she proved most skillful in deflecting questions about herself and her business by asking about the clinic and the personal lives of the other staff. She was blending in as one of them.

There were two routine surgeries scheduled that afternoon. She watched while two different surgeons conducted two different operations, one a hip replacement and the other a breast implant. The hip-joint replacement she found workmanlike and the breast implant, given the size of the enlargement, a bit obscene. Yet she complimented both surgeons on their work. When she made it known that she was a Harvard-trained surgeon, they basked in her praise.

The orthopod who did the hip bought her a coffee that afternoon and wanted to talk shop. He was an American-trained surgeon in his mid-fifties, and it soon became evident that he would like to move this conversation into something more than a professional discourse.

She nicely put him off for the time being, feeling it advantageous to leave the door partly ajar.

———

While Grace Davidson was establishing herself at the clinic, the other members of the team were making their last-minute preparations.

Garrett Walker made a final pass through each room of the wing that was to be occupied by their special patient. The janitorial staff was also there for a final cleaning. Walker made it a point to exchange pleasantries with each one. In those rooms that were vacant, he whistled a tuneless version of "Spanish Harlem."

Across the street, in a rental van that sprouted nearly invisible aerials, Brad Gregory and Bill Owen recalibrated their monitoring and recording equipment. Days earlier, Walker and Owen had carefully planted micro listening devices in each room. Later in the day, Owen and Gregory would be joined by a linguist who was fluent in Pashto and Arabic, and skilled enough to simultaneously translate either to English in real time. The van itself would be replaced daily by another vehicle so as not to give away the obvious.

Bijay Gurung and Akheem Kelly-Rogers would relieve Owen and Gregory to give them a break over the course of their vigil.

The purpose of the audio surveillance was to alert the team of any suspicions that might be raised by the target's security element. If, for some reason, they smelled a rat or caught on to what was being planned, they would have to get Grace Davidson out of there quickly. It was for that reason that Garrett Walker would never be far away while she was at the clinic.

"So, what do you think?" Brisco asked.

Fagan paused in reflection as he considered the depth of the question. The two of them sat in a small bistro, over coffee and a brioche, just a few blocks from the Bonsucesso Clinic. It was late morning.

"I think we've done all we can. And I don't think we could have a better team in place—nor could the team be better prepared. Now it's just a matter of waiting and execution. We have to let things play out and hope that Grace can do what she has to do after our Egyptian friend does his thing. What do *you* think? Have I missed anything?"

Steven Fagan was not asking out of idle curiosity. While he was in overall charge of this bold venture and had examined each aspect of what was to take place with the keen mind of a covert-operations expert, he knew he was not infallible. Furthermore, he valued Janet Brisco's opinion and instincts.

"I don't think so. It will work, or it won't. And if it doesn't, I'm confident we can get Grace out of there. It goes without saying, there's no way we can let this guy leave here like he arrived. One way or another, we have to take him down. But I'm still bothered by the donor. What's going to happen to this fellow once he's given up both his kidneys? What do you think they have planned for him?"

Fagan raised his eyebrows in conjecture. "We have no idea. My guess is that they will take him back with them and hospitalize him in Islamabad until the end—maybe with dialysis treatments and maybe not. Or they may choose to euthanize him and leave him behind. That will be their decision—not ours. Janet, you have to get past this. This is a high-stakes operation. We have to stay focused on what we came here to do."

She took a tentative sip of her coffee. "I suppose."

Following a brief stop for fuel in the Canary Islands, the Gulfstream touched down at Galeao International Airport five minutes ahead of the scheduled arrival on their flight plan. As the sleek jet taxied to the corporate terminal, Atiyaht Abd al-Rahman touched a key on his satellite phone. After momentary interchange clicks, he was connected to the front desk of the Belmond Copacabana.

Dr. Hosni Hasani had slept poorly. Normally, he would have enjoyed a bottle of Argentine Malbec with his evening meal before bedding down with a buxom sleeping companion. His sexual encounters were active to the point of violence—but mercifully brief for his paramour. And they did allow him to sleep soundly. On this trip, he took no more than a glass of wine with dinner and slept alone.

Throughout the night he had awoken with the sexual fantasies given only to Arab males who have infrequent encounters with western sexual antics. These exotic images were quickly extinguished by the thought of the medical procedure ahead of him. He had finally just gone into REM sleep when the phone jolted him awake.

"Yes, yes. Hello?"

"Doctor Hasani, this is Shakir. Are you awake?"

It took Hasani a moment to get his bearings—first where he was, then why, and finally with a stab of recognition, who he was talking to. "Yes, of course. Where are you?"

"We are here and will soon be headed for the clinic. Is everything in readiness?"

"Yes, yes of course. You are here already?"

Al-Rahman's voice was laced with impatience. "Did I not just say we were? Your patient will be available to you for examination late this afternoon. Is that acceptable?"

"Why, yes, that will be most acceptable." He looked at his watch. "May we say four o'clock at the clinic? An examination room has been held in readiness."

"Until that time then, Doctor." The man Hasani knew as Shakir rang off.

Through the window of the bistro, both Janet Brisco and Steven Fagan watched as the three Lincoln Town Cars with tinted windows rolled past the café, en route to the clinic. Fagan nodded in admiration—secure but ostentatious.

"Now it begins," Brisco said. It was not a question.

"Now it begins," he replied.

Chapter Ten: Osama

After the Gulfstream had come to a stop, two men made their way from the plane into the terminal. There, they met a driver retained by the clinic to lead a three-car motorcade through the late-morning traffic to their destination. The cars, all rented Lincoln Town Cars that had been parked in the lot adjacent to the corporate terminal, pulled up beside the aircraft as the entourage deplaned.

As they piled into the vehicles, some were dressed in western attire that, for the most part, were ill-fitting suits, while others were turned out in traditional Arab robes. A particularly tall man in Arab garb, his head shrouded in a *keffiyeh*, entered the rear of the second car. Luggage was hastily stuffed into the trunks, and the cars departed.

Following a half-hour drive from the airport and through the Bonsucesso District, the procession pulled to a rear portico entrance to the north wing of the clinic. The tall passenger emerged from the rear seat of the second car and made his way to the door. About half in his party rushed ahead of him, one holding the door while the others attended to the luggage. In a matter of moments, all were inside and the cars gone. They would be parked offsite, far enough away so as not to attract attention to the clinic but close enough to be on call if they were needed.

The tall man was shown to his ample but Spartan quarters—a bedroom, a sitting room, bath, and small kitchenette. After a slow pirouette, he imperceptibly nodded his satisfaction, and with a wave of his hand, dismissed the others. He wished to be alone. Once he was by himself, he slumped into a padded armchair.

While he took great pains not to let it show, Osama bin Laden was very tired and very much afraid. He had a morbid fear of the medical procedure that he now faced and tried not to think about it.

Not for the first time, nor the last, he wished he had not agreed to the operation. For a man who had been pursued throughout Africa, Southwest Asia, and the Middle East; had been wounded in Tora Bora; and had narrowly escaped death many times; he was more afraid now than at almost any other time in his long odyssey as the leader of al-Qaeda. He knew his fears were irrational, and that his best and perhaps only chance at a long life lay within this medical procedure. Yet he was still afraid.

As a Muslim movement's leader, he had also assumed the role of a religious leader—for in the Muslim world, leaders were clerics. Long ago, he had learned to take on the aloof demeanor of a Muslim cleric, hiding his emotions at all costs. He no longer spoke; he made pronouncements. He might seek counsel from others regarding the operation of al-Qaeda or on matters that related to the struggle, but he had no true personal confidantes. Even though he had several wives, no Muslim male, and certainly not one of his stature, took counsel from a woman.

So, he was very much alone with his fear and bore it with a stoic countenance. Yet, periodically, especially when he was alone with no immediate diversion, he found himself on the edge of panic.

Had not his kidney function begun to deteriorate over the last few months, he would never have agreed to this. He had recently come to a point where he was not sure if it was his failing kidneys or the debilitating fear of the operation that had all but immobilized him. If he thought too long about what was to take place, to visualize what was going to be done to him, he would begin to tremble uncontrollably.

He tried to think of the cause, the organization he led, and how much his presence was needed—what he himself meant to his followers. When he prayed, he asked Allah the Merciful to give him strength. Sometimes it helped, but most of the time it did not.

In his rational moments, bin Laden knew his fears were largely unjustified—that he would come through the surgery just fine. In the end, he was simply a mortal man facing a difficult but necessary operation.

Yet the prospect terrified him. At times, he felt he might not be able to go through with it—or hoped that his presence would be discovered and they would have to race back to the airport. As another tremor coursed through his large, awkward frame, there was a soft knock at the door.

"Enter."

The door opened, and Atiyaht Abd al-Rahman slipped inside. "Greetings, *Imam.* I have just had a visit with the clinic director, and he assures me that all preparations have been made for your procedure. He said that this kind of operation is often carried out here, and that the surgeon will be here later this afternoon to complete his final examination. Your procedure is scheduled for the day after tomorrow at ten o'clock."

Bin Laden nodded but said nothing. Because he was by nature a reserved individual and so revered by those around him, few knew or guessed that their tall, outwardly serene leader harbored this morbid fear of the transplant operation.

But al-Rahman did. As his chief of staff and most trusted advisor, he knew of bin Laden's reservations. They had been together since well before the World Trade Center bombings. More recently, the exodus from Afghanistan and the seclusion and sanctuary within the Federated Tribal Area of Pakistan had further galvanized their relationship. He knew how much al-Qaeda needed bin Laden—not the tentative, hesitant leader he had become but rather the dynamic visionary who had orchestrated the attacks of 9/11.

Yet, while he knew all this, he could do little to allay or even acknowledge bin Laden's fear. He could only appeal to his vanity, which—at times—was the only thing that could override the dread bin Laden felt about the upcoming medical procedure.

"I know this will be a trial for you, *Imam*, but when it is over, you will have your old strength back. And then, who knows what mischief we will be able to create for the Great Satan. You will see. Your followers will rally to the cause in great numbers and, with your guidance, again go forth to attack the West. And your name will be spoken in the same breath as the Prophet, praise be his name."

Al-Rahman spoke reverently, with head bowed, but snatched an occasional glance at bin Laden to see if his words were having any effect. The cleric—although he was no cleric in the strict Muslim sense of the word, as he had neither the religious training nor the bloodlines that would qualify him as a holy man—seemed unmoved and almost indifferent. It was as if he had given himself over to his fate.

This was just fine by al-Rahman. Al-Qaeda needed this man and needed him healthy and vibrant, as he had been in the 1990s when they were building the al-Qaeda networks that had challenged the great western powers. The loss of the sanctuaries in Afghanistan had been a setback, but the Americans leading their so-called coalition into Iraq had been an unexpected blessing. Iraq had proved to be something of a quagmire for their enemies and had spun off jihadist affiliates across the Middle East and Southwest Asia.

But now, this man—and *this* man alone—had the stature to serve as a unifying force for these Muslim offshoots. Only he could do this. Al-Rahman had known the bin Laden of those passionate early days of the struggle. And that was the bin Laden the organization now so desperately needed.

"Rest, *Imam*. A lunch is being prepared for you, and then you may rest until it is time for Doctor Hasani's examination. All will be well. *Inshallah* [if Allah wills it]."

"*Inshallah*," bin Laden repeated, but it was a listless, automatic response.

Al-Rahman inclined his head in a show of respect and left the room.

Only about half of those who had arrived that day were members of bin Laden's security team. There was his personal nurse, who attended him and would see to his personal and medical needs during his postoperative recovery, and there was a cook to prepare meals for the *Imam* as well as the rest of the detail.

There was also a communications specialist, who monitored the al-Qaeda internet sites and kept up routine communications that normally emanated from al-Qaeda Central headquarters. Al-Rahman had gone to great lengths to preserve the notion that bin Laden and al-Qaeda were still in tribal-controlled mountains of western Pakistan. The illusion that he was just another wealthy Arab in need of an illegal organ transplant was their best chance to remain undetected by the western intelligence services. That was why there were only five bodyguards who accompanied them. Their best security was the smallest possible footprint.

At the rear of the wing, on the next level above bin Laden's, quarters was a similar suite of rooms, which was occupied by a single individual. He was much younger than bin Laden, almost as tall, with rich dark features and a calm demeanor. When shown to his lodgings, he had been treated with almost the same deference and respect as bin Laden. Once he was alone, he unfurled his prayer rug, paused to discern an easterly direction, and knelt to pray.

Tahir Shahzad had been a medical student in Lahore before he joined al-Qaeda shortly after 9/11. When a kidney transplant operation was being contemplated for bin Laden, a search for suitable donors had been quietly initiated. The search had two criteria, one medical and one theological. The donor had to have the requisite tissue and blood characteristics, and he had to be a devout Muslim man. No woman's organs would be suitable.

Bin Laden's blood type and tissue-matching requirements had been specific but, given the modern drugs that aided in a patient's positive acceptance of a new organ, they were generic. So, among the potential donor pool, a premium was placed on the faith of the individual. And it was indeed a test of faith. A great many of those who were medically suitable stepped back when the full extent of their sacrifice was made known to them.

Tahir Shahzad had known better than most of the ordeal ahead for him. When he had been told that he would be asked for *both* organs, he had only asked that he be allowed to pray on the matter. Then he had humbly submitted that, as a true believer, he would be honored if a part of him could serve the *Imam* in this way.

At first, the ever-skeptical al-Rahman had questioned a faith strong enough to allow someone to submit to giving over both of their kidneys. It was one thing to strap explosives to one's body and walk into a crowded mall. In one instant, it was this life—and in the next, it was paradise everlasting. But the slow death that awaited the ultimate poisoning of one's own blood over time was another matter.

It was Shahzad himself who had sought al-Rahman out and asked if it could be arranged for the surgeon who performed the transplant operation to end his life when he was no longer needed. The answer to why he wished it to be this way had surprised and impressed both al-Rahman and bin Laden. He had simply said that he was being afforded a singular honor. To quietly go to sleep in the presence of his *imam* and be resurrected in paradise was more than any man could hope for. He felt that God had singled him out to serve in this way, and so he embraced the quiet death once he had fulfilled his service.

Tahir Shahzad's serenity and faith had impressed al-Rahman and all of bin Laden's inner circle. Al-Rahman too was a pious Muslim, and he both respected and admired Shahzad. But he was also a pragmatic man with a secret terrorist organization to run. He needed a healthy bin Laden and only wished some of the courage of this devout young man would rub off on their esteemed leader.

As soon as they had landed in Brazil and reached the Bonsucesso Private Clinic, Al-Rahman had breathed a sigh of relief. Bin Laden's right-hand man wanted the operation to be over with as quickly as possible.

———

Most of what was being said by al-Rahman, bin Laden, and the others was being recorded and transcribed. Fagan's team now knew the operation would take place in less than forty-eight hours, and it was intended that only one man of this two-person procedure would leave the operating theater alive. Neither Janet Brisco nor Grace Davidson were comfortable with this, but both knew there was nothing that could be done about it.

The person who would be the last to know of this was Doctor Hosni Hasani. Later that afternoon, he again examined his patient and placed him on a regime of antibiotics and antigens that would bolster his immune system and better dispose him to accept the new organ. On al-Rahman's insistence, a strong relaxant had also become a part of the pre-op regime.

It was only after the exam that Hasani met with al-Rahman and learned it was to be *two* organs. Al-Rahman joined the physician in the exam room after bin Laden was escorted back to his quarters.

"You wish me to transfer *both* of the donor's organs!" Hasani blurted. "Of course, I can do this, but what is to become of the donor? How is he to live with no kidney function?"

"You have done this in the past, have you not?" Al-Rahman asked, knowing the answer.

"Yes, but that was with a terminally ill donor. This is a healthy young man. And a man can live a long and healthy life with a single kidney. It is not necessary. Why was I not told of this earlier?"

"Is not two organs better than one, in case one should encounter a problem? You know our leader has other medical issues. What would happen if the single organ should fail him in the future?"

"All that is perhaps true, but this donor is young and very healthy. His one organ is more than adequate to sustain life."

Al-Rahman had purposely kept this from Hasani, concluding that he could more easily deal with any of his objections on the eve of the procedure. He had found Hasani a greedy and self-centered man, but not an unreasonable one. But if reason did not work, then there was always the prospect of a threat. Al-Rahman hoped it would not get to that. It was for that very reason that one of the more thuggish-looking of bin Laden's bodyguards had quietly posted himself in the corner of the exam room.

"You must understand, *Doctor*," al-Rahman began in a low, menacing voice, "that we have come here at great risk to all concerned and that, in taking this risk, we will seek the best possible outcome—again for all concerned. This means that the *imam*, having come this far, will leave here with two fully functioning kidneys. Are we clear on this?"

Hasani, noting the suddenly serious tone taken by al-Rahman, hesitated but only a moment. "Yes, yes. But what about the donor? What is to become of him?"

"Wait right here."

Moments later, al-Rahman returned with Tahir Shahzad. With al-Rahman and the bodyguard standing nearby, the young man—in clear and no uncertain terms—told Hasani what he wished him to do once the transplant had taken place.

Hasani had to ask but a few questions to convince himself that this zealot was not only serious, but compliant, uncoerced, and completely unafraid. Mechanically, it made little difference to Hasani. The extra time needed for the transfer of the additional organ would offset the time it would have taken to suture the connective tissue of a live donor. And, he would have to concern himself only with the postoperative recovery of a single patient. He was still not totally comfortable with the arrangement, but he had only to glance at the stern features of al-Rahman to know that he had no choice in the matter.

Later that evening, Steven Fagan gave copies of the transcribed conversation to Janet Brisco and Grace Davidson. The only comment was from Briscoe. "It makes you wonder," she said in a resigned tone, "if we can ever beat these people? If they have young men and women willing to sacrifice like this for their cause, how can we stop them?"

Fagan shrugged. "I can't answer that one, but if we can pull this off, we have a chance to hold back the tide of extremism—at least for a while. In the long run, maybe that's all we really can do. Fight a holding action until some form of secularism takes hold in succeeding generations."

Grace Davidson looked grim but determined. "I certainly never thought I'd be a party to a procedure that ended a human being's life. But then I never thought I'd lose my husband to a maniac in a commandeered jetliner."

"I've been giving that some thought," Fagan replied, "and I really see no way around this other than to abandon him to his fate. If Hasani terminates him, so be it." He looked at Grace Davidson. "But I certainly cannot ask you to do it. If he's alive when you enter the picture, then do what you can to see that he survives the procedure. We can do no more for him."

The day before the scheduled operation passed quietly and without incident. Dr. Hasani again called on his patients—the one who was to live and the one who was not. Both were resting quietly. The organ recipient required the assistance of mild sedatives and the organ donor required only his faith.

If Hasani thought this odd, he gave no indication of it. He was very accomplished at his job, and he'd had enough experience with donors and recipients to have learned that each case was different; each organ exchange a drama in itself.

Yet this one was different. Never had he performed an operation on so important a personage as Osama bin Laden. Seldom had he experienced the calm demeanor of this donor. And never had he been a part of a procedure where a donor asked that the giving of his organ or organs be his last act on earth.

It was true that Hasani had previously received illegal organs from terminally-ill patients for compensation—donors who willingly surrendered an organ so their family would get the money. But they had died later from their terminal illness—not the transplant. This would be the first time where, by the donor's request, the dying was to immediately follow the giving.

But Hasani was a mechanic—and a good one. In his own opinion, the best there was. And he was confident he could do what was required.

After again inspecting the operating theater, he would retreat to the hotel and try not to think of the good Argentine wines and generous Latin women he would be enjoying *after* the procedure was completed. He would give little thought to the postoperative recovery of his patient. That, for the most part, would be in the hands of the clinic staff and bin Laden's nurse. He would make a daily appearance, but barring any complications, he would not be needed.

Grace Davidson quietly moved about the clinic that day and was in attendance for the only scheduled operation, a facial plastic surgery. But there was, she sensed, a subtle difference about the clinic and the medical staff—a tenseness in the air like that in anticipation of an electrical storm. And the anxiety was not caused by the reduction and rebuilding of this woman's slightly oversized nose.

While the occupants of the clinic's north wing kept to themselves, there was an undercurrent of speculation about just who this special patient was. The janitorial services to the wing had been suspended. Food carts were loaded and prepared, then left at the door, where they were collected and taken inside by serious men who neither spoke nor made any acknowledgment when spoken to. The Muslim cook who had prepared the food in the clinic kitchen spoke neither Spanish nor Portuguese.

This was not the first time the Bonsucesso Private Clinic had treated patients with special needs and who wanted total anonymity, but seldom had security and privacy issues been carried to this extent.

That evening, with the exception of Brad Gregory and Bijay Gurung, who were in a mobile listening post not far from the clinic, the team again met in Brisco's apartment for a final briefing. With the preparations in place, there was little to be discussed, but they reviewed the day's upcoming events one last time.

Tom Gardina was again there, as he was the team's link between them and official U.S. government support. Past Gardina and his boss, the CIA station chief in Brazil, no one else knew of the team's presence or their mission.

Gardina himself would serve as liaison to an unwitting squad of FBI agents who were ready to respond in the event the target became spooked and left the clinic. The vehicles that served the patient and his contingent had all been fitted with tracking devices so any use of the Town Cars could be monitored. The agents had not a clue about the person with whom they were dealing. They only knew he was a high-value person of interest.

Despite the popular notion that the FBI and CIA did not get along, when dealing with potential terrorist targets overseas, the two agencies worked well together. Steven Fagan and his team had the backup they needed and hoped would not be necessary.

Bill Owen and Akheem Kelly-Rogers would relieve Gregory and Gurung at dawn and move the mobile listening post to a position where they would have eyes on the clinic.

This was not the first rodeo for either Steven Fagan or Janet Brisco, but both knew it was, by far, the most important of their covert undertakings. They stayed up late, Fagan drinking coffee and Brisco smoking cigarettes.

———

On the day of the procedure, Dr. Hosni Hasani was joined by Dr. Roberto de Silva just after 0700. Shortly thereafter, they were joined by another physician, the anesthesiologist. As there were to be two patients, they would be assisted during the procedure by a nurse anesthetist, but this pre-op meeting was just for the three doctors.

After going over his checklist, Hasani told the others that the procedure they were about to assist would be for the transplant of both kidneys. Before they could object, he went on to tell them that the donor was suffering from an inoperable brain tumor and had only a short time to live. His family was to be well compensated, and it mattered little whether his few remaining days were spent with a single kidney or on dialysis. Hasani said nothing of the donor's wish not to survive the operation. When the time came, he would personally attend to that.

The anesthesiologist simply shrugged at this. As an attending physician, he was simply responsible for the takeoff and the landing. The inflight mechanics of this medical flight were Hasani's responsibility.

As for de Silva, knowing what he did, he seriously doubted that the donor had a terminal condition. This did little to assure him that this procedure would go as planned, at least for the donor patient.

At 0900, Doctor Hasani made his way into the first of two pre-op rooms. Bin Laden was on the mobile gurney, face up with an IV drip going into each arm, one fast and one slow. Their combined effect had left him barely conscious, which was what Hasani wanted. Monitoring this was the attending anesthesiologist, whose eyes now shown wide and bright. Even with his beard cut short, his was one of the most recognizable faces in the world. Hasani saw at a glance that all was in order. And as the surgeon moved this one step closer to the operating theater, he became more sure of himself. This was his element, and he indeed had few peers for this kind of surgery.

The anesthesiologist left his station at the head of the one pre-op gurney and motioned Hasani to one side. "Do you know who this is?" the doctor hissed.

"I know, and at this juncture, it does not matter, Doctor. He is but another patient who needs our skill and attention. If you feel you cannot proceed, I will do this with the nurse anesthetist." Hasani, knowing his man, had counted on his ego and his professional pride.

The doctor stared at him for a long moment and then looked away. "Very well. Let's get this done. I wish to be away from here."

Hasani placed a hand on his shoulder. "Thank you. I knew I could count on you. He is but another patient for whom we will do our best. Nothing more, nothing less, eh?"

"As you say, *Doctor*. I will await you in the OR."

The second pre-op visit was much different. The donor patient was in the company of the nurse anesthetist, but he himself was on his prayer rug, forehead touching the polished linoleum floor. The nurse merely looked at Hasani and made a helpless gesture.

Hasani spoke to him quietly in Arabic. "My noble friend, it is about time for us to begin. May I ask you finish your prayer and place yourself on the table so we can prepare you for your part in this procedure?"

At first, Hasani was not sure Shahzad had heard him, but after a moment, the young man rose and eased himself upon the gurney. He calmly looked around the room with a serene, almost bovine expression, as if he were seeing the room and those in it for the first time. Then, the former medical student's eyes settled on Hasani. "Doctor, I wish you a successful procedure with no complications. Perhaps when we meet in the next world, we can talk about your work this day. *Inshallah.*"

"*Inshallah,*" Hasani echoed involuntarily. The courage and sincerity of this youth almost penetrated Hasani's surgeon-in-charge facade—almost. He nodded to the nurse, and she started the drip that would put Shahzad under for the operation. As he passed from consciousness, the calm smile remained pasted on his handsome features.

The two patients preceded Hasani into the operating room, where each of the two anesthetists sat at the head of their respective patient's gurney. Then, Hasani—like a high priest making his way to the altar—led Roberto de Silva into the operating room. Both were scrubbed and gowned and held their hands in front of them like a pair of sleepwalkers.

As the surgeon glanced around the room, he again saw that all was in order, but for a gowned and masked woman standing on the far side of the room. She was not part of the normal surgery staff. Noting that this was the only anomaly, he made straight for her. "Who are you, and what are you doing here?"

"My name is Doctor Davidson, and I am here with the permission of the clinic director. I represent the All-Americas Insurance Group. As a part of the clinic's medical coverage, we have to observe a certain number of operations each year."

Hasani was about to protest when she stepped forward and lowered her voice. "Imagine my good fortune when I learned you would be conducting this procedure. I've seen enough face lifts and tummy tucks. Now I get to watch a master surgeon conduct a difficult procedure."

Hasani was on the verge of ordering her from the room, but decided that might call unwanted attention to his patient. And he was anxious to begin this operation. The sooner he began, the sooner it would be finished. She may be a doctor, Hasani thought as he turned away without another word, but she was still just a woman. Let her stay.

He moved back to between the two operating tables. "Very well, let's get them into position, face down."

While Hasani looked on, four surgical nurses who were standing along the wall converged on the two prostrate forms. With gentle, practiced motions, they moved both patients from gurney to table, turning them face down in the process. With the two men lying on their stomachs, shaved backs exposed and bathed to a pale orange tint with anodyne solution, they retreated back to their on-call positions along the wall of the operating theater.

Hasani looked at the anesthesiologist tending bin-Laden and then his assistant. "Are we ready?"

Both nodded.

Then, Hasani asked for a scalpel and turned to bin-Laden for the first incision. There was no hesitation, nor did he take a deep breath before he put knife to flesh. In confident, workmanlike fashion, he simply made the cut.

Back along the wall, Grace Davidson did, in fact, take in a deep breath. She had scarcely moved since her brief confrontation with Hasani. Now, she began to take steady, regular breaths.

Much the same could be said for Steven Fagan and Janet Brisco, thanks to Brad Gregory, who—escorted by Garrett Walker and posing as an electrician days earlier—had installed both video and audio surveillance in the operating theater. The video feed, relayed to them in Brisco's apartment from the van parked across the street from the clinic, was a grainy, fish-eye presentation of the room. But the audio was amplified and clear, right down to the clank of the used scalpel Hasani dropped into the sterile metal receptacle.

"I can't believe," Brisco whispered, "that we are sitting here watching this arrogant Egyptian ass hack into the world's most wanted man."

"Interestingly put," Fagan replied, permitting himself a grim smile. "But is that not what we planned for all along?"

The procedure that removed bin Laden's kidneys and replaced them with those of Tahir Shahzad took just under four hours. The operation was not unlike removing the engine of a new car and inserting it into an identical but older automobile of the same make and model. The main component, or in this case components, were relatively simple to section, remove, and reinstall. The art was in the details of attaching the vessels and connective tissue that would serve and support the transplanted organs.

Hasani removed and attached one of Shahzad's organs, and then the other. With the basic installation made, and the major vessels sewn in place, he then busied himself with the tedious details of suturing the myriad of connective tissue and minor vessels that served each transplanted organ. While he attended to bin Laden, de Silva took care of the relatively simple task of closing off the major vessels that had taken the blood to and from Shahzad's kidneys.

While the two surgeons went about their tasks, Grace Davidson quietly moved to a position behind and to Hasani's left. As a part of her preparation for her role in this, she had observed several transplant operations, so she was not unfamiliar with what was taking place. A part of her had to choke down the moral aspects of the young life that was being sacrificed to extend that of this thoroughly evil man, and watching it unfold before her did little to stanch the anger that burned deep within her.

Yet the medical practitioner in her could not help but admire the speed and skill with which Hasani worked. He had moved like a ballet dancer from one patient to the other. Now that he focused on the organ recipient, his hands moved with the grace and speed of a veteran conductor coaxing the William Tell Overture from an amateur but eager orchestra.

"You are indeed a gifted surgeon." Davidson spoke quietly at his side. "I've observed some great surgeons, but seldom have I seen such good work. You have marvelous hands."

Hasani grunted in acknowledgment, but brokered no hesitation in the flow of his work.

But that was not why Davidson spoke as she did, though—with a moment's reflection—she realized that her compliments were quite truthful. She spoke as she did for one reason and one reason only. She needed to get close to Hasani and remain close to him. As he worked, she occasionally commented on his handiwork.

"Good. Good."

"Excellent."

"Well done."

Hasani had often been observed in close quarters by medical students. He was also used to being admired and having his work complimented. He proceeded without missing a beat.

If Steven Fagan and his team were to succeed in this complex undertaking, there would be a short window in the procedure in which Dr. Grace Davidson would perform her assigned task. But before she could do that, Dr. Hosni Hasani would have to be removed from the operating theater.

That would be a timing call and a call that she and she alone would have to make. Davidson sensed that Hasani was just about to that point in time, more from his slightly hurried movements and shortness with the two nurses handing him instruments than from the mechanics of the procedure. While Fagan and Brisco held their breath, they watched as Davidson stumbled and slightly bumped Dr. Hasani. Abruptly, he turned on her.

"You clumsy cow, watch what you are doing. Step back, now!"

Davidson took two paces back, mumbling an apology.

So intently was Hasani focused on his work that he failed to register the pinprick of a vented needle inserted into his hip. Within seconds, he was back at work, snarling at one ER nurse to hand him the next tool and another to blot the sweat from his brow.

For her part, Davidson stepped back, with her head lowered. Before she did so, she looked up at the hidden camera and nodded slightly. Fagan and Brisco caught this brief acknowledgment and sighed in relief.

In two minutes, give or take a few seconds, Dr. Hasani would find that he would have difficulty remaining on his feet and would be incapable of continuing. As it turned out, due to his powers of concentration as he focused on the procedure, it was close to two and a half minutes before he stood up and away from the prostrate form of Osama bin Laden. Knowing that something was terribly wrong, he managed a step back before his legs buckled. It was Grace Davidson who caught him by the shoulders and eased him to the floor.

A surgical team in an operating theater is much like a well-drilled squad of soldiers assaulting an enemy position. Everyone in the OR has a job, including the surgeon squad-leader. But soldiers are conditioned to handle combat losses; if the leader goes down, the second in command takes over and the soldiers carry on with the assault. Surgical teams are not trained for this; they are solely focused on their individual responsibilities. So, when Dr. Hasani suddenly passed out, it was beyond the training and experience of everyone in the operating theater.

But not unlike soldiers, members of the surgical team are slavishly adept at following the direction of the high priests of their profession—the surgeons. Or in this instance, the high priestess—Doctor Grace Davidson. "You!" she said in a calm but commanding voice, pointing to one of the male scrub nurses along the wall. "And you. This man is sick, and we must get him out of the operating room." Then to de Silva, "Doctor, are you ready to finish this operation? If you are, then I will assist you."

As if to document her new role as the assisting surgeon, she took a set of surgical binoculars from under her scrubs and pulled them on. Then, she bent over bin Laden. "It would appear that Doctor Hasani has completed the transplant portion of the procedure, and it is but for us to close—for both patients. Would you agree?"

For the first time, Roberto de Silva pivoted so he had a clear view of bin Laden's new organs. He had already begun to suture up the connecting vessels from rents left from the removal of Shahzad's kidneys. He had been surprised at the seemingly amateurish removal of the organs, but then de Silva had no way of knowing that it was Hasani's intent to terminate this donor. Now, he looked closely at the re-attachment of those organs in the slightly larger frame of bin Laden. All appeared to be in order.

"Take your time, Doctor," Davidson said quietly. "We need to make sure the procedure is complete before we close."

After a moment's inspection, de Silva spoke with a calmness that he did not feel. "It would seem that Doctor Hasani has completed the transplant of both organs. If you will be so good as to close the recipient, I will attend to the donor patient. He is currently in no danger, but is still at risk. I will do my best for him."

Before she bent to her task, Grace Davidson turned to the two wide-eyed anesthetists. "Are both patients stable?"

Both nodded.

"What has happened to Doctor Hasani," the anesthesiologist managed.

"Apparently, he has suddenly taken ill," Davidson replied. "But as the organ transplants have been completed, we will attend to the follow-up measures and close the incisions."

Both anesthetic practitioners, as well as everyone else in the operating theater, were screened from the exposed internal tissue by a wall of absorbent gauze that encircled the patient surgical openings. For the moment, both Davidson and de Silva labored in privacy, their work screened from view from their elbows down.

De Silva carefully sutured the blood vessels that had served Shahzad's absent kidneys.

Grace Davidson took a small case from the pocket of her scrubs, sprang the catch, and gently laid the open case along the crack of bin Laden's hairy ass. The rushing kaleidoscope of events that brought her to this point in time flashed before her. Then she went to work. As she had done so many times in practice, she pulled back the flap of skin along the sides of bin-Laden's spine and carefully fitted the two cylinders along either side of his spine.

She carefully took the gold filament antenna and laid it along the spinal connecting tissue, looping it twice between the T7 and T12 vertebrae.

When she had completed this, in close to her Virginia-clinic best practice time, she glanced up to meet de Silva's gaze. He too had finished with Shahzad and was closing the first of the two long incisions in his back. They silently exchanged a look of relief. Then, Davidson—her work now masked by muscle tissue and skin—began the task of sewing up the world's most wanted man.

By the time Dr. Hosni Hasani began to wake up from the sedative, both of his patients were in post-op recovery. Neither had yet regained consciousness. When he came to, he bolted upright, almost causing himself to again faint. "What is going on? Where is my patient?" When told that he had passed out in the OR, but not before completing the transplant of both organs, he was both angry and relieved.

Grace Davidson had quickly changed and was in another part of the clinic, leaving de Silva to handle Hasani's seemingly unending string of questions. When de Silva told him the American insurance doctor had helped him close, he seemed to accept this.

Assisted by de Silva, he looked in on bin Laden, who was still unconscious and resting on his stomach. The sutures on the two incisions across his back, he noted, were neat and well finished. "And you are sure that all the vessels and connective tissue were in place before you closed?"

"Yes," de Silva replied. "I personally inspected your fine work, and before your—your accident—you had completed the transplant. It was only for me to make the closure on both patients."

"So, the donor came through the procedure well?"

"Yes, doctor, other than the fact that he no longer has any kidneys."

Hasani frowned. His instructions from al-Rahman were that Shahzad was not to survive the operation. Well, he told himself, that cannot be helped at his point. Being a doctor, Hasani had never been in favor of ending the donor's life, and he had been saved from that detail when he fainted. Now it was for al-Rahman and his security team to decide what to do. It was out of his hands.

Hasani once again checked on bin Laden to see that his postoperative vitals were as they should be. The Egyptian doctor seldom prayed, but he did ask Allah to spare the al-Qaeda leader from a staph infection. Then, he was off to the physician's locker room to shower and change clothes. He had a long day ahead of him to ensure that this most important patient experienced a normal recovery and that his new organs were accepted by a new host and performing as they should. He thought about finding the attractive American doctor to thank her for stepping in to assist de Silva, but that could wait. He had other things to do.

Grace Davidson, under the guise of stepping out for a late lunch, met Steven Fagan and Janet Brisco at a café several blocks from the clinic. Both were camped out over coffee and wreathed in smiles when Davidson arrived. "My gawd," she exclaimed as she slumped into a chair, "I feel like I'm the one who's been three and a half hours on the operating table. But we did it! At least I think we did it."

"You did well," Fagan said. "It was a very, very nice piece of work. Do you think the organ transplant was a success?"

"It certainly appeared to be. Only subsequent blood tests will show if the recipient's new organs are doing their job. For now, the post-op recovery team's task will be to keep him quiet and pumped full of antibiotics and antigens that will help with any potential rejection of the new organs. Only time will tell about that; but it appeared to be a successful transplant operation. The tissue match going in was good to begin with, and Hasani, in spite of being a self-important ass, is a first-class transplant surgeon. And the donor provided us with two very healthy organs."

At her mention of the donor, a cloud seemed to pass over Davidson. "As for the donor—well, his life with no kidney function is going to be short and not terribly pleasant. I've been thinking, since we're in the illegal organ transplant capital of the world, maybe we could see about getting this kid a new kidney. As it stands now, and God help me for saying it, it might have been more merciful had Hasani euthanized him on the operating table."

"How about it, Steven?" Brisco asked, warming to the idea. "You think your operating budget could pop for another kidney?"

"Ladies," he said, "I take no pleasure in this, but any attention we give to Shahzad's plight will only call attention to us, and that is most certainly not in keeping with our objective. We simply can't risk the attention. We have to consider the background of this young man. He's a zealot and has a violent past; he's not just a passive sympathizer. We could probably find him a new kidney, but we can't find him a new heart. He's the opposition—and the opposition's responsibility. And Grace, as to our objective, it seemed to us from what we saw that all went as planned with the implants, correct?"

"Yes, I believe so. I followed Brad Gregory's instructions to the letter. Past that, only he can tell you how things are working."

As if on cue, Fagan's encrypted cell phone purred. He looked at the caller ID and accepted the call.

"This is Steven...yes, ...yes, ...that's good to hear. Let's get ready to close things up—and great work." He looked from Brisco to Davidson. "That was Brad. They just made contact with our subject and the initial interrogation and transmission checks are within specs. Our tall bearded friend is now essentially wearing a wire. You're both to be congratulated for your part in this project. Now we have to tie up some loose ends and leave this lovely city."

The day following the operations, Grace Davidson returned to the clinic but only to check in with the clinic director to say that the Bonsucesso Clinic, per her cover story, was to be given high marks for both its administrative and medical procedures. She asked that Doctor Hasani be told that she considered it an honor to have been some assistance to such an esteemed surgeon during this very complex procedure.

Janet Brisco remained in the area while bin Laden recovered. She continued to have lunch with the clinic surgical nurse she had befriended.

The woman had this extraordinary tale about a private and well-guarded patient who came for a transplant operation that was conducted by a famous Egyptian surgeon. It seems the physician fainted just as he completed the transplant portion of the operation, and the assisting surgeon and an American woman doctor, who happened to be on hand, had to complete the procedure and close. After a full week of recovery, both the patient and the Egyptian surgeon had left—the doctor by Air France and the patient by private jet. The surgical nurse had a friend who worked at the Belmont Copacabana and said that the surgeon had a taste for good food, good wine and big Latin prostitutes—apparently the bigger the better.

Brad Gregory had stayed on for a few days to recalibrate their equipment. Just before he had left Rio and prior to bin Laden's departure, an Air Force liaison team had paid a visit to the Brazilian Air Force Base at Santa Cruz, just outside Rio de Janeiro. The team had arrived in a C-17 transport, along with a *Predator* drone that they demonstrated to the Brazilian Air Force brass. In fact, a senior Brazilian military officer had been at the controls when the drone made a pass across the Galeao International Airport at about 1,500 feet, causing the air traffic controllers to momentarily divert two inbound commercial flights. The general at the controls didn't particularly care about the ruckus he had caused at the airport, nor had he seen the icon blink on his flight-presentation monitor that indicated the drone had captured a faint ground-based burst transmission as the *Predator* was over the Bonsucesso Private Clinic.

Before leaving Rio, Steven Fagan had a quiet meeting with Dell Maxwell and Tom Gardina to thank them for station support. While the two CIA men were not given the full details of what had taken place, they knew who had visited Rio, and that this eclectic but thoroughly professional team of covert operators had accomplished their mission. Sometimes in the intelligence business, success was measured in incomplete knowledge.

The last two of the deployed Rio team to leave were Janet Brisco and Garrett Walker.

Before she left, Brisco had one last dinner with Robert de Silva. She gave him the contact information that would put him in touch with a liaison officer at the U.S. Marshals Department. The officer would see to the mechanics of his relocation. Once settled in his new apartment in Pasadena, he would be introduced to the cleared and witting staff member at the Huntington Memorial Hospital, which was in receipt of his medical records—records that would hold up before the standards board and admit him to practice there. And there was a vascular surgery group nearby that was interested in talking with him.

Walker's last call was to a policeman he still only knew as Alehandro. He was somewhat puzzled when Walker asked him if he could use a reliable, if reluctant, informant within the *Comando Vermelho* crime organization. When Walker handed him a simple remote device and explained its use and its connection, literally, to one Ricardo Esteban, he looked at Walker in a new light. He had long suspected that this American was not just a hired retainer with a prominent NGO (nongovernmental organization) who operated free clinics; he was much more than that. But, he did accept the remote device, and after leaving the meeting with Walker, he made plans for yet another meeting with Ricardo Esteban on his turf in the Bonsucesso District.

Following a week of seclusion and rest, bin Laden had been pronounced fit enough for travel. Doctor Hasani had been on hand for a few hours each day for tests and follow-up blood work. The patient had shown no signs of tissue rejection and it had been determined the kidneys were functioning properly. With the successful transplant operation behind him, the al-Qaeda leader was now free to resume his duties with increasing vigor.

Tahir Shahzad, on a full dialysis regimen, had left Rio with bin Laden on the Gulfstream. He had sat in the rear of the aircraft and had been permitted no contact with the man whose blood was now filtered with his kidneys. On reaching Islamabad, he had been met by the leader of an al-Qaeda cell and taken to a safe house. The following day, in a weakened condition and fitted with an explosive vest, he had sat in a café that was across the street from a Shiite mosque. When he had triggered the vest, it had failed to explode. While he struggled with the detonation device, he had been shot dead by a Pakistani policeman.

CHAPTER ELEVEN: GEORGE W.

The Federally Administrated Tribal Areas in northwestern Pakistan, and North and South Waziristan in particular, have been a burden to the government of Pakistan since the Paks won their independence from the Raj in 1947. The total tribal population is only three and a half million—about two percent of Pakistan's population. This loose confederation of Pashtun tribes, when not fighting with the central government, were just as content to fight with each other. The only stabilizing influence in the area seemed to be the tribes' collective resistance to any outside authority and their universal support of the Taliban. Al-Qaeda, they tolerated, and actively supported, after 9/11.

These tribal societies, while fiercely independent, do have three things in common. The first is Islam and a strict adherence to *sharia* law. The second is revenge. It is said that if it takes a century to avenge an insult or an issue of family honor, then the revenge taken is made sweeter by the long, intervening period of time. The third is hospitality. Once hospitality is granted, and it is granted liberally by the tribes to individual outsiders, it must be honored.

It was on this third tribal tenet that Osama bin Laden traded. When he escaped from Tora Bora into Waziristan in early 2002, he had been granted sanctuary and collectively welcomed by the tribes. To offer shelter to the man who had so successfully attacked and humbled the Great Satan was an honor, and he had been made welcome.

What little news they had received from the West in this remote mountainous region greatly exaggerated the successes of 9/11. They felt it would take years, even decades, for America to recover. But what the Americans had accomplished in Afghanistan in but a few months was what the Russians had failed to do in a decade. With the aid of the Northern Alliance, they had quickly swept the Taliban from power. Now, with the world's most wanted fugitive hiding in their midst, and their villages serving as sanctuary for the Taliban, the tribes of Waziristan had invited an armed presence along the Afghan/Pakistan border.

Taliban irregulars, fighting to regain control of Afghanistan, were free from close pursuit by both the Afghan National Army and Coalition forces–on the ground. Yet they were not free from continuous American drone strikes. The tribes might have tired of providing sanctuary for Taliban fighters, or even the extended hospitality they afforded Osama bin Laden, had it not been for the drones.

The deeply embedded warrior's ethos that is so much a part of tribal culture viewed this new form of remote warfare as both indiscriminate and cowardly. Men who hid in bunkers, hundreds or even thousands of miles away, and sent these aerial machines to do their fighting were not men at all. The drones simply made the Waziri and associated tribes that much more staunch in their support of the Taliban and in their determination to hide bin Laden.

Bin Laden seldom remained in one location for more than a few months at a time. Following his transplant operation, the al-Qaeda leader had been flown to Lahore and then to the city of Bannu, in eastern North Waziristan, by a private aircraft. From there, he had been driven by Land Rover to a compound well into the mountains west of Bannu.

This remote compound is where he had completed his recovery and had begun to pick up the threads of his diverse al-Qaeda organization. By January of 2006, Al-Qaeda Central was back in business, and with each day, a more revitalized Osama bin Laden took an increasingly active part.

Now that bin Laden was himself an electronic transmission entity, an agreement was brokered by Jim Watson, still the interim director at CIA, and the National Security Agency to help with the mechanics of the collection, as well as sharing, of the product. Turf issues between CIA, NSA, FBI, and DOD still existed, but the necessities of 9/11 had done much to create interagency cooperation. *Predator* or *Global Hawk* drones, both CIA and military, now made regular reconnaissance passes over Waziristan and the Federated Tribal Area, sometimes armed.

Now, there was an additional requirement to seek out a weak homing signal that periodically emitted from a compound west of Bannu. Once the aircraft was in range overhead, a coded burst transmission was uploaded to the passing drone. The product was then uplinked to an orbiting satellite and passed to NSA for processing. The processed transmission was then passed to a small, autonomous team of analysts at CIA. From there, the information and corroborating intelligence went to a single end-user—one unknown to those who made the necessary electronic handoffs to get it to its final destination.

If those along the line thought this carefully guarded information was destined to some secure vault in the bowels of the CIA's headquarters at Langley or a secret targeting cell in the Pentagon, they were wrong. It went to the highly secure electronic repository that was Steven Fagan's den office.

There, I-4's covert-operations master decided how best to use this intelligence product. Often, this meant who would live and who would die. On occasion, Fagan would consult with Janet Brisco by their secure SCAP (Security Content Automation Protocol) link, but for the most part, he decided what information would be passed along for a possible direct-action strike and what would not. He alone decided what could be done without endangering this unique source of intelligence.

———————

One of the first trusted lieutenants bin Laden received on his return to western Pakistan was Muhsin Musa Matwalli Atwah. Atwah was Egyptian born and had been a member of al-Qaeda since the early 1990s. Early on, in his late twenties, he had received training in explosives and bomb making in Afghanistan and had proven adept at both.

He was a highly intelligent operative, and seemed to move freely in and around the Middle East and Africa using multiple aliases and passports. He had constructed the bombs used to attack the American embassies in Dar-es-Salaam and Tanzania. This earned him a place on the FBI's terrorist watch list. After seeing al-Qaeda duty in places like Somalia and Nairobi, he had found his way back to Pakistan, where he provided training and logistical support for al-Qaeda operatives in Waziristan—operatives who were targeting western cities.

In the early spring of 2006, Atwah was busy preparing Taliban fighters for their return to Afghanistan for the summer fighting season when he was summoned to bin Laden's compound.

Bin Laden asked that Atwah redirect his efforts to the training of Waziri fighters for operations against the Pakistani Army, which was then challenging the leadership of the certain tribes in the Federated Tribal Area. As their guest, bin Laden had been asked by the Waziris to help with this, and he felt duty bound to do what he could. His conversation with Atwah was recorded, word for word, and uplinked in a burst transmission during the next scheduled drone pass.

Atwah promptly set up a training camp in North Waziristan and began operations. Having been alerted, U.S. spy satellites were able to monitor Atwah's activity and progress. After waiting a reasonable length of time following the bin Laden/Atwah meeting, this information was passed to the Pakistanis, who—on April 14— bombed the training camp, killing Atwah and close to a dozen Waziri fighters. A subsequent sweep of the area by the Pakistani Army confirmed the death of Muhsin Musa Matwalli Atwah.

The regenerated al-Qaeda organization was now enjoying a resurgence in northwestern Iraq. With Saddam Hussein in jail and awaiting the verdict of his trial, the Shiite majority in Iraq, under the protection of the U.S. military, was exerting control over the country to the exclusion of the Sunni tribes in al-Anbar Province and northern Iraq.

Throughout 2005 and into 2006, the Iraqi Sunnis, under the urgings of a rambunctious Jordanian al-Qaeda zealot named Abu Musab al-Zarqawi, had laid siege to the cities of Mosul, Fallujah, and Ramadi.

But al-Zarqawi's brand of al-Qaeda intervention in al-Anbar was brutal and vicious—and not totally directed at the Coalition forces. He insisted that the Sunni tribes in al-Anbar submit to his will, and tribal leaders who resisted were publicly and brutally killed. Al-Zarqawi demanded tribute from the tribes and tried to influence tribal governance by insisting that the daughters of tribal elders marry loyal al-Zarqawi followers. This proved most unpopular, and spawned a revolt of the tribes.

While bin Laden applauded the success of al-Zarqawi in Iraq, he was informed by his advisors that al-Zarqawi was overplaying his hand and the tribes were seeking help from the Americans. A visit to al-Zarqawi in Damascus by al-Rahman did little to curb the Jordanian's excesses. Finally, it was at al-Rahman's insistence that an encrypted satellite call was made by bin Laden to al-Zarqawi.

The call lasted for close to a half hour. At the end of the call, al-Zarqawi had agreed to curb his excesses and to cease his purge of the Anbari tribal leaders.

While the encryption had held up, enough was decoded to know it was a conversation with al-Zarqawi. Immediately following the call, a *Predator* drone had flown over bin Laden's compound in Waziristan and received a weak but audible burst transmission. The transmission was passed by satellite relay to an NSA cutout in Fort Meade, Maryland, where it was decoded and sanitized. At Steven Fagan's direction, it was passed to Central Command Headquarters at MacDill Air Force Base in Tampa.

From there, it was analyzed, and a set of target coordinates were sent to Task Force 145, whose mission in Iraq was to find and kill or capture al-Zarqawi. The task unit wanted him alive, but above all, they wanted him. The target coordinates put him in a northwest suburb of Baghdad. But it was a hostile Sunni neighborhood, and the task force had no quick-reaction teams in the area. So, the requirement was passed to the Air Force.

Less than four hours after bin Laden had lectured al-Zarqawi on the excesses of his leadership, two F-16C Falcons lifted off from Balad Air Base and made the short flight south to Baghdad. The coordinates placed the target in a small house in a residential neighborhood.

Shortly after the F-16s arrived on station, two five-hundred-pound laser-guided bombs crashed into the house, immediately killing five al-Qaeda operatives. Al-Zarqawi himself lived for another hour, but died when Iraqi forces reached the target location and removed him from the rubble.

Since the operation had moved to what Steven Fagan and his I-4 staff called the exploitation phase, they had been very careful in just what targeting information they passed along for direct action. They had done their best in the selections of response elements, spreading the targeting assignments among the U.S. military and the Afghan, Iraqi, and Pakistani militaries.

Fagan, working at his secure home office in Larkspur, had carefully sifted through the coded intercepts coming from Waziristan, looking for just the right opportunity—potential targets that balanced operational utility with security. He knew that bin Laden, al-Rahman, and the senior al-Qaeda leadership were paranoid about security. While it was inconceivable that they would link the utterances of bin Laden himself with U.S. operational success, Fagan was careful that no correlation be made between bin Laden's having recently talked about or with an al-Qaeda leader, and that leader becoming a target. So, Fagan had looked for those opportunities where there were multiple al-Qaeda leaders present so as to expand the potential sources for an al-Qaeda-generated security leak.

Such an opportunity came in late October of 2006.

With U.S. forces bogged down in Iraq, al-Qaeda had stepped up its efforts to reestablish itself in Afghanistan. Bin Laden himself had a great fondness for the country, for it was Afghanistan where the Taliban had sheltered him for so many years—and where he had planned and executed the 9/11 attacks. He dreamed of returning there in triumph, helping the Afghans to oust the Americans, as they had done to the Russians.

But the Americans and their puppet regime, headed by Hamid Karzai, were proving to be difficult. In mid-October, Fagan learned of a meeting of al-Qaeda leaders in Pakistan to discuss the campaign for retaking the northern provinces in Afghanistan. The data coming from bin Laden in this instance was unique in that it came not from anything bin Laden said or was said in his presence. It came from an email.

One of the features Brad Gregory had built into the implants was the ability to electronically scan for computer keystrokes in close proximity. It had worked in the lab, when he was designing and building the micro-transmission suite, but this was the first time it had been put to the test in the field. Bin Laden's outgoing email correspondence was encoded before transmission, but the text of communiqués as he keyed them into a laptop computer could be gathered, processed, and uplinked as well as his spoken words.

There was little insurgent activity in Afghanistan during the winter months. Most of the mid- and senior-level Taliban leaders routinely abandoned their rank-and-file fighters for sanctuary in Pakistan. Those fighters left behind had instructions to harass the Afghan governmental and Coalition forces. The leaders would then return in the spring to direct the next season's campaign.

In 2006, having just retreated to their sanctuary in Waziristan, a meeting of these leaders was called to talk about the preceding summer campaign and to plan for the next one. Nothing from the bin Laden email alluded to the location of this meeting, but with its wide dissemination and the popularity of such a gathering among the expat Afghan Taliban leadership, it was being widely talked about. Once alerted by the listeners at NSA, the location of the meeting was quickly pinpointed.

Given the number of Taliban and al-Qaeda operatives involved, the targeting team at U.S. Central Command felt that any involvement of the Pakistani military or the Pakistani ISI would alert the opposition. So, a rare cross-border tactical air strike was authorized, with notification sent to the Pakistani army only at the last minute.

On October 30, four American AH-64 Apache gunships left Jalalabad, in northwestern Afghanistan, for Chenagai, in the Bajaur tribal region, just across the border with Pakistan. The Apaches launched a total of six Hellfire missiles at a Chenagai madrassa—a Muslim compound that taught fundamentalist Muslim doctrine and basic infantry tactics to young men of various ages. When the Hellfires hit, the carnage was pervasive. Close to eighty militants, students and instructors, were killed.

The missiles, with their slight delay, penetrated the roof and exploded in the interior of the dirt-floor classrooms. The overpressure kicked out the walls and dropped the roofs on the occupants. Many who survived the initial blast had their eardrums imploded and died in the dust of the rubble before they could be rescued.

Aside from removing a cadre of seasoned Taliban combat leaders and the psychological damage of death without warning, there were several mid-level al-Qaeda leaders known to be in the compound—leaders who were on the coalition hit list. One was a cleric named Liaquat Hussain, a close associate of Ayman al-Zawahiri. If bin Laden could be said to have a deputy leader—or number two—in al-Qaeda, it was Ayman al-Zawahiri.

The other was Faqir Mohammed. Mohammed was a senior official in the Pakistani Taliban umbrella group, Tehrik-i-Taliban. He was a much-wanted man by American intelligence agencies and the Pakistani government. The Apache missile strike killed Hussain instantly, but Mohammed had left the compound moments earlier and escaped the carnage. He would be captured by Afghan intelligence officials several years later as he and a band of supporters tried to cross back into Afghanistan from Pakistan.

―――――――――

It was just after 0700. As was his custom, Steven Fagan was at his desk with a mug of coffee, reading intelligence summaries from official and nonofficial sources. Apart from the responsibility of handling this important product, he had to monitor the flow of intelligence-collection activity from all sources, foreign and domestic.

The art of it, from Fagan's perspective, was to protect this source not only from the opposition, but from U.S. and allied intelligence services. This meant carefully analyzing potential targets and balancing the operational gain with the chance of detection. He was doing this very thing when his secure phone line buzzed.

"Good morning, Ambassador."

"Good morning, Steven. How goes the battle against the forces of darkness?"

"It goes well, sir." The voice quality was excellent, and there was only the slightest delay while the encryption engaged. "And, as you might imagine, we are developing more targeting information than we can really act on; but, over time, I believe we can seriously erode their command-and-control function. Then—it's only a matter of time before the rank and file begin to lose faith in their leadership. What can I do for you today, Ambassador?"

Fagan noticed the momentary pause on the part of Joseph Simpson, and it was not encryption linkage.

"Steven, the president has just named a new director of Central Intelligence, and as you might imagine, it was a political appointment—a capable man, but still a politician. So, we'll not have Jim Watson providing top cover for us going forward. While the appointment won't be public for a few days, I'd like to get out in front of this as soon as possible. The new director will have to be put in the picture sooner or later. So, the question is—who is going to tell him, and how do we go about it?"

"So how would you like to handle it, sir?" Fagan knew from the tone of his voice that Simpson had chosen a course of action, and this was really a call to let him know what he had decided.

"It is a matter of whether we should take a bottom-up approach or a top-down approach. Jim Watson said he'd be happy to make this a part of his turnover, but that might open the door for this information getting into the hands of some of the new staffers he's bound to bring with him. So, we thought it might be better to have this come down from above. And the sooner the better."

Fagan knew where this was going, so he waited for Simpson to continue.

"So, Steven, do you own a pair of blue jeans?"

Joseph Simpson was aboard the G-5 when it landed in Oakland to collect Fagan and take on fuel. It was another three and a half hours to Waco, Texas, where the two men deplaned and boarded one of the Simpson Foundation's helicopters. The Sikorsky S-76 was expected at the ranch just outside the tiny town of Crawford, and the large helipad, which had been constructed to accommodate Marine One, was more than adequate to handle it.

One of the waiting Secret Service agents boarded the helicopter for a careful inspection of the cabin and cockpit before Fagan followed Simpson out onto the pad.

It took a moment for Fagan to realize that the man in faded denims, Eddie Bauer shirt, and straw cowboy hat leaning up against a dusty Jeep Waggoner, was the president of the United States. He shook Simpson's hand with both his own and then turned immediately to Fagan.

"Mister President, I'm Steven Fagan."

"I know who you are, Bro. The ambassador's told me a great deal about you, and I'm looking forward to a sit-down with y'all. But before we get down to bidness, let's get up to the house. Miguel's fixin' to burn some prime beef, and he knows how to cook a steer. If you like a good steak, Steven, you're in for a treat."

Fagan found himself sitting in the front seat of the Jeep while the president drove. On the way to the house, they took a half-hour windshield tour of the ranch while their host kept up a running dialogue of the workings of the spread. Unlike Joseph Simpson,

Fagan knew little or nothing of ranching, which delighted the president. Fagan wasn't sure who was enjoying this mini Texas travelogue more—George W., who was going on about the mechanics of artificial insemination, or Joseph Simpson, who liked to hear a man talk about his land and breeding stock.

For his part, Fagan couldn't help but reflect that not in his wildest dreams would he ever have thought he would find himself feeling conspicuously overdressed while wearing chinos and a sweater in the company of the president of the United States and the former ambassador to Russia.

After an informal dinner that featured thick, rare, melt-in-your mouth beef, southwest style beans, coleslaw, and homemade apple pie, Simpson, Fagan, and the president encamped around a shallow coffee table in a small library setting, just off the main living area. Laura Bush, who had joined them for dinner, quietly disappeared and left them alone. The security, like the kitchen and wait staff, was ever-present, but knew when to retreat and allow the president his privacy.

"Okay, Steven, I know Joe here didn't have you come all the way down here for some good beef. I know there are fine steakhouses a-plenty in San Francisco. What's on your mind?"

While the voice and the mannerisms were still down-home Texas, there was now a focus and seriousness about the man across the table that was not lost on Fagan. The preliminaries were now over; the president was ready to listen. Fagan glanced at Simpson, who imperceptibly nodded his head.

"The ambassador, and by extension myself and our Intervention Force organization, were given a mission by the late director of Central Intelligence, Armand Grummell. It was a deathbed request and one that we undertook within the operational constraints as outlined by the former director and within our own I-4 charter."

"I had the greatest respect and admiration for Director Grummell," the president interjected. "He was a gentleman and a patriot. Please continue."

And Fagan did. He spoke quietly for close to forty minutes. President Bush interrupted infrequently, and then only to ask for clarification. He made no notes, and he did not touch his drink. His total attention was riveted on Steven Fagan.

"That's where we find ourselves today. It has led to some important operational successes, and so long as we don't overuse this source, it should continue to be a unique and reliable source of operational intelligence."

When Fagan had finished, he provided no summary and did not ask if there were questions. He simply stopped talking. After a long moment, the president absently reached for his whiskey and took a measured sip.

"Well, I'll be damned. You've got audio surveillance on the person of Osama bin Laden. The son of a bitch is wearing a wire!" After another moment of silence, he extended a hand across the table. "Sir, I'd like to shake your hand." When he did, he did not let go. "You've done your nation and your president a great service, Steven. Indeed, you have. I'll sleep a lot easier tonight knowing they're not about to make a move without our knowing about it. Hot damn!" The president sat back and, rightly sensing this was to be more than a briefing, continued. "So, what is it that I can do for you?"

"As you can well imagine, sir, we have needed and still need the support of the military, NSA, the various intelligence agencies, and especially the CIA. We can remain on the intelligence grid so long as we have a witting and compliant senior governmental sponsor. Jim Watson had been that for us; and to date, the buck has stopped with him. That's why no other agency or the Pentagon knows about this..."

"Y'know, Steven, I've been aware of I-4 and been briefed on a few of their operations. Not all—but a few. Tell me why I'm just now learning about this operation?"

"Uh, well, sir—it was simply a matter of security and a need to know, and to preserve your deniability. Now that Jim Watson is about to be replaced, we have no top cover, so to speak. We need that benign interface at CIA to facilitate the collection and correlation of the intelligence product; but the fewer people in the loop who know about this, the better. The new director will bring in some of his senior staff, and it will be difficult to keep this from them. Only a limited number of people are read in on this, and they are all seasoned intelligence professionals or members of our organization. We need the buy-in and help of the new director, but we would prefer him to know as little as possible."

"And how would you like to do this?" Another sip of whiskey.

"Let me brief him on this with a presidential warrant that he is to be told only a part of the story. He will have to know that a cell outside normal intelligence channels has a highly placed source in bin Laden's inner circle—but no more. Past that, he must be directed to continue to support us as has Interim Director Watson. But that direction can only come from you, sir."

"What about the congressional intelligence oversight committees? I assume they have been, and will continue to be, kept in the dark?"

"That is correct, sir. Director Watson felt that, since this was not technically a CIA operation, they had no need to know. That same interpretation will need to be observed by the new director." Fagan had not mentioned the incoming director by name, but that was about to change.

Bush paused before replying. "Y'know, General Seth Thomas is a good man, and good American. I think he'll do well at CIA. I picked him because I wanted to see the improving relationship between the military and CIA continue. So, he's the right man for the job. He'll not like being kept in the dark on this one, but I'll personally have a chat with him. And you'll get your presidential warrant to that effect. Anything else?"

Fagan glanced at Simpson and back to the president. "Just one thing, Mr. President. It's not just knowing an important and vital secret here, but the exploitation of the information. Right now, myself and a handful of individuals on my I-4 staff are aware of the situation. Even fewer are privy to the information coming from the source. To date, it has been my decision and mine alone as to what information is passed to the military and other agencies for direct action. It weighs quite heavily on me as to what information may or may not lead to revealing our source. There will be great pressure at CIA and other places to not only learn about our source but to also have input on how to use this intelligence product. I'm asking for continued control of what information is to be released and what is not released."

The president digested this and permitted himself another sip—this one more generous. His reply greatly surprised Fagan. "Alrighty then, you have it. This is your ballgame and your rule book. I'll back you one hundred percent; you've earned it. But there's just one issue I can't delegate to you. If you have any actionable intelligence that would clearly prevent the loss of American life, but you think it's best not to act on it for security reasons, I need to know about it. I may or may not take your advice on the matter, but if American lives are to be forfeited for some future greater good, it'll be *my* call, not yours. We clear on that?"

"The Coventry dilemma?"

"Exactly."

During World War II, the allies had broken the German code with the capture of the Enigma encoding/decoding machine. With its capture, the allies were reading German message traffic. But they had to exercise great care on how they used the information, lest the Germans change their encoding protocols. Churchill knew the Germans were planning a massive bombing raid on the City of Coventry. He could have put up the RAF in force to intercept the raid and save the city—but there was a high probability that this would alert the German high command that the British were reading their coded traffic. So, Churchill let the Luftwaffe turn Coventry into rubble, thereby saving the Enigma secret.

"Mister President, you have my word on it." They again shook hands.

President Bush recharged Simpson's glass, then his own. Fagan had hardly touched his. "Tell me something, Steven. Had I appointed Jim Watson to continue on at CIA, would we be having this conversation?"

"Sir, had Director Watson remained in place, you just might have completed your second term without knowing any of this." He paused for effect. "It was on Director Grummell's instruction that you be kept in the dark during the preliminary workup and the transplant operation. This was to afford you a measure of deniability if something went wrong. Once we were up and running, it was my recommendation that only those who needed to know the full story would know it. As primary operations officer, it was my call. But now, sir, you need to know."

Bush glanced at Simpson for confirmation and then chuckled. "I suspected as much. And remind me not to get in a game of Texas Hold'em with you."

Two weeks later, Steven Fagan, accompanied by Jim Watson, was shown into a spacious office that, until a few days ago, had belonged to Watson. It was now occupied by retired General Seth Thomas.

Thomas was a capable general, having recently served as the Commander, U.S. Central Command. But like all new directors of

Central Intelligence, even those occasionally promoted from within the military, he was drinking from a fire hose. Watson's request for a meeting with some nonemployee would have been tabled indefinitely had it not been backed by a presidential warrant—a piece of paper signed by the president and granting the holder, within limits, presidential powers.

Thomas motioned them to the two chairs that had been positioned in front of him and took his place behind the big mahogany desk that was now his—the DCI's desk. A glance at his watch told the visitor and the former interim director that his time was limited.

"Jim, you weren't kidding when you said I would be months finding my way around here. Candidly, it's been a humbling experience. And before we get started, thanks again for your time and courtesy during our transition." Then to Fagan, "I've read your file, and you left a very interesting and compelling résumé here at CIA. From what I've been led to believe, your service has continued after you left the agency. But a presidential warrant? If you don't mind my saying so, that seems a little extreme. You want to tell me about it?"

Fagan obliquely sketched out their possession of a high-level al-Qaeda source—and its perishability. He did not have to go into issues of sensitivity or compartmentalization. Nor did he have to account for why he, and not the CIA, was in sole control of this operation. The warrant meant that he did not have to. He did go into what he needed from Brad Gregory and a few other CIA staffers who were involved in the operation, and what CIA assets he would be calling on. Implicit in the discussion was that CIA would serve as a cover and an interface with other government entities and with the military. Thomas listened without interrupting.

"Okay, then," he said with a shrug. "I do have questions, but I'm not going to embarrass either of us by asking. This is the kind of thing that gets my nose out of joint; but then what the hey, I'm the new kid on the block. You'll get what you need and no questions asked—but one." Then turning to Watson, "Jim, why can you know about this and I can't? I now sit where you once did. If things come undone, can you guarantee that I'll not be sitting before some Senate investigative subcommittee with egg all over my face?"

Watson met his gaze. "No, Director, I cannot. There were things Director Grummell never told me before I took up my duties as interim director, and this is one of the things I cannot discuss with you. This is not the military. Our successes go with us to the grave; our failures are often paraded in public. I pray to God what Steven and his people are doing never comes to light. But if it does and I'm subpoenaed, I'll deny that even this conversation took place. Past that, I'll take the Fifth. Then it'll be on me—not you and not the Agency."

Thomas looked from one to the other. He was less comfortable now than when the meeting began, but he also knew he had little choice. He would file a memo for the record, along with the tape recording of the meeting. Thomas had not risen to four-star rank without being able to read people. Neither of these men were the least bit arrogant or condescending. Both emanated sincerity and humility. So be it. But within bounds of *his* agency's support for this unknown operation, he would be watching and looking for clues, lest he be hauled into Congress to give testimony. But his compliance would be in keeping with the presidential warrant.

He walked them to the door but offered neither man his hand.

———

Throughout the end of 2006 and the beginning of 2007, Steven Fagan was able to pass on some low-level targeting information that led to successful military strikes, but he was very careful about it. First, he made sure there was little chance of linkage to al-Qaeda

Central, let alone to bin Laden. He also wanted to make sure that the existing interfaces with CIA, NSA, and the Pentagon were functioning properly and that the cutouts that he and Brad Gregory had in place blocked anyone in the chain of information transfer from exceeding their role.

All looked to be in order.

To help him in this analysis, Janet Brisco came to his home office in Larkspur for one or two days each week. While she had a hyper-secure communications suite in her East St. Louis home office, it sometimes helped them to be in the same room to pass ideas back and forth. There was something about video teleconferencing by secure Zoom that was not as effective as the face-to-face.

"Here's one we might take a look at," Brisco said. "He seems to be moving freely about in al-Anbar Province, and he's a guy who is definitely overdue for a bullet."

Muhammad Abdullah Abbas al-Issawi was known among the Sunni tribes in western Iraq as the security emir for al-Qaeda. He had a long and brutal career as an al-Qaeda enforcer and had carried out much of the tribal intimidation efforts of the late Abu Musab al-Zarqawi.

With al-Zarqawi out of the picture, al-Issawi had assumed more of a leadership role in the al-Qaeda in Iraq organization, or AQI, and was now leading the ongoing effort to subjugate the tribes. It was al-Issawi who had perfected the really large vehicle car bombs that could take out a city block. Often, he recruited eleven- and twelve-year-olds, usually those with learning disabilities, to drive the vehicles to a target location and detonate themselves with the car bombs.

With the death of al-Zarqawi, his followers had stepped up their random killing in Sunni tribal neighborhoods, attacks that were pushing tribal leaders into league with the Americans. Like al-

Zarqawi, al-Qaeda Central and bin Laden himself had sent word to al-Issawi, directing him and AQI to curb these excesses.

Fagan pondered Brisco's observation that al-Issawi was ripe for the picking. "That's true enough," he said to Brisco. "And with al-Zarqawi out of the picture, this guy is probably the number one al-Qaeda thug in al-Anbar. We know that bin Laden is in regular contact with him, so we have to be very careful so as not to link him to al-Issawi."

Brisco pondered this. "Or maybe not. We know that AQ Central is not all that happy with al-Issawi, and how he's handling the AQI franchise in al-Anbar. As you recall, right after al-Zarqawi's death, bin Laden appointed Abu Ayyub al-Masri as the head of AQI. And from our intelligence feed and other sources, we know that al-Issawi is challenging al-Masri for AQI leadership. Since we don't know the location of al-Masri but we have a good chance of predicting the whereabouts of al-Issawi, let's make this an internal issue."

A smile crept across Fagan's face. "You mean that we have al-Issawi taken out and make it look like it was al-Masri who fingered him. I like it; I like it a lot."

The bin Laden intercepts had uncovered al-Issawi's Achilles' heel. It was his predictability. He often traveled to the same locations with an entourage of a dozen or so hardcore al-Qaeda fighters, usually to carry out the punishment of a tribal elder or for a show of force in a village.

In the early spring of 2007, the tribal Awakening in al-Anbar was well underway, and the remnants of the AQI hardliners were unwelcome in Fallujah and Ramadi. But al-Issawi and his thugs were still terrorizing the outlying villages. Through his contacts with al-Qaeda Central and bin Laden himself, Steven Fagan and Janet Brisco had been able to track al-Issawi's movements in al-Anbar by a pattern of cell phone calls.

On April 24, at a compound just northwest of Ramadi on the Euphrates River, al-Issawi and his security team had gone to ground for a few days rest and to plan their next move. But one of his retainers made one cell phone call too many.

Navy SEALs and Army Special Forces advisors working with the ISOF (Iraqi Special Operations Forces) were alerted. Within hours, they were kitted up and aboard MH-60L/M helos from the 160th Special Operations Aviation Regiment—the Night Stalkers. It was a predawn raid with the attackers having the benefit of night vision goggles and close American special operations supervision.

The attack was a complete rout. Muhammad Abdullah Abbas al-Issawi and eleven of his followers were killed in the one-sided engagement.

A few days later, Al-Qaeda Central began to receive scattered reports that al-Masri had given up al-Issawi to the Americans. When AQ-Central asked the AQI leader about this, he denied it. But bin Laden and those around him, including al-Rahman, assumed that al-Masri had had enough of his lieutenant's brutality, and had provided his location to the enemy. And since the ISOF was a Shiite force, but with contacts among the Anbari tribes, no one seemed surprised at the raid. Nor was there any suspicion that al-Qaeda Central knew anything.

President George W. Bush was at his desk the following day reading his daily intelligence summary. The death of al-Issawi was the third item on the summary. Not for the first time, the president wondered if this was the work of Steven Fagan and his miraculous intelligence coup.

He was tempted to reach out to Fagan to see if this was the case, but he resisted. It was, however, noted by Condoleezza Rice, his National Security Advisor, that there seemed to be a general upswing in the targeting and neutralization of senior al-Qaeda leaders.

Al-Masri would continue on as the al-Qaeda minister of war for the Islamic State of Iraq until his death in May of 2010—also on a tip from the targeting team of Steven Fagan and Janet Brisco.

CHAPTER TWELVE: BARACK

Steven Fagan and Janet Brisco continued with their careful analysis of the periodic intercepts from their al-Qaeda leader/human-transmission source. They used these intercepts to carefully target senior al-Qaeda leaders, but only when there was a reasonable expectation that the information could have come from multiple sources, or they could falsely attribute the sourcing to another al-Qaeda leader. This had the dual benefit of eliminating a senior AQ operative and eroding trust within bin Laden's inner circle and senior leadership.

The operation was working, and Steven Fagan was being more than careful not to overuse his source or to be tempted by a target that might reveal his source. He worked with a certain amount of anxiety that a time would come when bin Laden would sanction a strike that specifically would endanger American lives, and he would have to involve the commander in chief. This had not happened, but there was always the possibility.

That it had not happened, Steven deduced, was due to two things. With the deaths of those around him, bin Laden had taken steps to decentralize his organization. Those in the scattered al-Qaeda franchises might target Americans, but they needed no approval from al-Qaeda Central. The other factor was luck, which could end at any moment. For now, the fighting and the dying was at the tactical level in Iraq and Afghanistan.

Then, Fagan received an early-morning call from Brad Gregory on his encrypted line. "Yes, Brad. What can I do for you?"

"Sir, we've had a development and I need to talk to you about it. And I'd rather not do it over the phone—even on a secure line."

"Sure thing, Brad. Would you like to come here?"

"I think that might be best. There's some good news and some bad news, and I'll fill you in when I see you. I'm booked on a noon flight out of Dulles for SFO. I'll catch a cab and should be to you by mid-afternoon."

"Very well, Brad. I'll see you then."

While Fagan's major concern with the operation was all about security, Brad Gregory sweated the technical details. Would the nano-circuitry in the implants hold up? Were the periodic burst transmissions that uploaded the product vulnerable? Gregory knew bin Laden's quarters were swept periodically for listening devices, and he could only hope that such a sweep was not underway during the micro-second transmissions. But most of all, he worried about the batteries. They were recharged by bin Laden's movement through the mild electric field induced by ordinary house current and augmented by the host's body heat.

The power demands of the implants were minuscule, so his day-to-day passing through this household current grid was usually enough to keep the sensor and transmission functions operational. On one or two occasions, bin Laden had been housed in a compound with only periodic electric power or no power to a room where he spent much of his time. Then, his body heat powered the devices.

Yet, for some reason, they tended to lose contact with him when he was traveling. The implants could, at best, go for about forty-eight hours without induced power. If an interrogation of the system by an overhead pass showed the batteries to be below half, Gregory would put the system on receive mode and not seek a data transmission for several days to allow for the *imam* to charge his batteries. But Brad Gregory lived in fear that if or when the system failed, it would be due to batteries.

When Gregory arrived that afternoon by taxi, Fagan was there to greet him. After dropping Gregory's bags in the guest room, his host led him to the office. If there was any anxiety in the reason for Gregory's making this sudden journey, he did not show it. Yet, Fagan knew something major had taken place or Gregory would not be here.

"The cleaners from NSA were just here this morning, so we can speak freely. Oh, would you like some coffee?"

"Thanks, I had plenty on the plane."

Clutching his briefcase, Gregory lowered his considerable bulk into an armchair and got right to the point. "We lost contact with our source for a day, and I figured he was on the move to another compound in the western Waziri Mountains. It usually takes a *Predator* a few hours on a grid search to pick him up. But this time it was different. We exhausted the fuel reserves on two drone missions without finding him.

"Then, we flew a mission further inside Pakistan, close to Abbottabad. There, we found him. The signal was strong, and we were able to get an uplink from the *Predator*, but not before the aircraft was illuminated by a Pakistani air-defense radar. They didn't fire on the drone, probably due to their sloppy command and control communications, but if we continue to go back to the same location, it's only a matter of time before we attract a surface-to-air missile or a Pakistani fighter comes up to investigate."

"Tell me about this new location?"

"That's part of the bad news. It's in a suburb of Abbottabad and near several Pak military installations. It's a mile or so from the Pakistani Military Academy in Bilal. A great many retired Pakistani military officers live in the neighborhood."

Gregory opened his briefcase, removed a photo, and handed it to Fagan. "I checked some old satellite footage and it seems that he's taken refuge in a recently constructed compound. The compound is a three-story affair on an acre-sized piece of land that's protected by a ten-foot cinder-block wall. It's only a guess on my part, but it looks like this is not a temporary arrangement. I think he's gone to ground and plans to stay there for an extended period of time."

Fagan studied the satellite image for a few moments. "And you say there is some good news?"

Gregory gave a slight shrug. "Perhaps from my perspective. The place has modern wiring, and the batteries supporting the implants are fully charged. We have a good system and a good signal. The problem is getting a drone or some other collector in the area to receive the signal."

"Could someone on the ground do it?"

"They could, but they'd have to get within a quarter mile of the compound. They might do it once, but not on a recurring basis. I did not ask if we have any assets there on the ground in that area. Right now, only you and I know the whole story. The comm techs and the drone controllers know only that there is a signal to capture and that signal is now in Abbottabad—deep in Pakistani airspace."

"Let me think about this a bit. Meanwhile, Lon has dinner waiting for us. You'll stay the night, of course, and Janet is due in tomorrow. Let's, the three of us, put our heads together and see what we can come up with."

Steven Fagan went through the motions of participating during dinner and for the balance of the evening, but he continued to turn the issue over in his mind. The entire operation had depended on aerial access to the source and not high-altitude or satellite over flights.

The recorded computer keystrokes that led to a hacking of bin Laden's email had been the source of some targeting, but that targeting had been risky from a security standpoint. The real actionable intelligence had come from the voice prints. In the planning and execution of the operation, it had always been assumed that bin Laden would *not* take refuge in an urban area.

Who would shelter him? Save for the tribal societies in Waziristan or possibly the Sunni tribes in northern Iraq or western Afghanistan, there were few safe harbors for this most wanted of men. Any national entity that would offer him sanctuary risked a ruinous military response by the United States, still on a war footing from the attacks of 9/11.

As Gregory and Lon exchanged pleasantries across the dinner table, Fagan thought hard about the complication that now threatened his prize operation. *A suburb of Abbottabad, a picturesque city of 1.5 million with a robust Pakistani military presence. This is totally unexpected.*

But then, as Fagan reminded himself, his job was to plan for all eventualities—even the unexpected. In his line of work, *especially* the unexpected. *How*, he asked himself not for the first time, *could he have failed to foresee this turn of events?*

The next morning, Steven Fagan, Brad Gregory, and Janet Brisco sat before a Google Maps presentation of Abbottabad, zooming in and out and switching from the street-map presentation to the relief view.

Once Gregory IDed bin Laden's compound, they visually walked around the neighborhood and then the general area. It was flat, open, ethnic, and all the surrounding homes were similarly walled compounds, though most were on smaller tracts of land. Basically, it was an ideal location to hide in plain sight.

"I can check with ops at CIA," Fagan offered, "but I doubt they have an asset who can move into the area and do what we need. We haven't the equipment for ground support, and there'd be a lot of questions I'd have to answer if we ask the Agency for more help. If this is doable, it has to be done from the air. Any ideas?"

Gregory again shrugged his massive shoulders. He was a techie; this was all about operations. Brisco pursed her lips, and then smiled. "You know, I just might see a way out of this. I stay in contact with some of my colleagues at the Air Force Intelligence

Command. It seems they have a new toy in the inventory. But it still might require that you go to them or to the CIA and beg for a favor."

The RQ-170 *Sentinel* was a stealth drone developed by the famous Skunk Works at Lockheed-Martin. Its appearance was that of a one-third scale model of the Northrop Grumman B-2 *Spirit* stealth bomber. The B-2 had joined the Air Force inventory in 1989 in small numbers and had proved itself quasi-invisible to all but the most sophisticated air defense radars.

The RQ-170, while very similar in looks, was a generation newer in its performance and stealth capability. In addition to being smaller and unmanned, it had an on-station capability of close to two days. The *Sentinel* program was a joint effort by the CIA and the Air Force, and it was to the CIA that Fagan again made his pilgrimage. Once again, he found himself in the office of the director of Central Intelligence.

This time, instead of former Director Jim Watson, they were joined by a man in a poorly cut civilian suit who introduced himself as Colonel Lee Markum. Markum was the Air Force liaison officer to the CIA.

After being introduced to Markum, Fagan turned to Seth Thomas. "Thank you for seeing me again, Director,"

Both the director and the colonel knew what Fagan needed and why he was here. A confidential memo outlining this new requirement had preceded him. Neither as of yet knew why he needed the on-call use of this new drone, of which there were only four in existence.

The RQ-170 was barely out of the prototype stage. Together, Director Thomas and Colonel Markum stood as guardians of this new reconnaissance tool. Fagan, who had just come from the White

House, had briefed President Bush on bin Laden's latest retreat and the difficulties this move now presented. When he had informed the president what he needed, Bush had told him that the presidential warrant would cover such a request.

Fagan was shown a seat across the desk from Director Thomas. Colonel Markum stood at the director's side. Both men were positioned to look down on him. He was not offered any refreshment, but Fagan asked if he might have some coffee and remained silent while Thomas had some brought in. After the steaming mug was place in front of him and the server withdrew, Fagan pushed it gently to one side and leaned forward.

"Gentlemen, I know this is difficult for you. I can imagine you're wondering where I get off making demands for support and providing little or no justification for those demands. And it's probably crossed your minds that I might be working at cross-purposes from you, or at least infringing on your charter. Let me answer that in this way. I represent a small organization that is privately funded, operates within the guidelines of national command authority, and does things that would exceed the statutory guidelines and rules of engagement of both the military and the intelligence community. Basically, in certain situations, we do what you cannot do.

"We were tasked by our government with a mission and came up with a plan to execute that mission—a complex and rather unorthodox plan that has proved successful to date. We think it has been highly successful. It's an intelligence source that, if carefully exploited, is a game changer. I'll not insult you with a lecture on security or the sensitive nature of this source. I will ask that what I'm about to tell you go no further than the two of you in this room. Basically, I think the time has come for me to pull my pants down, so to speak, and fully brief you on this project. But I will remind you that the presidential warrant that I carry stands behind that drone request. Fair enough?"

The director and the colonel exchanged glances. "You may proceed," Thomas replied.

"Then let me tell you of our project and the support we will need to continue to exploit this source of intelligence." With that, Steven Fagan laid all his cards on the table.

Two days later, an RQ-170 *Sentinel* drone was delivered by C-17 jet transport to a military airstrip in Jalalabad, Afghanistan, along with a team of Air Force technicians. The following evening, the *Sentinel* took off from Jalalabad and crossed into Pakistan, headed for Abbottabad.

The controller, sitting at her console at Nellis Air Force Base just outside of Las Vegas, knew only the coordinates over which her bird was to fly and the altitude at which it was to make the pass. She did wonder why the *Sentinel* flew a roundabout path to the target coordinates, made a single run over the target, and then returned by a circuitous route back to Jalalabad. But that was all she knew of the mission.

The signal-capture aspects of the mission were handled by an NSA technician at another console.

Over the next several years, a great many targets were passed over, as attacking them would have jeopardized their source. Steven Fagan and Janet Brisco worked long hours to vet potential targets or to create false trails or misdirection as to the true source of the targeting information.

But targets—senior al-Qaeda leaders and periodic gatherings of mid-level al-Qaeda operatives—that met their operational requirements were found and passed along to the military strike elements. These were usually addressed by a missile or smart bomb from a drone or a manned aircraft. On occasion, a ground-force special operations element was assigned the mission.

The al-Qaeda leadership, especially that of al-Qaeda Central that accounted for many of Osama bin-Laden's close associates, continued to be decimated. This, in turn, forced a continued decentralization of bin Laden's organization.

One such al-Qaeda franchise, a radical and headstrong offshoot of the loose al-Qaeda brand, took hold in northeastern Syria. It was an aggressive, Salafi jihadist militant group headed by a minor Iraqi religious scholar named Abu Bakr al-Baghdadi. They would later call themselves, among other titles, the Islamic State of Iraq and Syria.

During 2009 and 2010, Iraq was a nation in transition. The surge of thirty thousand U.S. troops in 2007 had helped to stabilize the country and dampen sectarian violence.

The death of Abu Musab al-Zarqawi in 2006 and the Sunni tribes banding together in what was then called the Tribal Awakening had been a watershed event. The tribes, hard pressed by al-Qaeda in Iraq, had joined the Americans against al-Qaeda and brought some stability to al-Anbar Province.

After taking office in early 2009, President Obama announced his plans for withdrawal of American troops from Iraq. His plan was for all combat troops to be out by the end of 2011, leaving behind a transitional force of some thirty-five thousand to continue to work with the fledgling Iraqi army, which was now largely a Shia army.

This transitional force went to zero when the United States failed to reach a status-of-forces agreement. The Shiites in Baghdad went back to a systematic campaign to repress the Sunnis in western and northern Iraq.

The presence of a coalition force, which by 2008 had largely become an American presence, had done two things. It had provided a creditable armed force to prevent the resurgence of al-Qaeda, which was now primarily a contingent of foreign fighters and hardline Sunni militants.

Secondly, it had forced the government of Nouri al-Maliki to include the Sunni minority with a seat at the table in Baghdad. In addition to countering sectarian strife, the American military leadership was there to continually broker something of a truce between the al-Maliki's majority Shia government in Baghdad and the Sunni tribes prevalent in the northwestern portion of Iraq.

With the Americans pulling out, al-Maliki and his government began to dismiss or arrest all Sunnis holding government positions. The tribes in al-Anbar Province and northern Iraq once more became a haven for insurgents. The Iraqi Army, backed by a diminishing number of American advisers, was keeping a lid on insurgents in the Sunni provinces; but by the beginning of 2011, violence in these areas was clearly escalating. By the end of 2011, Iraq was virtually on its own.

With the drawdown in Iraq, President Obama bolstered the U.S. presence in Afghanistan. Combat action in Afghanistan, first under the leadership of General Stan McCrystal, and then General David Petraeus, began to escalate as the reconstituted Taliban came across the Afghan-Pakistan border in increasing numbers.

The mini-surge of troops originally ordered by President Bush, and increased by President Obama, brought NATO force levels to close to thirty-five thousand by mid-2009. In a surprise move in February of 2009, the president authorized the deployment of another seventeen thousand American troops, an augmentation that was less than McCrystal or Petraeus, then commander of U.S. Central Command, wanted but was hopefully enough to do the job.

It was a difficult summer fighting season for the Taliban, but time was on their side. Plans were already in place for a phased withdrawal that would leave a NATO advisory force of ten thousand, eighty percent of which would be Americans, in the country by the end of 2014. The Taliban had only to hang on and continue to create American combat deaths.

From his compound in Abbottabad, bin Laden continued to guide al-Qaeda Central. But the decapitation of al-Qaeda leadership was ongoing, both those close to bin Laden and within al-Qaeda Central. Senior leaders in the al-Qaeda franchises in the Middle East and Africa also suffered.

Bin Laden, his loyal chief of staff (al-Rahman), and his security staff all watched with horror as one senior lieutenant after another was killed by air strikes or targeted by a special operations team. They suspected a leak in the organization and took additional security measures. With the threat of penetration, few of the capable, lower-level followers were promoted to senior rank, which greatly restricted the execution of al-Qaeda-sponsored operations against the West. With each of these precision strikes, al-Qaeda's command, control and influence were reduced. And both al-Rahman and bin Laden knew it.

The various al-Qaeda franchises were holding their own because much of the time they functioned by consensus leadership, with no one individual the key to the success of the local movement. They terrorized a regional area, took up residence, and under the guise of *sharia* law, exploited the countryside.

Al-Qaeda under bin Laden did not function that way; they were a more centralized, top-down organization, and they were far more idealistic.

Al-Qaeda was a political movement, and its aim was to influence right-wing, western-friendly governments like Saudi Arabia and the Gulf States to become more theological and to implement strict *sharia* law. They did not want to govern—but to influence governance.

To this end, they supported attacks on the West or sponsored attacks on governments friendly to the West. Then, they went into hiding to plan the next attack. Al-Qaeda influence helped to bring about the Arab Spring, but other than backing a theological successor, their leadership had no plans about what was to come next.

Unfortunately, there were others who did—men like Abu Bakr al-Baghdadi, who rose to leadership in the Islamic State of Iraq and eventually broke with al-Qaeda to form ISIS. ISIS, also known as the Islamic State of Iraq and the Levant, or Daesh, used both terror and *sharia* law to subjugate local populations with the intent of total control and domination in the name of the Prophet. Al-Qaeda advocated the killing of Westerners and nonbelievers. ISIS advocated the killing of Westerners, nonbelievers, Shia Muslims, and anyone who did not subject themselves to ISIS rule.

Steven Fagan and Janet Brisco continued with the business of finding, isolating, and killing senior al-Qaeda leaders or bands of mid- and junior-level leaders when they gathered in sufficient numbers to warrant a disruptive, direct-action mission.

But even with their impeccable source of intelligence, viable targets that met their nondisclosure criteria were becoming increasingly hard to come by. Still, their efforts continued to degrade the reach of al-Qaeda Central and prevent the central organization from recruiting new leaders. Those who huddled in the Abbottabad compound, or were allowed to come and leave, lived in constant fear of penetration and betrayal.

Brisco now only visited Fagan on occasion. The two were able to continue their targeting efforts from their respective secure home offices, and when they occasionally did come up with a viable target, it was quietly passed through CIA channels for execution.

Then—one day—as Fagan was sifting through this increasingly less-than-target-rich environment, he fielded a call from Joseph Simpson. "Good morning, Mister Ambassador."

"Good morning, Steven. How goes the battle?"

From previous calls, along with the clicking noises generated by the encryption interlocks, Fagan knew he was on a secure line. "We're on the hunt, but the target population is getting smaller and harder to find. We're confident they know nothing of where we're getting our information, but they are taking security precautions that are making things more difficult. But we're keeping after it. What can I do for you, sir?"

"To be honest, I'm not sure. I just received a call from the White House. It seems the commander in chief would like me to call back to schedule a meeting at my earliest convenience. He requested that you attend that meeting as well. Are you available for a trip to the capital?"

Fagan's mind was racing, but he answered immediately. "We all serve at his pleasure, sir. When would you like me there?"

"Let me try to set something up for tomorrow afternoon. If that can be arranged, I'll send a plane for you. Can you fly out tomorrow morning?"

"Yes, sir. Just let me know the details. Is there any indication as to what this might be about? I mean, we know what it's probably about, but do you have any specifics?"

"None whatsoever, but it might just be that the president is going to take a hand in the operation. I guess we'll know what he has in mind when we meet with him."

After Simpson rang off, Fagan pondered the situation. Since he had taken office, President Obama had asked only that any targeting go through CIA, specifically the office of his appointed director of Central Intelligence, Leon Panetta. Otherwise, it had been business as usual. They had not been pressed for more aggressive targeting, and only on one occasion had the CIA deferred taking action on a recommended target. It was a mid-level al-Qaeda functionary in AQAP–al-Qaeda in the Arabian Peninsula. Fagan had rightly concluded that the individual was either a source or a source in development.

Now this.

Fagan had long ago purged from within himself the urge to worry about what he could not control. He told Lon that he would be gone for a day or two, that he would be leaving tomorrow morning, and that he would need a dark suit for a formal, high-level meeting.

While she scurried about to make ready, he went back to rereading an intelligence summary that tried to make sense of the tribal entities in eastern Syria.

Late the following afternoon, Steven Fagan and Joseph Simpson, both in dark suits and crisp white shirts, found themselves waiting outside the Oval Office. Both had submitted to a TSA-like scanner and now waited patiently for their presidential meeting. Neither had a briefcase or a notepad.

Just after 1700, the president himself came to the outer office and showed them inside. "Mister Ambassador, good to see you again." Simpson and Obama had met briefly several times at state and fund-raising functions. He turned to Fagan.

"Mister Fagan, I'm honored to finally meet you and to personally thank you for your service to our nation. Words cannot express the debt we owe you."

"Thank you for your kindness, Mister President."

Obama retreated to behind the massive Resolute Desk—so named because it was constructed of English oak salvaged from the HMS *Resolute*. The desk had also been used by Bill Clinton and

George W. Bush. Standing behind the desk and to one side was his national security advisor, Tom Donilon.

After Fagan and Simpson declined coffee, the president got right to it. "One of the two reasons I asked you both here was to thank you for your service. Your work in helping to fight global terrorism has been significant. The other is to inform you personally of a decision I've made. After much discussion with some of my key advisors and a great deal of thought on my part, I've decided to terminate this operation."

The president paused to gauge their reactions to what he had just told them; both Steven Fagan and Joe Simpson remained impassive, revealing nothing. "To that end, our Navy SEAL special missions unit is at a secret location outside Kandahar. As I speak, they are rehearsing for a cross-border operation to kill or capture Osama bin-Laden."

Still no reaction.

Obama glanced at Donilon and continued. "My reasoning is this. Most of the more dangerous senior al-Qaeda leaders have been killed or captured. In other words, we seem to be running out of high-level targets. Secondly, there are variables. We don't know how much longer the source of these transmissions will remain operable, or if bin Laden himself may move farther east into the interior of Pakistan. He's no good to us unless we can conduct regular overflights.

The president's tone and facial expression became noticeably more intense. "And finally, whether he's being harbored with or without the permission of the Pakistani government, I cannot let this stand. We must take action. I've considered a precision drone strike, but our national interests will be best served if we can capture him or kill him with certainty. And we can't do that with a drone. So, within a week's time, I will authorize the SEALs to go in and get him.

The president looked up and cued his national security advisor. "Tom?"

Donilon stepped forward and picked up the narrative. "We've been working with Leon Panetta's people at Langley, and they've created a pretty convincing legend about a known courier who has been tracked to bin Laden's compound in Abbottabad on multiple occasions and an agent who has come forward with information for the reward. They're prepared to backstop these stories for a year or more to show that bin Laden has been hiding there for some time."

Donilon was about to go into the ruse they had developed about a female analyst who had first discovered the courier and had marshaled the resources to confirm that bin Laden was, in fact, hiding in the compound and had been there for some time. This was to protect I-4 from public scrutiny about their part in the operation. But Obama raised his hand to cut him off.

Fagan glanced at Simpson, slightly lifting his eyebrows, and Simpson nodded imperceptibly.

It was a subtle exchange but one not lost on the president. "Am I missing something here? Is there more to this than we know?"

Fagan cleared his throat. "Mister President, there is in fact more to this than we've shared with you to date. It may or may not influence your decision. From the beginning, we thought there might come a time when bin Laden would outlive his usefulness to us—or become worth more dead than alive. We further assumed that there might be good reason to deny him martyrdom. So, we built into the implants the ability to kill him. On your direction, he can simply just die in his sleep.

"Since it is Muslim custom for the remains to be interred within twenty-four hours, there's little chance of an autopsy. We will know with absolute certainty that he is dead, as we've been monitoring his bodily functions for more than five years now. He will not be seen to die by our hand, so he will not—in the strict since of the word—die a martyr. In this way, we deny him and those who come after him to use his death to further their cause. In fact, if I know Atiyaht Abd al-Rahman, his chief of staff, his death will not be announced by al-Qaeda for quite some time—at least until they can vacate the compound and move back into the mountains."

Fagan leaned forward. "And I will do this on my own initiative. I'm prepared to walk out of here, right now, and end it on my own accord—independent of any knowledge you may have. You, sir, will have nothing to do with it. End this meeting right now, and a very evil man will die quietly in his sleep without a named successor. It's a lot better than he deserves, but it is an efficient way to terminate our operation and kill an enemy of our nation."

"And why would you undertake this on your own initiative?" This from Tom Donilon.

Fagan glanced up at Donilon and then back to the president. "Sir, as you know, we—along with our allies—observe a protocol that prohibits the direct targeting of a head of state. Few of them would consider bin Laden in that light, but a great many in the Muslim world would. Such a move could generate security issues for yourself, as well as creating a recruiting tool for al-Qaeda and their franchises. It's a risk we don't need to take."

A silence descended on the Oval Office and lasted for close to a full minute. "If I might suggest," Donilon finally said quietly, "can we table this for the moment so we can reevaluate the issue in light of this new information?"

Again—silence, this time broken by the president. "Steven, Ambassador, will you be available tomorrow?"

Simpson answered for the both of them. "We serve at your pleasure, Mister President."

Obama glanced at his desk calendar. "How about ten o'clock tomorrow morning?" He looked from Simpson to Fagan and then back to Simpson.

"Again, sir, we serve at your pleasure. Ten o'clock will be just fine."

The president rose but did not come from behind the desk. "Thank you both for coming. And, Mister Ambassador, might I ask you stay behind for a moment?"

"Certainly." Then to Fagan, "I'll see you later this evening."

As Fagan made his way into the outer office, he was surprised that Tom Donilon had followed him out. He gave Donilon a questioning glance.

"Election coming up," Donilon said in a low voice and with a wink. "Maybe he wants to hit him up for a campaign donation?"

Fagan shot him a grin. It was nice to see that the national security advisor had a sense of humor.

Steven Fagan met Joseph Simpson in the elegant lobby of the Watergate Apartments. The ambassador had seen to it that Fagan was booked into an efficiency not far from his own suite of rooms. The car service took them to the Army-Navy Club on Farragut Square, where they were shown to a private table.

"The president wanted me to thank you again," Simpson began, "both for the work you've done for the last several years and for giving him an option that did not involve a risky direct-action raid—and a cross-border operation at that."

Fagan nodded. "Donilon jokingly thought he might be hitting you up for some money."

"No joke. I contributed to last campaign. He knows he can count on me to make a generous contribution this time around—and that I will also make an equally generous contribution to his opponent. I always do. No, his questions were about the I-4 organization and about the number of people in and out of government read into the operation. I think he's playing the odds, militarily and politically, on what he may or may not get away with. He did ask me why you would want to end it this way. I told him that the case you just presented said it all—that it had to do with winding things up in the most advantageous way possible. Did I miss anything—is there some other reason?"

Fagan considered this while they were served. Simpson had ordered a well-prepared porterhouse with new potatoes and broccoli. The waiter placed a swordfish steak with cauliflower and asparagus tips in front of Fagan.

With the waiter gone, Fagan answered Simpson's question. "I've given that some thought," he replied before touching his food. "And I suppose there is—another reason, I mean. I'm a covert operator, and the inherent beauty of a covert undertaking is always the back door. First, you have to get in and accomplish the mission, which is hard enough. But to get out with the opposition none the wiser...well, it's the sublime end to a good covert operation. It's an elegant conclusion to a nice piece of work."

Fagan picked up his knife and fork, only to rest his now-filled hands back on the table. "I certainly understand that the longer we run the intercepts, the more risk we run. There's no question that we've crippled the opposition, almost to the point that looking for additional targets will create more and unneeded exposure. Of course, there's always the chance that the implants will fail or our source will move to a location that's inaccessible to overflights."

Fagan placed his utensils back down on the table, not ready to interrupt his train of thought by taking a bite of his dinner. "There's all of that. And yet, to me personally, there's a certain amount of closure in ending the operation on our own terms. A raid, which will amount to a mini-invasion of a sovereign nation, just seems like a clumsy, heavy-handed way to undo something that we assembled and managed with such care." He made a helpless gesture. "Am I the one who's missing something?"

Simpson chuckled. "No, other than our food's getting cold. This operation will get wound down in a way that serves the political and military stakeholders. It's out of our hands. We'll learn what's to be done tomorrow. What that will be, I couldn't say."

They ate in companionable silence with an occasional server coming within earshot to see if they required anything.

After the plates and service were cleared, Joe Simpson regarded his operations officer with no small amount of admiration and pride. "Steven, they keep a very superb twenty-five-year-old Talisker Single Malt behind the bar here for me. I know you're a temperate man, but I'd be honored if you'd join me for a splash."

"Mister Ambassador, it is I who would be honored."

After they were served, Simpson raised his glass and met Fagan's eye. "Confusion to our enemies."

"Confusion to our enemies," Fagan echoed.

<hr />

They were shown into the Oval Office at the appointed time. They were again met by the president, only this time he escorted them to a settee, where Tom Donilon waited for them in one of the four armchairs. Fagan and Simpson sat on one side, and President Obama joined Donilon on the other. Coffee was offered and accepted.

Then the president spoke. "Steven, Mister Ambassador, I appreciate your coming back for a second meeting. Once more, I'm doubly indebted to you—both for the successes of this operation to date and for providing me what I guess we might call an alternative exit strategy. That said, I have decided to go ahead with our planned raid on the bin Laden compound."

He paused to let that sink in.

Both his guests showed no outward reaction.

Obama continued. He was speaking to them both, but his eyes were on Fagan. "I wanted to explain why I elected to disregard your recommendation to quietly terminate bin Laden. You see, I or my successors may not have the luxury of the Intervention Force in the future—or your capable services, for that matter."

The president, still looking at Fagan, nodded toward Simpson. "The ambassador tells me that you wish to step back from this work and return to your well-deserved retirement. Therefore, I need to send a message to our enemies and our allies alike. That message is: Anytime, anywhere—even if we have to cross borders to do it— there is no such thing as a safe haven for terrorists. While such a mission will not be without risk, I have given the green light for the raid to go forward as planned. The Navy SEAL special missions unit that is to conduct the raid is in isolation as we speak. They will launch into Abbottabad on a kill or capture mission pending weather, final preparations, and last-minute intelligence on the ground."

The president again paused. "I'm sorry if this is perhaps not how you would like to terminate this operation, but that is my decision."

Fagan stared back at the president with a neutral expression. "It is your decision to make, Mister President."

President Obama, who himself was very good at reading people, could not get past the pleasant mask of the quiet man sitting across from him. So, he changed to another tack. "Steven, and I hope you don't mind my calling you Steven, is there anything I can do for you?"

Fagan gave this some thought, and the president was not sure if he was really thinking or simply giving the impression that he was.

"Sir, since you are going to put a special operations team on the ground, may I ask that one of our I-4 operators, who is himself a former Navy SEAL, accompany the raid and that he be allowed to retrieve the devices implanted on bin Laden?"

President Obama sat back, not sure how to respond to this request. "May I ask why?"

"Sir," Fagan began, leaning forward, "it was not until 1970 that we learned of the German Enigma Machine captured on the U-505 and the enormity that that source of intelligence had on the duration, perhaps even the outcome, of that war. Breaking the German codes and the capture of that Enigma shortened World War II and saved tens of thousands of lives. There is a rare *Abwehr* machine, number G312 to be exact, on display at the Bletchley Park Museum in London. It is thought to be the one from U-505."

Fagan paused and took a measured sip of coffee. "I think it would be a good idea to recover the implants. Events may prove that these devices shortened this war on terror and saved many lives. And who knows, sir? They may make for an interesting museum exhibit some twenty-five years from now. Perhaps, when you've joined me in retirement, they might even make an interesting exhibit in your presidential library."

The president sat back, smiled, and imperceptibly nodded. *The man is good–very good.* "Very well, Steven—let me see if that might be arranged."

Also from Braveship Books...

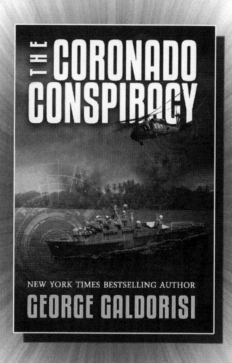

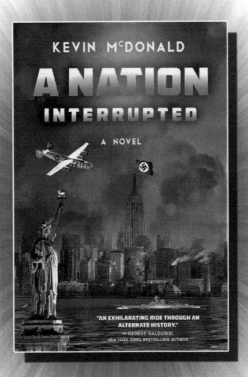